Pra

"Burnsworth nails the voice of new Southern noir. This talent~~ author will win you over with his engaging and multi-faceted hero, then keep you turning pages with his suspense."

– Hank Phillippi Ryan,
Mary Higgins Clark Award-Winning Author of *Say No More*

"Hop on board for a hard-edged debut that's fully loaded with car chases (particularly Mustangs), war veterans, old grudges, and abundant greed. A choppy start belies a well-executed plotline enhanced by the atmospheric Palmetto State setting."

– *Library Journal*

"This second case for Brack is marked by a challenging mystery, quirky characters, and nonstop action."

– *Kirkus Reviews*

"In Brack Pelton, Burnsworth introduces a jaded yet empathetic character I hope to visit again and again."

– Susan M. Boyer,
Agatha Award-Winning Author of *Lowcountry Book Club*

"Burnsworth is outstanding as he brings out the heat, the smells, the colors, and the history of Charleston during Pelton's mission to bring the killer to justice."

– John Carenen,
Author of *A Far Gone Night*

"If you have always suspected there is more to Charleston than quaint Southern charm and ghost stories, then David Burnsworth's noir series, featuring ex-soldier, tiki bar owner, and part time beach bum, Brack Pelton may just be the antidote to a surfeit of sweet tea."

– Michael Sears,
Shamus Award-Winning Author of *Black Fridays*

CAUGHT UP IN IT

Books by David Burnsworth

The Blu Carraway Mystery Series

BLU HEAT (Prequel Novella)
IN IT FOR THE MONEY (#1)
BAD TIME TO BE IN IT (#2)
CAUGHT UP IN IT (#3)

The Brack Pelton Mystery Series

SOUTHERN HEAT (#1)
BURNING HEAT (#2)
BIG CITY HEAT (#3)

CAUGHT UP IN IT

A BLU CARRAWAY MYSTERY

DAVID BURNSWORTH

HENERY PRESS

Copyright

CAUGHT UP IN IT
A Blu Carraway Mystery
Part of the Henery Press Mystery Collection

First Edition | April 2019

Henery Press, LLC
www.henerypress.com

Trade Paperback ISBN-13: 978-1-63511-475-1
Digital epub ISBN-13: 978-1-63511-476-8
Kindle ISBN-13: 978-1-63511-477-5
Hardcover ISBN-13: 978-1-63511-478-2

Printed in the United States of America

To Patty, with all my love

ACKNOWLEDGMENTS

Thanks to my wife, Patty, for all her love and support and for basically putting up with me when I'm not at my best.

Thanks so much to the tireless efforts of Henery Press. This is my fourth full-length book with them and they continue to be wonderful to work with.

My publicist Rowe Carenen has always had my back throughout my writing career.

Jill Marr of the Sandra Dijkstra Literary Agency is simply awesome. Just as they did for the previous two Blu Carraway Books, my parents, Mom and Ron, gave this book a thorough review. Thanks for always being there!

My other beta reader, Cheryl Sherman, found a lot of details requiring attention which was exactly what I was looking for.

Special thanks to Lori McCracken and Cory Ritsko for their efforts in helping with research for this book.

Finally, thanks to all you readers. You are the reason I keep writing.

God Bless!

Chapter One

Kuala Lumpur, Malaysia, Mid-July, Saturday late night

Blu Carraway, Private Investigator and sometimes, like at present, private security consultant, handed off his client to her boyfriend's security team. In truth, there wasn't an actual handoff. It was more of a formality since Jennifer Kincaid started seeing Mandel, the industrialist's son. His security team was rivaled only by the Secret Service.

The exclusive club they were in had several levels, each with their own VIP list. Thanks to being a one-percenter and the aforementioned wealthy boyfriend, Ms. Kincaid was at the top of every list which meant Blu was at the top of every list. He parted the strings of beads hanging down as a curtain that was some decorator's bad idea of kitsch and entered the innermost bar, a darkened room made up of marble, mahogany, gold, and leather—the best of materials.

The only other person in the room was the bartender, a pretty-boy type with short, styled hair, a trimmed beard, a starched white shirt with knife-edge creases, and a nod. He said, "What can I get you, Mr. Carraway?"

It had been a long thirty-six hours. The last batch of Millennials, those currently in their early twenties including his client, apparently did not sleep. Blu had been on the job the whole time along with Mandel's team. Even with exclusive VIP lists, he did not trust his client's protection to anyone else while in public places.

Blu took a seat at the bar, the soft leather stool offering comfort for his tired glutes. "Black coffee—iced."

"You got it."

This being *the* club in the city and Blu being on *the* list meant he could do pretty much whatever he wanted. Right now he wanted—needed—nicotine. As the bartender set a glass of chilled coffee in front of him, Blu pulled out his vape pen and took a few hits. The coffee and the vapor had been the two things keeping him going but he knew he was set to crash soon.

The bead curtains parted again and C walked in. Twenty-seven years old, shoulder length hair an unnatural shade of orange, various tattoos down her arms, and the prettiest face Blu had seen all evening, C was the reason he was at this particular club. Ms. Kincaid had talked her boyfriend into contracting C for a private show. As the girl whom *Rolling Stone* called the hottest act of the decade with Grammys and platinum albums, C was in high demand.

Here, this morning, at what Blu felt was the end of a hellacious run, the pop star was alone.

With a loud sigh she took the seat next to him. He was not really a fan of her music, some form of synth pop with a mixture of Arabian and Latin influence. He preferred eighties alternative and punk, but she had talent and a pretty face.

To the bartender, she said, "Get me a Guinness, Jesse."

Blu took another hit on his vape pen, realized he was staring, and stopped.

She said, "I saw you with Jennifer and Mandel. I'm Ariel."

C was her stage name.

He shook her offered hand. "Blu."

Jesse the bartender set a pint of dark liquid in front of her with a perfect shamrock in the head.

Raising her glass, she said, "To new friends and quiet bars."

As he clinked her glass of stout with his iced coffee, Blu said, "To the end of a long night and a soft bed with my name on it."

With a smile, she said, "We're both on the job, aren't we?"

Something wasn't right about the scene, and if Blu hadn't been so exhausted he would have picked up on it sooner.

She was alone.

Twenty million albums sold, two Grammys, and no personal security at the moment. She had a unit assigned to her. Blu knew the man in charge of her safety, didn't like him, but thought he was competent. Except that he didn't have her covered at the moment. It was not professional and left an opening for something bad to happen to C. With as much subtlety as he could muster, Blu checked to make sure he still had his Glock.

As he did that, a clipped sound came from the other side of the beads just before they parted around a suppressor, the kind screwed on the end of a firearm.

Blu had his Glock out and aimed. To Ariel, he said, "You better follow me."

She saw the look in his eyes and did not question.

Because the entrance covered by the beads faced the right side of the room, and he and Ariel were seated at the front, he had time to take Ariel's hand and guide her to the other end of the massive wood bar. They ducked.

The suppressed automatic fired twice, bullets ricocheting off the bar's marble surface.

Blu leaned out from the lower part of the bar, sighted in a figure in a black suit holding the gun, and fired. His Glock barked twice and the figure, a young Asian man, went down.

A second figure, another twentyish male, dove for cover on the other side of the bar.

Blu climbed onto the marble surface to give himself a better sightline.

Jesse the bartender lay on the floor behind the bar, two red holes in his chest. His eyes were open but not seeing anything anymore.

The second figure rose up.

Blu saw him first and blew him away.

An alarm sounded from somewhere in the club.

Hopping off the bar, Blu asked, "Where's your security detail?"

Ariel, obviously in shock by the blanched color of her already white skin and bloodshot eyes, shook her head. She sat on the floor.

This wasn't good.

"We need to move," he said. "In case they have friends."

"Friends?" she asked.

"More guys with guns," Blu said.

With an arm around her waist, he lifted her up and guided her to the side door of the club, the one he'd seen on the architect drawings of the building when he'd scouted the place two days ago. He kept his gun pointed where he looked, glancing back periodically to watch their six.

Another alarm started blaring when he kicked the door open but he didn't care. They needed to get out. Who knew how many of the gunmen there were?

Through the door, they found themselves in a narrow landing with stairs leading up and down from where they stood. Blu closed the door behind them and led her down, his gun pointed directly ahead.

No one met them as they descended the stairs.

Blu pulled out his phone and hit redial.

The call was answered with, "Yo, you on your way or what?"

"I need a car at the back entrance to the club. Now."

"What? I thought Goldilocks left with the baby bear?"

He didn't have time for this. "Give me an E.T.A. Now."

"Yeah, um, hold on."

What the hell? His team had been on point the whole day and a half. An hour off the clock and they fell apart?

The man came back on the line, "We're on our way. I hope two is enough. Are we coming in hot?"

"Safeties off. Don't shoot until I say otherwise."

"E.T.A. ten minutes."

"Roger." Blu ended the call.

At the bottom of the steps, Blu leaned Ariel against the wall and inched the door open, slipping his pistol out the slight opening as he got a read on the situation.

Two men with submachine guns stood guard facing the street along with a waiting van, its side doors open. They were all dressed like the two he'd capped upstairs—nice dark suits, ties, expensive shoes.

He fired twice, taking them both out with single head shots.

The van took off down the street, its open doors swinging shut.

Blu kicked the back door to the club fully open and unloaded his clip into the speeding vehicle as it bucked and bounced around a corner. When the magazine was empty, he ejected it and jammed in a full one.

He checked the street which was really an alley, saw no one else around, and slipped back inside the building. Sirens wailed in the distance.

Ariel still leaned against the wall. He put an arm around her and guided her to the exit, slipping the door open as before, training his pistol out first. He didn't see anyone else around besides the two downed mercenaries with the machine guns.

The walkie talkie app on his phone chirped with, "We're two blocks away."

"I'm in the alley on the south side. I've got a female with me. Safeties still off. Four unfriendlies down. Maybe more around."

"Roger that."

Thirty seconds later, a black Mercedes SUV charged around the corner and screeched to a stop in front of them.

The front passenger, a man with a military build, got out holding a submachine gun. He opened the back door.

Blu pushed Ariel inside the truck and dove in after her.

The armed passenger jumped back in and the driver accelerated away.

The passenger, the one Blu had called on the phone, a man named Colton, said, "What the hell, Blu? I thought we were clear for the night?"

Blu peered out the back window. "So did I."

"Who's th—" Colton looked at Ariel and stopped himself. "You're C. Jesus, Blu. What the hell is going on?"

"Not sure," Blu said. "Get us to the compound and we'll figure it out from there."

The driver, a man named Brack Pelton who'd recently joined Blu's team as a wheel man, knew to keep quiet. His skills as a mercenary were many, but they paled in comparison to his driving. He hustled the two-and-a-half-ton SUV through the back streets like an ace. Of course it helped that the truck was the AMG model with 600 horsepower.

Brack didn't drink any more but Blu couldn't say the same for Colton whose reflexes were not one-hundred-percent at the moment.

While they rode, Blu called the compound to give the new details. He didn't begin to relax until they'd crossed the Klang River and were almost there. His client's father, Adam Kincaid, had homes around the world. With his daughter spending more time here since she'd met the prince charming, he'd reinforced the barriers and increased the security detail. Blu had been contracted to make improvements and had complete authority.

Ariel seemed to come out of her shock. She looked over at Blu, then the men up front, and then back at Blu.

He said, "You're okay. We're going to Jennifer Kincaid's house."

"Can you take me to my hotel?"

"Where's your security detail?" Blu asked. "I'd feel better handing you over to them."

Looking down at her lap, she said, "I don't know. I thought they were at the club."

Blu said, "There wasn't anyone left besides you, me, Jesse, and some of the wait staff."

She looked up. "Jesse? Where is he? Is he okay?"

"Jesse didn't make it."

"Huh?" she asked.

"They shot him."

"Oh, God."

With that, she collapsed in her seat again.

The first traces of daybreak peeked out of a halo on the horizon as they arrived. The Kincaid compound was a bungalow in the hills just outside the city. Jennifer had wanted an apartment in town but Blu and her father felt it was safer here. The home sat on the top of a hill overlooking the city.

Pelton circled the fountain and eased to a stop at the entryway of the home.

Colton got out first and opened the rear door. Blu exited and then helped Ariel get out, her tight dress preventing her from too much mobility.

She looked around. "I still don't know why I can't go back to my hotel."

Blu said, "Call Teller. Find out where the h—" He caught himself. "Find out when he can be here to collect you."

Jack Teller was supposed to be her head of security.

While Ariel made her call, Blu phoned Adam Kincaid and explained what had happened. The man had enough money to fix anything. Four dead mercenaries in a foreign country were no big deal. After Blu explained that Kincaid's daughter was safe, he described the situation. Adam listened and then said he'd call back after he found out what the authorities were doing.

Jack Teller showed up at the Kincaid compound four hours later. Blu watched him exit an Audi SUV, all six-foot-five of himself, blond hair, blue eyes, and tanned muscle.

Blu met him at the door.

Before he could speak, Teller said, "I don't need you butting in on my job, Carraway."

No "thank you for saving my client" or "I'm glad my client is alive."

"Really," Blu said. "I'm sorry. I didn't see you in the room when the two mercs with suppressed automatics came in blasting."

Teller scowled.

It seemed to Blu that the man was somewhat embarrassed and was trying to save face, but this was a stupid way to do that.

"Where's Ariel?"

Blu motioned toward the sitting room just off of the entryway. The flooring and walls were stone and the ceilings stretched twelve feet at the lowest points. Their footsteps echoed as they walked.

Ariel, sitting on one of the leather couches and hugging a pillow, looked at Teller. Without saying a word, she stood up, tossed the pillow to the other end of the couch, and walked past her head of security.

Blu hadn't known her very long, but he got the feeling she was not happy with the service she was being provided. He'd used the opportunity of waiting for Teller to hand her a business card earlier in case she felt the need to make a change.

Teller eyed Blu one last time and then followed his client outside.

Ariel was waiting at the SUV for someone to open the door for her.

That showed a couple of things. The first was she was letting Teller and his men know that they still had a job to do, and opening the door for her was part of it. The second was that she was telling them that she was still willing to submit to being in their care.

Blu had dealt with Teller before. He might do things differently than Blu, but he wasn't known for being sloppy. Ariel should never have been alone in that club.

At the sight of the Audi SUV's exit off the compound and the closing of the gate, Blu turned to Colton and Pelton.

"I'm taking a shower and hitting the sack. We are back on in six hours. I suggest you rest up."

And with that, he retired to his room.

Chapter Two

Three days later, Wednesday, Barrier Lowcountry island south of Charleston, South Carolina, Residence of Blu Carraway

"I think it's Colic. We need to get him to his feet."

Blu Carraway didn't look at the man who'd spoken to him. He kept his eyes on the magnificent creature lying two feet away from him in the shade by his house. The black horse was older than Blu recollected and he was sick.

The man, a local vet named Dick Campbell, knelt by the horse Blu had named Murder and listened to his breathing with a stethoscope.

The other horses stood close by. Dink and Doofus, normally on post by the front door awaiting treats, seemed to be making the rounds comforting the other members of their ragtag herd.

Blu wiped sweat from his brow. "This horse saved my life."

Without an ounce of condescension, the vet gave him a nod.

For most of his life, Murder had chosen to live on the opposite side of the island. Blu's nine acre plot, depending on the tide, had been the place they both called home. Murder had made it his in his own way, leading the rest of the herd of Carolina Marsh Tackeys.

Dick raised himself up. "He's going to be tough to move, so we need to make him as comfortable as we can where he is. But we need to get him up. Keep him shaded and hydrated. I'll come back with an I.V."

Blu wanted Murder patrolling their island forever, not lying on his sickbed, which at the moment was a mixture of crushed shells and pine needles.

"If you want," Dick said, "I can get a canopy set up."

Blu felt his head droop. An involuntary sigh came out. He shut his eyes and opened them. "Yeah, okay. That would be nice, Dick. Thanks. How do we get him up?"

"If he won't stand on his own, we'll have to lift him." He put a hand on Blu's shoulder. "Don't worry. I have some friends who know what to do."

The vet gave him another nod and walked toward his Suburban which was parked in front of the house.

Murder's chest rose and fell. If Blu listened hard, he could hear how labored the animal's breathing had become. This was not something expected. It seemed like yesterday, this horse led the rest in a stampede in front of the house, running from one end of the island to the other. So full of life.

And now this.

"Hey, Blu?" Dick called from the tailgate of his truck.

"Yeah?"

"One of my assistants is on his way with the canopy and liquids. Should be here within the hour. The sun won't be on that side of the house until later so we have some time."

Blu didn't think Murder really had any time to spare.

It wasn't worth debating. Whatever's going to happen was going to happen. And it really sucked eggs.

Blu said, "Thanks." But he didn't really mean it.

At the moment, the rumble of a Harley Davidson could be heard in the distance and getting louder.

Mick Crome idled his way across the bridge and onto Blu's island paradise. He swung the bike in a semicircle and stopped next to Blu's four-year-old Nissan Xterra. Wearing his normal biker garb of a do-rag to keep his long hair under control and out of his face, aviator sunglasses, handlebar mustache, black T-shirt advertising a Harley dealership in Bangkok, ripped jeans, and biker boots, Crome looked at Murder and then at Blu.

"What the hell's wrong with him?"

"Campbell thinks Colic. He's going to get someone to lift him back onto his feet."

Crome took out a vape pen and inhaled a lungful. On the exhale, he said, "I guess you told him money's no object. Cause I'm gonna chip in whatever you need."

This vet bill could go real high in a hurry and still not save the horse.

Blu said, "Thanks."

Crome put an arm on Blu's shoulder. "I mean it. Whatever it takes."

Not knowing what else to do for the horse at the moment, and with Dink and Doofus and Sally, another horse from the herd, standing nearby keeping Murder company, Blu felt it was okay to step away.

As they turned to go into the house, the crunch of tires on the crushed shell drive stopped them. They waited to see who it was, Blu hoping and then not hoping it was Tess Ray, the woman in his life at the moment. She was great, but made him feel both younger and older at the same time.

It wasn't Tess; at least it wasn't Tess's convertible Beetle. The grey sedan had rental practically stamped into the doors and the shock of orange hair on the driver confirmed it wasn't Tess.

Crome said, "I could be wrong, but that looks a hell-of-a-lot like that pop star named C."

"So it is," Blu said, suddenly concerned because like the first time he'd met her there was no security detail present. She was alone.

Ariel waved and pulled in next to Crome's bike.

Blu and Crome waved back.

"You listen to C?" Blu asked.

"You get a look at her?" The biker said. "Remember those pictures?"

Of course. It had nothing to do with the two Grammys she'd earned and had everything to do with the nude photos leaked all over the internet a few months back.

"One question," Crome said. "Why's someone as famous as she is and worth thirty-million-bucks driving herself anywhere?"

"I'm guessing, once again, her security detail has come up short."

"Once again?" Crome asked.

"Long story," Blu said. "The short version is Jack Teller fell down on the job."

"Teller? Really? He's a tool, but I never thought he was incompetent."

Ariel got out of her car, looked at the horses, and then at Blu and Crome. "I didn't believe it when I heard you have an island in paradise with a bunch of horses." She swatted at a mosquito.

Dink and Doofus did not leave Murder's side. His illness had affected the whole island.

Blu approached her. "Nice to see you again. Um..."

"Why am I here?" she asked, flailing her arms at the full on parasite assault.

"Before you answer your own question, let's get you some bug repellant."

He led her, rather quickly, to his side porch, picking up a bottle of the good stuff. "Are you allergic to anything that might be in this?"

She swatted at her legs. "Spray me! Spray me!"

"Close your eyes," he said.

She did and he gave her a thorough dousing.

Ariel breathed a sigh of relief. She had a few welts forming, but otherwise looked like she did the last time he'd seen her.

Crome cleared his throat.

Blu said, "This is my business partner, Mick Crome."

Holding out a hand, Crome said, "It's a pleasure."

She said, "I'm sorry but I don't remember seeing you at the club. I was kinda out of it."

"He wasn't there," Blu said. "Can I offer you something to drink?"

Crome said, "He's got tap water and cold—I mean iced—coffee."

"Anything's fine," she said.

"What my partner's trying to tell you," Blu said, "is he's got beer in his saddle bags."

She looked at them. "You rode a horse?"

"Naw," Crome said. He lifted the lid on one of the bags mounted on the side of his bike. In it were an insulated pouch of ice and some cans of beer.

She took the offered can, popped the top, and took a long drink.

Crome said, "Honey, try not to make everything you do remind me of your videos."

Risqué would be a polite way to describe them. Pornographic might be how a certain demographic labeled them. Either way, Crome seemed to enjoy thinking about them.

She gave him a smile. "You're cute."

He popped the top of one of his beers, tapped it to hers, said, "Here's to your health," and drank half of it down.

"Back to the question you asked yourself," Blu said.

"Why am I here?" She smiled. "Because I fired Jack."

"He leave you high and dry or something?" Crome asked.

She looked at Blu. "You didn't tell him?"

"I was getting around to it," he said.

Not giving him the chance, Ariel said, "Your partner here saved my photogenic behind."

Eyeing Blu, Crome said, "You don't say?"

"He shot four men and got me to a safe house."

Blu said, "I meant to ask, where was Teller in all that?"

She huffed, took a drink from her beer, and swallowed. "Said he thought I'd told him I didn't need him anymore. I don't remember saying that. All I remember is seeing Jesse lying in a pool of his own blood as you shot the second one with the gun. Say, what's with that horse on the ground over there?"

"His name is Murder and he's sick," Blu said.

"He one of yours?" she asked.

"In a way."

Crome said, "They sorta came with the island. Blu might be afraid to, but I'd call them family. We're worried about Murder."

Still looking at Murder lying on the ground, Ariel said, "That's sad. Anything I can do to help?"

"I appreciate the offer." Blu pulled out his vape pen and took a quick hit to calm his nerves. "My vet's the best horse doctor in the lowcountry."

"The what? Lowcountry? What's that?"

"You're standing in it. The low lands of South Carolina. Marsh and pluff mud and fill dirt. That's what makes up most of Charleston County."

"Yeah," Crome said, swatting at a bug. "And parasites like Blu here."

She laughed. "And you, too?"

Crome bowed. "At your service, m'lady."

Blu took a last look at Murder and then motioned for them to sit on the chairs on the patio under the working ceiling fan. It was cooler than the inside which did not have air conditioning at the moment.

They sat.

Blu and Crome watched Ariel.

She said, "I guess I need to explain what I'm doing here."

"Only if you want to," Crome said. "We could always play a guessing game."

As if ignoring him, she said, "Teller is no longer on my payroll."

"Who's managing your security then?" Blu asked.

"You, I hope."

Crome said, "You mean you flew commercial from Malaysia, rented your own car, and drove yourself here all by yourself?"

She leaned in and gave him a blank look. "I can walk and chew gum at the same time as well."

"What he's doing a bad job of saying," Blu said, "is that

someone in your position puts themselves in danger when there is no plan accounting for risks."

She sat back and took a breath. "Sorry. There are a lot of men in this business who enjoy cutting women down. I have a habit of not letting things go."

Crome said, "Apology accepted. I can see you're tough. But part of the reason me and Blu are in business is because there are some real pikers out there that tend to take things up a few notches. Wouldn't want that to happen to you."

"So you'll take the job?" she asked.

"What is the job?" Blu asked.

"Handling my security."

Before Blu could say anything, but with thoughts of every reason his biker business partner would not want to have a long term commitment like this one, Crome said, "Hell yes."

Blu blinked a few times. Then he said, "What is the timeframe you are looking for, here?"

"Permanent."

Holding up a hand, Crome said, "We talkin' twenty-four hours a day and seven days a week?"

"Yes."

He looked at Blu. "I been looking for something a little more long term that our normal jobs. How about you?"

This coming from the man who vetoed a similar opportunity guarding a rich banker with six-figure paychecks for both of them and, frankly, a much easier task than trying to guard someone who books hundred-thousand-seat stadiums.

"No offense," she said, "but I want Blu on point. He already proved he's capable before I offered to pay."

"Of course," Crome said, and toked on his vape pen. The change in his demeanor was minor, but Blu could sense she inadvertently just threw Crome's ego in a blender and hit the high-speed button.

Blu said, "We work with a few contractors, handpicked by us of course. But without knowing more specifics, I'm not sure I can tell you we'll be able to handle the job."

Brushing strands of orange hair off her face from the ocean breeze in the air, she said, "What do you want to know?"

"If we're on the hook round the clock," Blu said, "we need to see where you live, what your studio and tour schedules are, and where you spend your leisure time, if you have any."

"Is that all?" she asked.

"No," Crome said, recovering from the brush off, "we need to know all of your friends and business associates. We like to do background checks on everyone."

"You're kidding," she said.

"I'm afraid not," Blu said. "You mean Jack didn't go through all of this with you?"

She said. "With him, I felt like luggage."

Blu inhaled a lungful of vapor, thought for a moment, exhaled, and then said, "How do you feel about handguns?"

"I don't mind them," she said. "But I've never shot one."

"Reason I ask," Blu said, "is because those guys meant business back at the club. We need to talk about them. And if you're agreeable, I'd like Crome to take you to the range and teach you handgun safety and how to shoot."

She looked at Crome as if to ask, "Him?"

Blu said, "Crome's rough around the edges—"

"Thanks a lot."

"But," Blu continued, "he's the last person to pull a handgun in a fight which makes him the best instructor for you."

As if finally getting what Blu was saying, Crome offered, "I'm more of a leg-breaker type."

"I see."

It was clear she didn't see or understand, but was going along with it. As Blu understood the situation, she was already here and asking for help. It would seem disingenuous for her to back out now, no matter how unsophisticated Blu Carraway Investigations appeared.

"Good," Blu said. "Now, about those four men with guns."

She sunk back in her chair. "I have no idea what they were after."

Blu got the feeling, and it wasn't the first time with a client, that she was not telling the whole truth. Or at least as much as she knew. He said, "I'm told they were contract killers. Not exactly high end, but killers none-the-less."

Kincaid had gotten the information from the local authorities back in Kuala Lumpur.

"Well I have no idea why they'd be after me."

Almost the same thing she'd said before.

Blu wouldn't get more out of her at the moment, but he would eventually. "Okay, then." He turned to Crome. "Mick, why don't you take her to Pop's place and get her started on her training?"

"What are you going to do?" she asked.

"There is a lot of work even before we review your schedule and lifestyle."

"What about a contract or something?" she asked.

"How about this," Blu said. "We sign on for one week while we figure the situation out. If a lot more killers come knocking, Crome and I won't be enough and I'll have to refer you to a bigger shop."

Chapter Three

Carraway Island south of Charleston, South Carolina

Crome sucked down vapor, wondering how this was all going to work. What started out as maybe something amusing and superficial had turned into a real job and not much of a fun one if you asked him. He thought someone with orange hair and a bunch of tats would be a little less formal when it came to rules and such. But apparently C was more than she appeared.

"Okay, Mr. Crome," Ariel said, "I hadn't planned on shooting guns today and probably am not dressed appropriately."

"Nobody except the military, cops, crazies or hunters plans on shooting guns," Crome said, "but I find their wardrobes lacking."

She laughed. "A joker. Now I'm beginning to figure you out."

"As far as your wardrobe," he motioned to her t-shirt, vintage jeans, and Doc Martens, "it looks like you take lessons from Blu."

"I was trying to travel incognito."

Her signature orange hair prevented her being incognito in any situation unless it was under a wig. Something to think about for later.

He said, "How about you hand me your car keys and I drive us to the range?"

"You're not on my rental plan."

Again traces of formality and rules.

"I think someone with your credit score wouldn't need to worry about things like that," he said. "But if it'll make you feel better, Blu tells me we have a pretty hefty umbrella policy in case I blow off the wrong person's head."

"Still," she said, giving him a smile that almost melted his guts, "I'd rather not risk it."

Crome couldn't believe it when she instead donned a ball cap, walked over, mounted his bike, raised the kick stand, and started it up.

Blu, who'd been silent through the whole exchange, laughed, patted Crome on the shoulder, and walked inside his house.

Blu listened as the rumble of the Harley's engine dissipated in the distance.

The first call he made was to Brack Pelton, a local Charlestonian and the wheel man he'd used in Malaysia. Starting right now, Ariel would no longer drive herself anywhere. She was as safe as could be expected riding on the back of Crome's bike, especially with no one the wiser that she was in town. While she was strikingly beautiful, she and Crome together looked the part of bikers, or something like that.

Pelton answered the call with, "Darcy doesn't believe me that we had C in the car with us while on the job with Jennifer."

"Listen, Brack," Blu said. "The last thing I should be doing is giving marital advice. But I'd recommend you let her win this one."

"Why's that?"

"Because you can prove your point when you bring your lovely wife over to my house for dinner tonight."

"Prove my point?" he asked. "What's that supposed—wait a minute. She's there isn't she?"

"No." It was a true statement.

"Then how am I going to prove my point?"

"Crome took her to Pops' range to teach her about handguns. They'll be back for dinner."

"Hot damn."

"Helping you impress your wife wasn't the goal of my call," Blu said.

"Sorry. What can I do for you?"

"I'm not sure yet, but I think Crome and I are going to take over her personal security."

"No kidding? You need a driver?"

"Yes, and may need a second home base if things go south here."

"No problem," he said. "How's Murder?"

"Not well."

"Man, I hate to hear that. Let me know if there is anything we can do for you there. Even if it's to come and sit with him or whatever. We're here, okay?"

"Thanks, Brack. Right now, plan on coming for dinner. In fact, can you have your restaurant cater it? I don't normally keep much on hand and don't have time to go shopping. I'm going to call my daughter. When Tess and Harmony get wind of it, the count's eight."

"We'll take care of everything," Brack said. "Darcy's gonna love this. Thanks for thinking of us."

"See you at six."

The call ended.

With dinner now planned, Blu contacted Adam Kincaid. Unbeknownst to Crome, Blu had signed an extended contract with the Kincaids. The sole purpose was to watch Jennifer Kincaid when she traveled outside of the country, which happened every couple of months. More often now that she was dating Mandel. Blu thought she could do better, maybe someone who wasn't afraid of actual work. Any kind of legitimate effort would suffice.

Crome congratulated himself on having the foresight to call ahead and ask for the private room. Ariel, or C, whichever name she went under, sold a bunch of albums with her picture on the cover. She'd also done a Super Bowl half-time show and a New Year's Eve party with a wardrobe malfunction that was broadcast on a major network. There was no way she was going anywhere without being recognized, which brought up another thought—if she flew commercial, people already knew she was in town. That might cause some problems.

Plug It and Stuff It, the taxidermy and gun range Blu and Crome liked to use, had been around a long time. So had its owner, Pops. Crome dropped the kickstand next to a twenty-five-year-old F-150 with new Trump decals and faded "W" stickers on the tailgate.

Ariel read the faded wooden sign on the front door: *"We can help you load it and shoot it. If your pistol still don't fire right, see a doctor."*

"Whaddaya think?" he asked.

She looked at the weathered and run-down building, the cracked asphalt parking lot that was mostly empty, and the surrounding buildings and lots that weren't any better. "I love America."

"Pops is good people," Crome said. "You'll see."

"You don't understand," she said. "These are my people, too. My family runs a hunting lodge in Michigan. Their regulars work in the car factories."

He felt like saying, "You ain't in Kansas anymore, Dorothy," but thought better of it. She had enough money to buy the rust belt, no matter how much she thought she was just like everyone else.

As Blu ended the conversation with Adam Kincaid, another call buzzed in. It was Tess. He and Tess were, well, he wasn't sure what they were. Since leaving the now defunct *Palmetto Pulse* news organization, she had worked as an independent news correspondent along with her cohort, Harmony Childs. Tess spent most nights on his island home in his bed but was gone by dawn. There was none of the usual new romance rituals of "couldn't wait to talk to you" or "just thinking of you" phone calls, jittery lunches, candlelight dinners, or bouquets of flowers. Okay, that last one was on him, but she didn't have an office he could send them to and wasn't home long enough to receive or enjoy them.

All that passed through the black hole that was his brain as the phone rattled and hummed with her number displayed on the screen. It was the middle of the afternoon and they weren't working on a similar story—the only other reason they talked during the day.

He answered with, "Hey, Tess."

She said, "Didn't you tell me you saved C's life in Malaysia?"

"I did."

"Well, there are several fan-selfie posts with her on a flight to Charleston. I wouldn't be surprised if she was on her way to see you."

He wondered how many other people knew. "Um…"

"She's already there, isn't she?" Tess asked.

"Not exactly."

"Am I going to have to play twenty questions or are you going to give me the story."

"She's at the shooting range with Crome. He's teaching her handgun safety. She came to town to contract me and Crome for her personal security."

"No kidding?"

Thinking fast, he said, "The Peltons are bringing dinner over tonight. Call Harmony and come over at six."

"C is going to be at your house for dinner tonight." She said it as if she were trying to convince herself it was the truth.

"That's right."

"Oh. My. God."

He thought he heard her give a slight squeal. It was times like this, and there weren't that many of them, when he felt the other side of their twenty-year age difference. Most of the rest of the time he played catch-up, her being so much more mature.

"So you'll be here?"

"Can I call Hope?"

That one caught him off guard. He wasn't used to—or better

yet—didn't expect Tess to want to have a relationship with Blu's twenty-two-year-old daughter. "If you want." It didn't come out with a whole lot of confidence, but he hoped she didn't notice. "Just don't tell her who's going to be here."

"Great! See you tonight."

The call ended.

Crome watched Pops help Ariel reload the clip for the thirty-two he'd set her up to use. The old man was patient with her, almost grandfather-like, and she showed him respect that only came with good upbringing. At least, what Crome imagined good upbringing would do. He wouldn't know for sure. His father walked out when he was nine and his mother worked two jobs just to keep the lights on. He pretty much grew up on his own.

Pops wore a ball cap with a confederate flag on the front, a red flannel shirt, and blue jeans and looked every bit of his seventy years. He was a Vietnam vet who chain-smoked cigarettes and Crome and Blu were like the sons he never had.

Ariel shoved the clip in, aimed at a fresh target twenty feet away, and put four holes center mass.

She clicked the safety on, turned to Pops, and said, "Yes!"

Pops accepted the gun from her and put it on the table.

She gave him a hug, almost knocking his hat off.

When Crome and Ariel had entered through the front door, Pops' ten-year-old granddaughter smiled from underneath a head of dark curly hair. She received her light-brown skin and African features from her father but she had Pops' brown eyes. Crome wasn't sure where the girl's mother, Pops' daughter, was.

Ariel had been a good sport and a better student than Crome would have thought. It helped that Pops became enamored with the young woman, taking a liking to her immediately, orange hair and all.

Crome thought he was going to have to do all the work, but all he had to do was carry a few boxes of thirty-two rounds to the private room where they were. After that, he was free to stand back and vape.

Pops lit a cigarette, inhaled, and blew out a puff of smoke.

Ariel did not seem to mind.

He said, "You sure are a good shot, young lady."

She curtsied. "Thank you, kind sir."

Pops ate it up. He had no clue how famous she was. His granddaughter, recognizing Ariel right away, squealed and tried to explain it to her grandfather but it all went over his confederate cap.

Crome said, "So what do we owe ya, Pops?"

The old man scratched his five-o'clock shadow. "The thirty-two and three boxes of shells. How about Ms. Ariel signs a poster for my granddaughter? She seems to like your music."

"I'll be glad to," Ariel said. "But we're going to pay you for the pistol and bullets."

"And the lane and instructions," Crome said.

"Hell," Pops said, "it ain't every day I got a celebrity in here. Donate some money to the V.F.W. and I'll call it even."

Ariel kissed his cheek. "You are too much."

Pops blushed for the tenth time.

It seemed to Crome as if everyone but him was getting all the female attention. Blu walked into a room and women swooned. Pops gets a kiss from the artist of the year. And all Crome ever got was blown off.

What was the world coming to?

Chapter Four

Blu stood leaning against one of the posts holding up the roof over his front porch. Dick Campbell and his crew had come back with an expandable canopy to put over Murder who hadn't moved on his own and refused to budge.

The canopy covered a much larger area, room for several horses to be underneath it and near their leader. Sally had decided to stand next to the black horse. Dink and Doofus stood guard.

Campbell had also said that he'd made arrangements to have Murder lifted to his feet in about an hour. In the meantime, he'd given the horse a sedative to get him ready.

Crome and Ariel rode up and parked, both all smiles.

Blu was about to ruin the mood. When they approached, he showed Ariel a selfie someone had posted with her in the Charleston airport. It had been liked and shared a zillion times. "The world knows you're in town."

She said, "My trip here was the most refreshing travel I've had in a long time. Nobody rushing me from jet to limo, limo to hotel, hotel to limo, limo to concert, concert to limo—"

"I get it," Blu said. "But there's a reason why it's done that way."

"Oh, yeah?" she asked.

"The four dead guys in Southeast Asia."

That seemed to stop her.

Blu said, "I don't like killing. In fact, I'd prefer not to be put in a position where men with guns are shooting at me." He held up his phone again. "It's acts like this that are going to bring those men with guns here."

Crome said, "Easy, there partner."

"She came to us," Blu said. "We're setting the rules. And rule one is she doesn't pose for selfies any more. Rule two is she needs to lose the orange hair."

Ariel opened one of the saddle bags on Crome's bike and took out a bottle of hair color. "Good idea. We stopped and picked this up."

She walked into the house.

The men watched her.

Crome said, "She's a good kid. Did you have to do that?"

"Yep."

After a brief pause, Crome said, "Okay, why don't we stash her at Kincaid's?"

It wasn't a bad idea. The man had ex-Secret Service agents running his home security. The place was like Fort Knox.

"Not yet," Blu said. "People may know she's in town, but they don't know she's here. Unless they recognized her on your bike."

"I think we're okay so far," Crome said. "She wore the ball cap and most of her hair had been covered. I just hope our friends don't talk."

"That reminds me," Blu said. "They're coming for dinner at six."

"What're we having?"

"Whatever the Peltons bring."

Crome took out his vape pen. "Hot damn."

"I don't feel like cooking. We really need to focus on who's out to kill her. And why Teller laid down on the job."

"The more I think about it," Crome said, "the less I like what he did."

An hour later, a pickup truck pulling a loader on a trailer crossed the bridge onto the island and parked. A man got out and Campbell met him at his truck. Together, they were going to get Murder onto his feet. It was bad for a horse to lie down for more than a few hours.

Campbell introduced the man as Jim.

Blu watched as the two men approached Murder, who did not look happy to see anyone but didn't put up a fuss, the sedative doing its work. This was the same horse that on a normal day did not let anyone get near him without galloping away.

After the men moved the canopy out of the way, they spread out two large slings behind the horse and then carefully rolled Murder over and onto them. Again, Blu expected the horse to kick and bite, but he stayed complacent. Nor did he move when Jim backed the loader off the trailer and drove to within ten feet of where he lay.

The men then "burritoed" the slings around the horse. Jim got back into the loader's driver seat and slowly moved in close to the horse until the bucket was above the animal. Campbell connected the slings to the bucket with hooks and chains and then backed away. Jim slowly raised the bucket, and eventually Murder was lifted.

The horse gave Blu a pathetic look, and seemed to tolerate the ordeal until he was standing, wobbly, on his feet.

There was no way he had enough energy to walk very far, much less run away. Blu had bought a 30 gallon barrel and moved it close to the horse. He then filled it with water from a hosepipe.

Campbell dropped off a bale of grass hay and the three men moved the canopy over Murder, who just stood there watching them. At least he was back on his feet, if reluctantly. Dink and Doofus, who had vanished at the sight of the loader, reappeared and stood beside their leader.

Blu watched Tess and Harmony arrive together but in their separate cars. Instead of coming to the porch to greet Ariel, Crome and him, they went over to Murder, a bag of something in Tess's hands. Dink and Doofus, standing guard, parted and let them through. They dropped apples next to the bale of hay.

Only after they had left the treat for Murder did Dink and Doofus approach the two women for their own apples. Sally, standing by, got one as well.

Tess came up to the group, kissed Blu first, and then introduced herself to Ariel. A true blond, she stood something over five feet and wore librarian's glasses over a pretty face and a sundress over a petite but in shape physique.

Ariel said, "You got yourself one hell of a man, there."

Putting her arm around Blu's waist, Tess said, "I know."

Harmony, the outgoing strawberry blonde siren that always left Crome tongue-tied, hugged Ariel. "I don't care if I sound like a groupie, I love your songs."

It made the pop star smile and hug her back. "Thanks. I needed that, groupie."

After they separated, Harmony said, "What have we got to drink around here?"

Crome said, "Tap water and cold coffee."

"Ah, yes," Harmony said. "The Blu Carraway staples."

Blu said, "What else is there?"

Crome held up a six pack of Shiner Bock. "There's beer."

Ariel raised a stemmed glass of red wine. "And vino!"

"Oh, my. Are you married?" Harmony asked.

"Not anymore," Ariel said and they both laughed. Her divorce had also made the tabloids. Her ex-husband was another recording artist who'd been caught cheating on her. Ariel had sent the divorce papers to his mistress' house.

Tess said, "I'll get us two glasses."

Harmony said, "So you've had the Blu Carraway Investigations treatment already I see."

"What's that supposed to mean?" Crome asked.

Tess returned with two glasses of red.

Harmony took her glass and raised it. "When you two come up against the bad guys, they die."

Last year, some psycho kidnapped Crome's girlfriend

Maureen, killed the mayor, and abducted Harmony. When Blu and Crome finally tracked down the women and the psycho, Crome blew his head off. As in, if the guy had had a funeral he would have needed a closed casket ceremony. None of them lost any sleep over his demise.

Ariel clinked her glass with Harmony's. "Yes they did."

Blu said, "This isn't over yet."

"I know," Ariel said, "but I feel safe being here. I haven't felt this way in a long time."

Tess raised her glass. "To Blu and Crome, the toughest men I know."

Harmony and Ariel said, "Here, here!"

Blu wasn't sure what to do. He wasn't used to having three beautiful women cheering him on at the same time.

Crome looked as if he were smitten with Ariel, which wouldn't help his focus on the job of protecting her.

Before Blu could finish the thought, the Peltons pulled into the drive in Darcy's SUV. Brack got out of the driver's seat and opened the back door. His dog, Shelby, jumped out and ran over to greet them. In general, the dog could care less about any men nearby. His attention was on making all the women in the vicinity swoon around him and he succeeded again. But, he broke off and went to greet Murder, who stood underneath the canopy watching everything. The horse did not startle when the dog approached. Neither did Dink and Doofus. They'd all met before.

Crome and Blu helped Darcy and Brack unload containers of food from the back of the SUV.

"What's for dinner?" Crome asked.

"Shrimp and grits." Darcy said.

"Perfect," Blu said. "Gives Ariel a taste of the lowcountry."

Pelton had a chef in his bar and grill on Kiawah that should have his own TV show he was so good. The guy crossed the border from his homeland of Mexico and Pelton had been helping him get his citizenship. By far he was one of the best lowcountry cooks in Charleston County.

After the food was set up on Blu's kitchen table, Darcy and Brack introduced themselves to Ariel and greeted Tess and Harmony.

Tess had told Blu that Darcy was not a fan of their relationship but she never voiced it to him. It could be because Darcy was friends with Blu's ex-girlfriend, Billie—the woman he'd asked to marry last year but who'd never given him an answer.

As they chatted under the relief of circulating air from a ceiling fan, another vehicle parked in the drive.

Blu, Crome, and Brack all looked to see who it was. Hope got out of her old Suzuki Sidekick.

Her smiling face beamed through the screen door. She carried two pies in her hands. Blu's daughter was the most beautiful woman, to him, on the face of the earth. She had her mother's features and his mother's Cuban heritage. From him she got her knack for looking beyond the surface to find the truth. And his stubbornness.

Blu let her in. She put the pies, key lime from Simmons Seafood—her and Blu's favorite—in the refrigerator.

Turning, she noticed Ariel, looked at her father who had purposely not told her who the special guest was, looked at Tess who also hadn't told her when she'd called, and then back to Ariel.

Ariel held out her hand and introduced herself.

For once, Hope was speechless.

Blu said, "This is my daughter, Hope."

"Nice to meet you, Hope."

Hope, star struck, managed a "You're C."

"My friends call me Ariel," she said.

"Wow."

The group chuckled.

Harmony put her arm around Hope. "I squealed when I saw her. It isn't every day you meet a superstar. I'm convinced God put your father on this earth to keep us on our toes. You never know what Blu Carraway is going to do next."

Crome said, "What about me?"

With a grin, she said, "I *know* what you wanna do next, Sugar. And I love you just as you are."

The group laughed again.

Hope hugged Crome. "I love you too, Uncle Mick."

Shelby, Pelton's dog, nudged his way in between them, convincing Hope to give him her attention.

"Mr. Shelby," Hope said. "My hero."

It was true. Some bad men had taken Hope a few years ago and Shelby had been the one to find her tied up in a closet. They had a special bond.

Everyone, except Blu who was impervious to the bloodsuckers, doused themselves in high-powered bug repellant. Life on the island had its ups and downs, the parasitic insect breeding ground being a major downer for most everyone.

The picnic table on the back porch overlooked the marshes and faced west where the setting sun began a slow drop over what Blu knew was heaven on earth. Rays of every color on the pastel chart bathed the tide pools, pluff mud, and salt meadows of the wetlands.

A squadron of twenty brown pelicans sailed overhead, their bodies and outstretched wings angled in the breeze.

Everyone ate in silence and watched the natural beauty, occasionally swatting at an insect hearty enough to withstand the odorous cloud of repellant hovering over the table. As the locals knew all too well, dusk was feeding time for more than just aquatic fowl. It was the worst time for mosquitoes and tiny sand flies called no-see-ums.

"I have never seen a more beautiful place," Ariel said, "but these bugs are the worst."

Hope said, "We learn to live with the one to have the other."

Ariel cocked her head. "That's a great line." She pulled out her Smartphone and typed something. Then, to Hope, she said, "You keep that up and you may have a future in songwriting."

Crome got another beer from a chest of ice on the porch.

The women drank wine, a barbera Blu heard all of them say

paired nicely with the tomato-based sauce in the meal.

Tess leaned into Blu, her skin slightly sticky from the salt air. If someone had told him a year ago that he would be sitting here with anyone other than Billie, he wouldn't have believed them.

Hope winked at her father which made him feel good. She was okay with how things turned out, Blu thought, because she was happy that he was happy. He had lost Billie but gained Tess.

Crome had only lost. Maureen, his ex-girlfriend, had packed up and moved away after they'd recovered her from the shackles of abduction. Mostly Blu felt she needed to get away from Crome. It was her association with him that had caused bad things to happen to her and she had trouble forgiving him.

Logically thinking, it wasn't fair. Crome was only half of the target. Blu was the other half. But Maureen had taken the brunt of the evil, something no one besides the two members of Blu Carraway Investigations should have endured.

To Ariel, Blu said, "You're welcome to sleep here but I'm afraid I don't have air conditioning."

"Yet," Tess added.

"Hell," Crome said, "you can crash at my place."

"That's what I was thinking," Blu said. "You've got four bedrooms, right?"

"Um, yeah," Crome said, obviously not liking where this was heading.

"Ariel can have a room and Harmony and Hope can have the other two."

Normally, Crome would jump at the chance to have three beautiful women staying at his house. Except in this situation, one was a client, one was Blu's daughter, and one already made it clear she would not be going to bed with the biker. Blu would have worried about Ariel staying there by herself which was why he volunteered the other two.

Harmony said, "His house is right on the beach. You'll love it."

"For tonight," Ariel said. "Tomorrow you're calling a guy and getting AC installed here. I'm paying. Call it a signing bonus."

For some reason, clients liked to give Blu things he should already have. Maybe it was out of pity. His first real client in three years got him a new iPhone and a phone number with the last four digits spelling out "BLUE." Crome had ribbed him about it ever since.

Now he had the opportunity for air conditioning. He felt his pride begin to take over until he noticed Tess nodding at him. While he was used to sleeping in the heat, others were not. It was past the time to get this done.

"Hope," Blu said, "set it up for in the morning."

She nodded, a big smile on her face. She was tired of working in the heat of the home office as well.

The men cleaned up the table and did the dishes while the women chatted. Blu put on a pot of coffee, while Pelton and Crome carried in saucers with pieces of pie. By the time the coffee was done, the pie was the perfect temperature, somewhere below atmospheric but not refrigerator cool.

Ariel patted her toned stomach. "I can see that I'm going to have to double up on my crunches. Is there a gym around?"

Blu said, "You get your hair color changed and tomorrow morning I'll pick you up and we'll go to the gym."

Tess said, "You'll get to meet Heath and Roger."

Hope laughed. "Those guys are a riot."

Chapter Five

Crome's house on Folly Beach

Crome had the pleasure of Googling the effects of salt water on hair color, not that he minded. Harmony and Hope were in the process of dyeing Ariel's hair a more traditional hue in the brown family and had already talked themselves into a late-night dip in the ocean. Crome was quite convinced it wouldn't be of the "skinny" kind.

His impression of Ariel was that of a strong business woman, much like their friend Patricia Voyels who recently sold her news empire for eight figures and now traveled abroad. Ariel was down to earth, mostly, knew what she wanted, and understood that money opened a lot of doors.

He'd been hounding his partner to get air conditioning since he'd first moved into his ancestral island home all those years ago. Then Ariel comes to town, makes it a contingency, and tomorrow Blu's going to have AC.

Of course, Crome saw Tess giving Blu the nod. He'd caved in to make her happy which was okay. Tess was good for Blu. She came to him as an open book. There was no hurtful history between them because they'd only known each other a year before they got together. Billie had made the mistake of running away from Blu and cutting off all contact with him, which had really hurt him and pushed him into the arms of another woman. It was her loss and Blu's gain, as far as Crome was concerned. Now if only he could figure out how to get a shot with Harmony.

As if reading his mind, Harmony turned to him and said, "Not a chance."

He gave her a mock salute and a grin. They had a connection that went beyond friendship. The problem was he didn't know what kind of connection.

Hope asked, "What did you find out about saltwater?"

"Inconclusive," he said, using a five-dollar word. "Some say it makes the color brighter and others say you should make sure you rinse it out as soon as possible. There's a shower at the bottom of the back stairs, by the way."

Thursday

The next morning, while Hope was arranging for the air conditioning to be installed and Tess and Harmony went to work, Blu picked up Ariel from Crome's. The orange hair had morphed overnight into a soft brown—very becoming if he had to give his opinion.

She walked out the front door in tight-fitting but low-key colored exercise clothes he'd noticed other women at the gym wear. With the hair color change and semi-conservative attire, she'd blend in. Hopefully, the person handing out the guest pass wouldn't recognize her name.

Turned out, it was his favorite meat-head, Heath. Taller than Blu's six-foot-three with an over-developed upper body, Heath was a monster. Perpetually dark thanks to tanning bed visits, Heath was always getting ready for the next body building competition.

As they approached the front desk, Heath said, "Hammer-time." He looked at Ariel, said, "Hello!" and then at Blu. "How's Tess?"

"She's good," Blu said. "This is my cousin from California."

"I'm just bustin' your chops," Heath said, grinning. To Ariel, he said, "Blu is *the* ladies man."

Ariel said, "For as long as I've known him."

"All I need is a driver's license," he paused, "and your cell number."

Blu said, "She's going to use my home phone while she's in town."

"As long as I can reach her," Heath said, flexing his pecs, alternating sides.

Blu wondered if Heath was aware he did it.

Heath looked at the license, then at Ariel, then back at the license.

"Heath," Blu said. "Before you say anything aloud, I need to tell you this is a job. Don't make a fuss."

"Holy cow," he said, his face flushing. "I mean, wow. I mean, like you're here."

This might have been a mistake, Blu thought.

Heath seemed to gather himself. He said, "Okay. Okay. Wow. I mean. Wow." He took out a sheet of paper.

Blu said, "Can you maybe misspell her name on the form?"

Heath said, "You mean like so no one else knows she's here?"

"That's right. It'll be our little secret."

"Can I tell Roger?"

Roger was his work-out partner. Below six-foot and African American, Roger was the stronger of the two, a real powerhouse.

But Blu wasn't sure who these two fraternized with outside the gym.

He said, "Not yet, okay?"

"Hey," Heath said, "anything for the job, right? I mean I'm part of the team and all."

"That's right."

Heath had helped Blu out on more than one occasion, thanks to his other job being a bouncer to both legal and not-so-legal clubs in the city. Blu had found Heath to be more than willing to give him access to places he would normally not have gotten into. But he never put Heath directly in danger and kept him away from anyone he was tracking.

The giant looked again at Ariel, this time with sheepish, puppy-dog eyes.

Another one struck by the shooting star.

Blu said, "Can you show Daisy around?"

Ariel said, "Daisy?"

"Absolutely," Heath said. "Fantagious!" He hoped over the front desk. "Right this way, Miss Daisy."

Blu said, "I'll be in the weight room. See you here in two hours."

Ariel gave him a "What the hell is this?" look.

He waved his goodbye, went into the changing room, put on shorts, t-shirt, and gym shoes, and hit the weights hard with Roger. Sometimes Roger or Heath would coach him through an ungodly workout. However, today, Heath seemed to be preoccupied with Miss Daisy. Blu caught sight of the two of them, Ariel pushing hard on the Stairmaster and then doing rounds of different exercises in the back room with Heath acting as her trainer. Even distracted by Ariel, Heath would not shortchange her on what he considered a respectable workout. Meatheads or not, Heath and Roger took their work seriously and were knowledgeable on most things fitness-related.

Exactly two hours later, Blu walked out of the changing room freshly showered and in a clean set of clothes.

Ariel's hair was still wet, but she wore a loose tank top over khaki shorts, simple gold jewelry, and tennis shoes. While the tank did not hide her tattoos, she did not look like the pop star C at first glance any more—what she looked like was tired. She sat slumped on the bench in the entrance. "Good workout?" he asked.

Heath was not around.

She said, "Jesus that was tough."

Blu smiled. "Heath and his friend Roger are the best personal trainers that I know."

He helped her up.

"You're not kidding. I pay my guy, well I don't want to tell you what I pay him, but Heath kicked my ass."

They got two steps toward the door when Heath called, "Uh, Miss Daisy?"

She turned around.

Heath handed her a shirt. "Me and Roger signed this for you. I told him it was for a new member."

"That's sweet." She held up the t-shirt and then kissed him on the cheek. "Thanks for the shirt and the killer workout. If you can keep my secret, I'll be back for more."

Heath pumped his pecks. "That's my girl."

They left.

Crome sat on the front porch and watched Blu and Ariel pull up. Blu got out, waved, and looked over at Murder who still stood under the canopy. A Range Rover was parked near the horse and Dick Campbell was connecting an I.V. An extension cord from the back porch powered two fans blowing on the sick animal.

Ariel said, "That is so sad."

"He'll pull through," Blu said, although he didn't sound convincing to himself.

They walked inside the house.

Crome said, "That horse has more chutzpah than the three of us put together. If that don't do it, nothing will. You two look tired."

Ariel opened the refrigerator and stood in front of the open door, eyes closed.

Hope, who'd been sitting at the kitchen table, said, "You must have introduced her to Heath and Roger."

Ariel nodded.

Blu said, "How's the air conditioning coming?"

"They'll be here after lunch. It was the soonest I could get anyone."

"I'm paying," Ariel said. "I want the best."

Hope nodded. "Okay. If that's what you want."

Crome said, "You all could always crash at my pad again

tonight."

Ariel said, "I loved swimming at midnight, but tonight I just want to sleep."

Blu did not want any details on Ariel or Harmony in swimwear. Crome probably had a field day.

"Me, too," Hope said.

Crome gave Blu a slight nod, indicating he wanted them to step outside.

Blu said, "You two stay here. We'll be right back."

The men walked to a small building a hundred feet from the house. It held various garden tools and a small tractor Blu used to move things around the island. At the back side of the building, facing away from the house, Crome said, "I got a location on Teller."

"Oh, yeah?" Blu said.

They both took out vape pens and inhaled.

"Still in Malaysia."

"I want to talk to him."

"I know," Crome said. "Hope's already got you booked on a flight out tonight."

"I only need a day there."

"That's how she's got you booked."

Hope had taken the job as office manager for Blu Carraway Investigations. She handled all the travel arrangements, invoicing, bills, and promotion. The skill she showed in the position convinced her to change her college major to business which was more than okay with Blu. She would be less likely to get shot sitting behind a desk than working jobs with him and Crome.

"Another thing," Crome said.

"Yeah?"

"Word is lately some of the girls Teller rents have been found beaten to death."

"Figures." It was a callous answer only because the news didn't surprise Blu. "Anything else?"

"Yeah," Crome said. "Ariel's rental car could have a tracker on it."

What Crome was saying was the car was in her name and anyone skilled in the art of tracking someone down might get all the way to his island.

"We've got to get rid of it."

"Like right now."

The biker leaned against the building. "I don't want her to think she's on house arrest or anything."

"I get it," Blu said. "We'll get a car for her to drive. I'll put it in the business name."

Crome smiled. "I've already got Jimmy bringing something by."

Blu had to give his partner credit. He was usually a few steps ahead.

"Should be here within an hour," Crome continued. "Three grand—what you've got in petty cash. And I told him it better be decent or I'd feed him to the alligators."

There weren't usually alligators around, per se, but that didn't mean they didn't drop by from time to time.

Speaking of alligators, Ariel wasn't enthused about giving up her rental car until they explained she could be tracked. After that, she volunteered to drive it back to the airport herself after Jimmy showed up with the other car. Some things had a way of working themselves out.

With the rental car dilemma resolved and Ariel the proud owner of a ten-year-old Ford sedan with working AC, Blu turned his attention to who hired the gunmen he killed at the club.

Through the private security grapevine, Crome had learned that Teller and his crew had screwed up another job in Barbados and disappeared. Except, as Blu learned early in his investigation career, no one could ever really disappear, especially someone with a background on file. Someone such as Jack Teller whom Crome had discovered had a known taste for expensive, young, prostitutes from a certain brothel with a menu limited only by the patron's wallet size. The same owners also ran an exclusive casino catering to the elite.

Blu, having been in the business for twenty years, had no idea how Teller could afford such expensive habits. Sure there was money to be made in private security. But not at the level required to support such an addiction, much less two if Teller also gambled.

He flew coach out of Charleston, through Atlanta, and landed in a hot and rainy mess 20 hours later. Ariel reluctantly agreed to stay behind with Hope on the island. The language could certainly be a barrier so he had Hope make arrangements for a translator, another contractor in the business. His name was Ring Anuwat and he met Blu at the Kuala Lumpur International Airport.

Anuwat was part Asian, part Anglo but did not blend in anywhere in Asia because he was six-feet-tall. His height helped him in his profession but not for sleuthing. Always a sharp dresser, Anuwat wore a dark sport coat over a starched white shirt, light khakis, and polished loafers. He kept his full head of hair neatly trimmed and his face clean-shaven.

Blu shook his hand. "Long time, my friend."

Anuwat grinned. "I missed working with someone fun. My clients are mostly stiff-necked suits with too much money."

"Wish I had that problem," Blu said. "I didn't check any bags so I'm ready when you are."

They walked toward the exit.

"Your challenge," Anuwat said, "is convincing Crome a steady paycheck is a good idea."

Another connection Blu had with Anuwat was they fought together in the Middle East along with Crome.

"That about sums it up. So how's Teller? I heard he jumped off the deep end."

Chapter Six

While his partner was jet-setting it to magical Southeast Asia, a place where Crome had spent one hell of a weekend hopped up on reds and strippers and blackjack, he was back on Blu's island watching Ariel sit in a chair under the awning with the sick horse.

She'd taken a liking to Murder who was getting hydration through an I.V. Dink and Doofus had already accepted her as family, giving her a nudge every now and then. She'd made the mistake of feeding them carrots and now had to keep something handy. Horses, particularly those two, could eat quite a bit of just about anything.

According to Ariel, she had no enemies and had no idea who might want her dead. As with most of their clients, she had left some things out which was why Blu was halfway around the world trying to fill the gaps and why Crome had made a few phone calls. Not wanting to tip their hand that Ariel was now a client, Crome danced around the specifics. A few of his contacts already knew about the gunfight in the club in Kuala Lumpur but hadn't linked it to Blu.

Not wanting any embarrassment, the club had released the footage to the local police and had kept quiet about the details to the media. The authorities might have come to the conclusion that Blu was acting in defense of the woman on their own, but Adam Kincaid had greased the right palms. The case was officially closed and the deaths were attributed to infighting amongst the victims. Blu's name was not in the report and the video footage had disappeared.

It paid to have someone like Kincaid as a friend.

Crome took out his vape pen, sucked in a lungful, and exhaled.

Ariel joined Crome on the porch.

He offered his vape pen and a cold bottle of Shiner Bock from a bucket of ice at his feet. She took both, inhaled vapor, returned the pen, and twisted the top off the beer.

They clinked bottles, Crome's third already half gone, and drank.

A small trash can stood against the opposite wall twenty feet away. Ariel flung the cap and made the shot into the can.

Crome said, "Show off."

"You're just upset I beat you at the range."

Pops had talked them into a little friendly competition, except it was impossible for competitive people to keep anything challenging from getting out of hand. Ariel had won by a single shot.

Of course, as Crome was about to nail the bull's eye, Ariel had raised her shirt exposing her bra. He missed the target altogether.

Some, okay most, would call that cheating. But he recognized it as doing whatever it took to win and he respected that. This was no timid fawn they had here. Ariel was as tough as they came. He was even more smitten with her.

Friday morning, Kuala Lumpur, Malaysia

Blu opened his eyes and realized immediately he did not know where he was. His mouth had the taste of vomit and his skin stuck to the floor. Peeling his cheek and then his arms off the sticky residue adhering him to the cold tiles, he raised himself up and checked the time—he had four hours to make his return flight. His gut told him not to miss it. As his mind slowly cleared the fog out of itself, he began to remember things like riding in the car with Anuwat and stopping at a strip club where Teller was supposed to be. That was the last thing he remembered.

Blu looked around the room. It was filthy and not air conditioned. He stumbled through the dirtiest kitchen he had seen in a long time and found the bathroom which might have been even dirtier. After relieving himself in a toilet that wouldn't flush, he turned and spotted a dead Asian man in the bathtub with a bullet hole in his forehead. His blank eyes stared into nothing.

Now he was positive he had to make his flight. Fielding questions from the local police with answers he didn't have about how a dead man ended up dead in the same apartment Blu found himself was not something he wanted.

Instead, he reached down inside his left boot. If traveling the world had taught him anything, it was to be prepared. That was why he kept two passports. A fake one that he carried in his pockets and the real one he stashed in the secret pocket inside his Dr. Marten boot after he cleared customs but before he'd met Anuwat. Anyone wishing to steal a passport, or more specific—his passport, would find the fake one and not think anything about its authenticity.

With his real passport accounted for, Blu looked in the mirror and found himself in need of a shower. Dirt was smeared on his face and his clothes were filthy.

None of that mattered. What he needed was to get to the airport immediately.

He checked his own pockets and found them empty. Looking at himself in the mirror again, he spotted the dead man's foot sticking over the rim of the tub.

Blu checked the dead man's pockets and found local currency equivalent to about five-hundred U.S. dollars. A more thorough search netted a pack of matches.

Blu stuck the money in his own pockets.

He reached around the man's waist and retrieved a nine millimeter with one round missing and now his own prints on it. There was a good chance things would go south between now and his flight leaving the tarmac in three and a half hours.

He ran water in the tap, found it to be clearer than he expected, and rinsed his face and arms. Not daring to taste it and end up with God knew what kind of parasite or stomach bug, he rinsed his hair and felt better.

There were no clean towels but he managed to shake himself mostly dry.

Looking out a grimy window, he found he was on an upper floor. He cracked open the door and peeked out. An empty concrete hall with rusty metal rails and steps stared back. Easing the door open more, he found more of the hallway empty of people but full of trash.

He slipped out and double-timed it to the nearest stairwell. Before barreling down the stairs, he checked to make sure it was clear. The basic structure of the building was in bad shape with deep cracks in the walls and concrete and a lot of dirt. In the US the building would be condemned. Maybe it was here also.

Blu didn't know and couldn't focus on that now. He needed to stay on task which was to get to the airport.

Unlike the building, the street in front of it was busy. And at six-foot-three, Blu was not inconspicuous. The locals did not hide their surprise at seeing the tall, filthy, tan-skinned man among them. As luck would have it, a grimy taxi turned onto the street.

Blu flagged it down and got in the backseat.

The driver, a young man with a thin mustache, said in English, "You look like hell."

"Take me to the airport."

"Sure thing. What happened to you?"

Blu rested his head back. "Just drive, would ya?"

"Sure thing, boss."

His English was better than some South Carolinians back home.

Blu must have drifted off because he awoke to a car beside them honking.

The kid driver yelled something that sounded like local profanity, raised his hands, and then accelerated around a stalled bus.

"Is there a place I can get a quick shower and change of clothes," Blu asked.

The kid said, "I know a place. You pay and I hook you up."

Blu showed the kid the wad of local currency. "And I need some bottles of drinking water."

The kid's eyes fixed on the rearview mirror and the wad of money Blu held and he almost rear-ended a car. After missing the car by millimeters, he looked back again. "You got it!"

By his watch, a Timex Blu used while traveling instead of his father's vintage Rolex, he still had almost three hours left. The kid drove him down a side street and double parked next to a doorway where several young women in various degrees of tight clothing stood.

"I wanted a shower and water, not my ashes hauled. Jesus."

"Ashes hauled?" the kid asked. "What does that mean?" He looked at the women. "Oh, I know what you asked for. Come on."

Blu got out. The kid left his car double parked and led the way inside.

Several women pawed at Blu as he did his best to follow the kid.

Deep inside the building, the kid stopped beside an older, bosomy woman who had to be the Madame—were they all like that?—and turned to Blu. "Money."

Blu handed him about a hundred dollars.

The kid turned to the woman and rattled off a bunch of words Blu would never understand.

He turned back to Blu. "More money."

Blu handed him another hundred. "That's it or I leave."

The kid said, "Okay, follow her. She will take you."

"I want a private room."

"You got it. I'll wait. Oh, and mister?"

Blu turned back to him. "Yeah?"

"I get the rest of the money or I leave you here."

"You got it."

The Madame took him down a narrow corridor with many doors and opened the last one. Inside the room were two young women. Each held a towel and gave him a sheepish grin. The room was tiled and had a shower in the corner, a sink, and a commode. He took the towels and told the women to leave. They didn't seem to understand what he was saying so he opened the door and pointed.

They got the hint and exited.

The door had a lock, a flimsy slide, but it would prevent someone from sneaking in. They would have to give the door a hard shove to get past the slide.

He removed his clothes, turned on the water, slid his passport and money inside the towel folds, and got in the shower. Because time was short, he didn't waste any as he lathered up and rinsed off. By his count, it took two minutes, tops.

He got out and dried himself off with one of the towels.

There was a knock.

Through the door, the taxi driver said, "I've got some clothes. Time to go."

Blu opened the door wide enough to collect the garments and shut the door again.

There were generic pairs of underwear and socks, Levi's jeans, and an olive-colored t-shirt. They were all clean and they fit, more or less, and he was ready to go.

He opened the door.

The driver nodded and walked away.

Blu followed out to the still double parked taxi. They got in and the driver drove like a crazier version of Brack Pelton to the airport.

At the departures drop-off, Blu gave the driver the rest of the money. "Thanks. Give me a card. If I have to return, you're my guy."

That seemed to make the young man happy. He handed Blu a card. "See you when I see you."

*   *   *

Inside the airport Blu felt someone's eyes on him, but he couldn't tell who it was. He did what he always did in situations like this, found the restroom and went inside. His flight was still an hour from boarding. So as not to look like he was stalling, Blu proceeded to spend time in front of the mirror combing his short-cropped hair, checking his face out, and smoothing out the wrinkles in his clothes.

People not used to surveillance got impatient. It was only a matter of time before they came looking for him.

Several Asian men entered the restroom but didn't seem to notice him as they headed for the urinals or the stalls. It was the sixth visitor that walked in, looking annoyed, spotted him standing in front of the mirror, paused as if trying to decide what to do, and headed toward the stalls.

Blu followed him around the corner.

When the man entered a stall, Blu popped him hard across the back of the neck, knocking him out. The man collapsed and Blu caught him, saying, "You okay, man? Here, you better sit down." He turned him around, sat him on the toilet and closed the door behind him.

The stall doors and walls went to the floor so there was privacy, which Blu needed so he could go through the man's pockets.

He came up with a cell phone, identification, and a nine millimeter pistol. The ID and phone went into his own pockets. He wiped his prints off this gun and the one he got from the dead guy in the dirty apartment, wrapped them in toilet paper, exited the stall while making sure to shut the door behind him, walked out of the restroom, and tossed the wrapped guns in a waste bin.

His plane was now boarding. He walked up to the ticket counter, got his boarding pass, made it through two security check points, and got to his seat with no other issues.

As the plane backed away from the gate, the phone from the

man in the restroom buzzed. Blu hit the accept button and listened. Someone spoke in a language Blu did not recognize but assumed was the local tongue.

He answered with, "Yo."

There was a pause, and then in fairly clean English, the voice said, "What have you done with Choen?"

"He didn't practice proper urinal etiquette. You should tell him to keep his eyes on his own package while relieving himself."

"I do not understand."

"Sure you do," Blu said. "I'm not sure how he thought he was going to get through security with a nine millimeter on him. I helped him get rid of it."

Blu opened the man's wallet, found a badge, and said, "Then again, Officer Peepers would probably be allowed through with the firearm."

"You have made a grave mistake."

"Tell you what," Blu said, "why don't you find me and tell that to my face."

"We have ways."

"And I have—"

Blu was interrupted by the flight attendant who told him he needed to end the call and turn off his phone.

"No problem," he said to her. Into the phone, he said, "Gotta go. Miss you already."

He ended the call, pulled the Sim card out, and slipped the phone in the pocket of the seat in front of him.

The plane took off and Blu fell fast asleep almost as soon as the wheels left the ground.

Chapter Seven

"You got set up," Crome said, thinking he was going to handle Anuwat personally when this job was all done.

He and Blu sat on Blu's back porch. Blu was filling him in on how he made it out of Malaysia.

Blu said, "The guy I popped in the bathroom had a badge. I'm just glad to be back home. Something's wrong with this situation and I'm not sure what we're into."

"I can tell you what you're into," said Ariel as she exited the house holding two cups of coffee by the handles. She set them down for the men and went back inside.

She'd caught them off guard. The last time Crome checked on her, which was about fifteen minutes ago, she was fast asleep on the couch.

Ariel returned with a cup of coffee for herself and sat at the table with them. "God it's beautiful here. And I don't care that I have to bathe in bug spray to enjoy it."

Crome said, "You gonna finish your statement or what?"

"Sorry," she said. "I had a deal that fell through. It was a lot of money and some investors got hosed."

"You screwed them over?" Crome asked.

"My manager at the time did." She took a sip of her coffee. "He's no longer my manager."

"And you didn't think of this before?" Blu asked.

"That's the business," she said. "And with the amount of money we're talking about, there are bound to be winners and losers."

"Yeah, but you're the winner," Crome said. "That makes you a target."

"I'm not always a winner," she said. "That same manager also swiped millions of my blood, sweat, and tears dollars. I hate his guts."

Crome looked at Blu. Millions.

It was more than they'd personally see in their lifetimes and here this twenty-seven-year-old was talking about it like a bad basketball bet.

Blu said, "Ariel, you mind writing down every bad deal you can think of?"

"I'm not sure I want to do that without my lawyer involved," she said.

"We'll sign a confidentiality agreement with you," Blu said. "In fact, we should take care of the contract as well."

"What we need," Crome said, "is as much access as you can give us into your life."

"Why would I want to do that?" she asked, suddenly sitting back in her chair all guarded up with hands across her chest.

"Because someone wants you dead," Blu said.

"Not just dead," Crome said. "Gunned down like a mob hit."

In Blu's mind, the story she told them did not help the situation at all. The money was more than enough to kill for. Someone benefited and someone lost. In murder cases, love or money were the sole logical reasons. There were always crazies killing for their gods or just because they liked the power that taking someone innocent down gave them.

This was no crazy they were dealing with. This was millions of dollars worth of motive. And whoever got burned didn't care about the money any more. They cared about getting even, or at least making someone pay for their loss.

This reminded Blu to ask, "What's the name of your ex-manager?"

"Why?" she asked.

As if reading Blu's mind, Crome said, "We need to find out if he's still alive."

It was apparent to Blu that Ariel did not grasp the situation and when their conversation steered toward educating her on how big of a problem she had, she failed to accept the reality.

She had already moved onto the next topic. "I saw that you have a boat. Can we go for a ride?"

The eighteen-foot Sea Ray cut a trench through the waves at thirty knots. Two hundred horsepower was overkill for the craft, but Blu liked it that way.

Ariel sat on the bow, the wind blowing her brown hair back, sunglasses protecting her eyes from the rushing air. The water was surprisingly calm, the surf breaking in small crests.

Blu saw movement to their right and pointed for Ariel to see three dolphins swimming parallel to them, their top speed about a tenth of what the boat was running. He eased off the throttle and their speed slowed as they approached the Intracoastal Waterway. The I.C.W. traveled from Boston all the way down to Florida. Every year, many a retiree sailed it, crossing off a bucket list item and stopping in Charleston along the way.

Capers Island was an uninhabited barrier island and State Heritage Preserve located north of the Isle of Palms. It had a nice, sandy surf populated by bleached tree stumps and was called Bone-yard Beach. At this time of day, they were the only ones there. Blu cut the motor and raised it out of the water as the boat slid to a stop on the beach. Ariel helped anchor the boat and they walked the surf.

She said, "Outside of the major cities, California is beautiful, especially driving up the coast to Carmel. We don't have anything like this. I mean, we're the only ones here right now." She turned to Blu. "You didn't bring me here to kill me, did you?"

Given her current circumstances, Blu forgave the question. "Not today. It's easier to guard you when there's no one else around."

She smiled. "You're a sweetheart. I don't know what would have happened if you hadn't been there for me." Her smile left. "I can't stop thinking about Jesse."

The dead bartender in the club—definitely an innocent just trying to do his job. This was healthy for her. She needed to be scared. People were surely out to get some kind of revenge on her or prevent her from doing something they didn't want.

Resting a head on his shoulder, she began to cry. It was the first time he'd seen her shell crack. He let her get it out, putting an arm around her in a fatherly gesture.

"So," she said, wiping her eyes after half a dozen sobs, "what do we do now?"

"You let me buy you lunch."

Backing away slightly, she said, "I thought you wanted to keep me away from other people."

"Don't worry," he said. "I know the owner of the restaurant. He's got guns stashed all over the place. Nothing bad will happen there."

She said, "My life is in your hands."

The response told him three things: Ariel had finally realized how dangerous her situation was, she trusted him, and her interest in him was purely professional. He needed all three from her.

Someone like Crome might not appreciate the third, but Blu had already made the mistake of getting involved with a client in the past. It made the job much harder than it needed to be and clouded his judgment.

He helped her get back in the boat, pulled the anchor, and pushed it off the sand. When it was free-floating, he hopped in, lowered the motor, started it up, and sped away.

The Isle of Palms marina was a class act. Blu spotted a prime slip and docked and he and Ariel rode on the back seat of a Pirate's Cove bar and grill golf cart to the restaurant.

They walked up the front steps and entered the pirate-themed establishment.

Right away, Ariel spotted the bullet holes Pelton refused to patch. Most tourists got their picture taken with them.

She said, "Can you take my picture here?"

Holding his phone out, Blu said, "Don't go and post it."

"Very funny," she said. "I won't."

Pelton, or one of his staff, had marked an X on the floor for where to stand to get the best pic. Ariel stood on the X and handed Blu her phone. He took the photo.

Paige greeted them, mouthing, "Oh my God. It's her."

Blu shook his head.

Lucky for them, Paige turned to him and soft-punched his arm. "Brack told me not to cause a scene. I'm not stupid. But I would love an autograph."

Ariel introduced herself to Paige. "Of course."

"In your office," Blu said.

Paige said. "I downloaded all your albums. But I went out and bought the disks as soon as I heard you were in town."

Ariel turned to Blu. "I love this girl."

The music industry, like everything else, was all about the money—ticket sales, album downloads, CD purchases. He'd even seen vinyl records make a comeback. While he'd migrated from cassettes in the eighties to CDs in the nineties, he hadn't really moved on from there. Hope had helped him download some hard-to-find tracks, but he still preferred the vintage media.

In fact, his home stereo was a thirty-year-old McIntosh unit that still worked perfectly. Top of the line in 1988, he picked it up at an estate sale a few years ago for pennies on the dollar.

Paige said, "The office is this way. And of course, order anything you want off the menu on me. I'm honored you're here and sorry it isn't under better circumstances."

Ariel hugged her. "Thanks so much."

They entered Brack's makeshift office better described as organized chaos. Paige had done her best to keep the piles low. Apparently Brack was less hopeless than the previous owner, his uncle, when it came to neatness. But he wasn't exactly what Blu would call rigid.

The bar used to be a real dive, but Paige and Brack had turned it into a nice place with some staged rough edges. Tourists visited places with good reviews and passing health inspection scores. Under the previous owner, Brack's uncle, it had neither.

Brack, sitting behind a desk covered with stacks of papers, stood and greeted them.

Paige shut the door.

Shelby introduced himself to Ariel again, who forgot all about why she was there and was rolling around on the floor with the mutt within seconds. Such was the magnetic attraction the dog had on any female.

Paige, Pelton and Blu watched the two-time Grammy-winning artist worth a fortune play-wrestling with the dog with not a care in the world.

After an extended period of time, Blu cleared his throat.

Ariel snapped out of Shelby's trance. "Sorry, he's just so cute."

"Tell me about it," Paige said.

Blu said, "I'm not sure what brings more people through the doors, Brack's antics or Shelby's reputation."

"For me it would be this guy here," Ariel said, standing but still petting Shelby. "You wanted me to autograph some CD's?"

Paige had a stack of Ariel's albums on disk, apparently all of them.

Ariel flipped through them. "You want me to sign them to you?"

Paige nodded, a girlish grin pasted on her face.

Brack said, "We also got posters of you for the bars, if you're so inclined. I won't hang them up until Blu and Crome solve all your problems."

Blu wondered how a poster of the pop star would fit the pirate theme, but one of C's album covers was of her standing on the deck of a yacht in swimwear and a buccaneer's hat with an eye patch and a parrot on her shoulder. With her orange hair and tats, it worked. Most any other artist couldn't pull it off like Ariel.

With the autographing duties accomplished, Blu led her to a

table on the back deck with a good view of the Atlantic. The ocean always calmed him. To change up his workout routine, he sometimes would come here and swim out as far as he could until his smoker's lungs began to scream, pushed another thirty seconds, and then swam back. By the end, he was physically exhausted but mentally refreshed. There was a public changing area with showers to hose off the salt and sand. If he needed to clear his mind, it worked every time.

Ariel ordered a "Harmony" sandwich, grilled chicken with avocado named after the actual Harmony Childs, along with a cup of "Blu" Crab Soup. The soup had been a recent addition to the menu and one Blu thought Pelton had added mainly to needle him.

Blu ordered the soup—sometimes he had to roll with the punches—and an Atomic Burger that had a heap of jalapeños and Heinz hot ketchup, the spicier the better.

He introduced Ariel to another southern staple, sweet tea. When the drinks arrived, he squeezed three lemon wedges in each glass.

She took a sip and said, "I think my teeth just started to rot from all the sugar."

"That means it's just right," he said.

While they waited for their food, Blu noticed Pelton standing behind the bar keeping an eye on the front door. For all his quirks, and there were many, Pelton was a loyal friend and a good wingman when Blu needed one, and was the only man he had ever seen not back down to Crome which said a lot.

Their food came and they ate, Shelby sitting at Ariel's feet.

She tried to give him part of her sandwich but he wouldn't touch it.

Blu said, "Don't take it personally. He's trained to only accept food from certain people."

Giving the dog another pat on the head, she said, "I really hate that it's taken a threat on my life to force me into this mini-vacation."

"We can't relax just yet," Blu said. "We've still got a lot of work to do."

Crome got a call while he waited as the bike shop serviced his custom Harley. The number was not in his call log and came from "unknown."

"Yo," he said, deciding to risk it given that it could be linked to the Ariel job.

"Mick."

Crome recognized the voice. It was an old acquaintance, one he'd hoped never to hear from again—for a lot of reasons.

"Thomas, what's up?"

"Tell me Blu wasn't in Malaysia two days ago."

"Okay," Crome said, "Blu wasn't in Malaysia two days ago. Why?"

"Because there are five dead bodies and a description of a suspect."

"Blu's not dead," Crome said, although he had a hunch Thomas already knew that.

His hunch was confirmed when Thomas said, "He fits the description of the suspect."

Crome didn't reply.

Thomas said, "What I'm saying is Blu's name has already been floated to the authorities over there. They're looking for him."

"How hard?" Crome asked, meaning how important was it to the local police that they find and question Blu.

"Top priority," Thomas said. "One of the bodies was a cop."

The guy from the airport, although Blu said he didn't kill him.

"How'd they die?" Crome asked.

"Gunshot wounds."

"All of them?"

"Yes."

Blu only mentioned the one dead guy with the hole in his head and the cop he beat up in the bathroom. Something wasn't adding up.

Thomas continued, "From the fact that you haven't already hung up or told me to piss off, I'd say this information is important to you."

"Gee, Thomas," Crome said, "you tell me the authorities are looking for Blu about five murders and then wonder why I haven't hung up yet. What kind of game are you playing?"

"No game. I caught wind of it and thought you'd like to know Also, you got about seventy-two hours before hell comes looking. Ninety-six if you're lucky."

"Thanks. Message received." Crome hung up.

Chapter Eight

Crome gassed up his Harley and called Blu. It wasn't a conversation he wanted to have.

Blu answered with, "Where are you?"

"On my way back to your house. We gotta talk."

"Okay."

Crome took a hit on his vape pen and exhaled. "They haven't linked you to Ariel yet but it's only a matter of time."

"Who's they?"

"Not sure, but that extra trip back to Southeast Asia wasn't a good idea."

"Who's your source?"

This was the question causing him heartburn at the moment. Thomas was the guy who got Crome set up with the mob in collections during his three year sabbatical from Blu Carraway Investigations. He was also the guy who always seemed to know more than he should. Crome's source was tied in to the old Costa Nostra, not the fresh crop of degenerates from Russia who thought of Americans as lambs for the slaughter. The Eastern bloc mobsters cared even less about human life than the Italians and gutted men for amusement. Crome hated them and had taken satisfaction in ridding the earth of more than a few in his time.

"A guy I know in Key West."

"I'm not going to ask how you know him, Crome."

"Better you don't," he replied.

"How long do we have before it all goes to pot?" Blu asked.

Inhaling more vapor, Crome said, "Seventy-two hours. Ninety-six, tops."

"Three days. I'll meet you at my house. We need to wrap this up."

"On my way."

Blu ended the call with Crome. While he wasn't happy about it, he'd suspected something like this was going to happen, especially since he had the Malaysian cop's wallet. His next step was to call his lawyer.

Lester Brogan was a short and stocky bald man about Blu's age who drove an Aston Martin. He was not cheap, but, in Blu's opinion, worth every penny. A real live shark of an attorney who'd also helped Brack Pelton out of a jam at one time.

Blu set up an appointment with Brogan's secretary.

Standing on Blu's front porch, both of them watching the horses stand by Murder under the canopy, Tess almost lost her balance when he told her about the seventy-two hour window. Not because of concern for him, not really. He knew her well enough to recognize the glint of a big story in her eye. This would be the biggest. A worldwide pop star being hunted down possibly by organized crime over millions of dollars.

"What can I do to help?" she asked. Again as much if not more for the story than concern for him or Ariel.

He knew this and still found himself falling more for her every day. At first, he'd tried to resist, keeping it purely physical—Tess was a beauty in any man's eyes. But she was faithful, didn't play games, and didn't waver from whom he knew her to be. Her dedication to her job could get in the way of what was normally a caring nature, but he understood how she thought and encouraged her to be herself.

She'd done the same for him. He had his daughter, his business, his partner, his island, and his horses. She didn't ask him to change anything. She spent nights at his house and tried to insist on paying when they went out. He wouldn't let her pay, of course, so she brought him gifts. As they spent more and more time together, the gifts got more personal.

She handed him a small gift-bag but he had trouble not looking at her, a band keeping her blonde hair pulled back and out of her face, sunglasses covering her eyes, white v-neck t-shirt, khaki shorts, and sandals. And a thick layer of bug repellant.

He reached in and pulled out a CD. It was a hard-to-get vintage New Order album. And it wasn't something she particularly enjoyed listening to.

"How'd you find this?" he asked.

"I have my ways." She kissed him. "So we have three days before Charleston blows up?"

"Yes."

"I'm in," she said. "Heck, I owe Ariel for getting the AC installed in your house. I was afraid we'd have to go all season without it, and I gotta tell you I wasn't looking forward to that."

He hugged her. "I know. I'm sorry."

She kissed his cheek. "No you're not. It's who you are. I accepted that already. I'm just glad we have air now."

Ariel walked out the front door, said, "Whoops!" and turned to retreat.

Tess said, "Your ears must have been burning. We were just talking about you."

"Uh oh," Ariel said, smiling. "Good things, I hope."

Blu said, "She's glad you got the AC installed."

"Girl," Ariel said, "you must love him. He's gorgeous but I don't think that's enough to live without air."

Neither Blu nor Tess had used the "L" word although he found himself heading in that direction.

While he hid his true feelings, it was refreshing to feel Tess tighten her hug, kiss him on the cheek again, and say, "She's right. Good thing you've got more than your looks going for you, baby."

Catastrophe averted, he patted her bottom, "You, too."

"Don't start something you can't finish," she said.

Ariel said, "How about if I drive into town and give you two some alone time."

Before Blu could say anything, Tess said, "He gets a rain check. You aren't going anywhere by yourself." She pushed away. "Time to get back to work."

"What did she give you?" Ariel asked.

Blu showed her.

Ariel took the disk. "Everybody says they like Joy Division better, but I prefer New Order."

"So you've heard of them?" Tess asked.

"Of course," she said. "It's my job, even the old stuff like this."

"Ouch," Blu said.

The women laughed.

Blu didn't think it was that funny.

Lucky for him, the rumble of Crome's bike distracted them.

Dink and Doofus turned but didn't leave Murder's side.

Crome idled up, dropped his kickstand, and leaned his bike on it. He pulled a paper sack from his saddle bag and walked over to the entire herd of horses standing around Murder and handed all seven of them carrots. Then he stroked Murder's mane and whispered something in his ear. The horse didn't back away, still under the weather.

For the first time since he found the horse on the ground, Blu thought he saw Murder's ear twitch as if some of the old wildness was returning.

Crome walked toward Blu and the women, balling up the empty bag.

Ariel asked, "What did you say to him?"

With a smile, Crome said, "That's between me and him. He'll make it. I can feel it."

Blu wasn't so sure. The last time the vet had stopped by, the news wasn't any better.

Tess said, "So we have three days?"

The men looked at her and then Ariel.

Ariel said, "Three days until what?"

Blu said, "Until word gets to the wrong people that you're here. But that's just a guess."

Running her hands through her colored hair, combing it back off her face, Ariel said, "I've been so selfish and now you're all in danger because of me."

"Are you kidding?" Tess said. "You made their summer."

"I don't understand."

"You think it was just luck that my boyfriend got you out of that place? No, ma'am. He's that good. And this is their specialty. They'll find out who's trying to do you harm and punch their ticket."

"Jesus, Tess," Crome said. "You make it sound like we enjoy violence."

Tess raised an eyebrow at him.

"Who'm I kidding?" Crome asked, pulling out his vape pen. "Of course we do."

"Now that we have that settled," Blu said, "I'd rather they didn't end up on my island. Not with Murder in the shape he's in."

"I agree," Crome said. "We gotta get back to work."

Crome boarded the plane for California with two objectives: to find out who in the entertainment industry out there wanted Ariel dead and, if possible, eliminate the threat. It wasn't exactly his forte, but he wasn't worried about the job.

What worried Crome was his travel partner.

Harmony took the seat next to him. "I still can't believe I had to use my miles to get us bumped to business class. When we get back, Blu and I are going to have a chat."

"You know," Crome said, stretching out, "when we're on a job, we should try not to make spectacles of ourselves."

They had a history, him and her. She liked to toy with him, be all flirty and such. He did his best not to let her have too much control over him with her feminine wiles. Like the time when she got mad that he'd gone around her to get some information a few years back, showed her tail, and got shot for it. Since then, they'd had this love-hate thing going on—he loved her and she hated herself for caring about him.

This California trip was exactly not what the doctor had ordered. But, the job required it. Blu had rationalized with him that while Crome was really good at working in the shadows and fringes of society, they needed someone good working in the light. That person was Harmony.

Even Crome couldn't argue with the logic. He just didn't like having to be responsible for her wellbeing. Especially since their weapons were in their checked bags.

Harmony ordered two glasses of champagne and they toasted to their endeavor. It didn't help that she wore a tight shirt and short skirt and made him feel every bit of the twenty years between them.

At the Atlanta airport while they'd waited for their connection seated at one of the bars, some Peckerwood tried to cut Crome out and make a pass at her. She politely informed the intruder that Crome was five seconds away from snapping the man's neck. The man looked at Crome, who gave him a maniacal grin in return. After that, no one seemed to bother them.

In business class on the plane, Harmony sipped her champagne. "You think Ariel's legit?"

"I do," he said. "And not because you think I have the hots for her."

"Okay," she said. "Then why?"

"The guys with the machine guns that Blu took care of."

"That whole Asian thing is disturbing."

The flight attendant, a woman Crome's age named Norma, came by to collect the glasses because they were about to take off.

Crome buckled his seat belt. "Someone set up Blu and they almost took him out."

As the plane lifted off the runway and leveled at thirty thousand feet, he fell asleep thinking about revenge on their enemies.

Harmony nudged him awake. It felt like he'd just gone under until he looked at his phone and saw he'd been out for an hour and they were about to serve the meal.

He ordered a beer from Norma and Harmony got a glass of white wine to go with the fish dinner. Norma brought the drinks, the wine in a stemmed glass and a can of Heineken.

They ate in silence, the food certainly better than anything Crome had in what Harmony called "boot-class" which was all the seats behind them. What she didn't finish of her meal, she offered to him. It had been a while since he'd eaten so he gladly accepted.

Afterward, they chatted mostly about places they liked to visit.

He caught himself reminiscing about Key West more than once. There was something about that town that got to him. The trips from there to Havana in drug runner go-fast boats, the marathon drunks that lasted three days, and the total lack of responsibility.

During his three year sabbatical in Key West, Crome did special jobs for one of the top east coast mobsters who lived there. The vig—interest on the loan—was the vig, whether the debtor lived in the same city as their loan shark or not. Payment was expected. When a particular out-of-state gambler began missing payments to the Key West mob boss holding the markers, Crome was contracted to go and collect ten grand or ten fingers.

He came back with nine and one and a steady job for the next two years where he personally managed to pocket three-hundred-thousand-dollars now sitting in a bank in the Caymans—his retirement fund.

Harmony preferred Hawaii. Her plan was to marry a rich guy, retire, kill him off—just kidding, and move there forever.

The conversation tapered off and they soon donned ear buds to take advantage of the in-flight entertainment. Crome settled on music, jumping between classic rock and country, while he saw Harmony load a movie.

Chapter Nine

Landing in LAX, it didn't take Crome long to decide there were just too many people in California.

At the car rental agency, they picked up the vehicles Hope had arranged for them. Harmony got a convertible Mustang while Crome received a Tahoe.

With different tasks at hand, they said their goodbyes and agreed to meet back at the hotel for dinner. Hope arranged for a suite for them to share as they would need space to spread out and work.

The first thing Crome did while exiting the airport was take out his vape pen and replenish his internal nicotine supply. He had a source to meet on the Sunset Strip, a place where he would actually fit in as well as he did his favorite dive bar in Myrtle Beach.

The drive gave him time to plan things out. An extra hour stuck in traffic allowed him to listen to Pink Floyd's "Dark Side of the Moon" album twice while he crawled along. He was glad he'd stopped at the first drive-thru coffee shop he'd come across, although by the end he was ready for a men's room.

California was a lot different from the lowcountry of South Carolina. Charleston embraced its southern heritage. Los Angeles represented urban sprawl and everything that came with it. Crome didn't have to worry about mosquitoes and sand flies on the west coast, but a parasitic element did exist here although more of the two-legged kind.

Crome found a parking spot and backed the truck in.

He got out, pressed the lock button on the key fob, and figured out where he was in relation to where he needed to be.

Key West might be his spiritual home, but he could live on Sunset Boulevard. His wardrobe was functional—leather and jeans to help prevent road rash and burns from the exhaust pipe of his bike, boots to keep his feet from getting torn up, and sunglasses to protect his eyes from bugs. These people here on the other side of the country wore things to get themselves noticed. A brand of one-upmanship had formed. In this mixture of misguided type-A personalities, Crome found himself invisible. What a treat!

His contact was an old Army friend from the nineties. Her name was Colette. Curly, shoulder-length blonde hair crowned an almost six-foot-figure. She smoked Marlboros and could beat up most men, and now she was a detective for the LA police department.

Crome spotted her sipping coffee at a table in front of the outdoor café where they'd arranged to meet.

He walked up. "Hey, Gorgeous."

She and Crome also had a fling back in the day. It had ended badly—she wanted a marriage proposal and he wanted a Harley-Davidson. He got what he wanted and she didn't.

She looked at him. "Hey, yourself."

"I been in traffic for two hours," he said. "Give me a minute to take a leak and I'll be right back."

"Still the charmer," she said.

He found the restroom, relieved himself, and returned. The seat across from her had a steaming cup of Joe ready for him.

"You remembered," he said.

"It was either that or beer but I figured this was business so I went with the coffee." She looked him over. "Aside from your weathered face, you haven't changed a bit, Mick. For good and bad."

To him she looked better than she had in her twenties. She wore her life experience in the confidence she exuded. "You look great, Babe."

Hooking an arm over the back of her chair, she said, "That line worked back then. It doesn't work now. What do you want?"

"Can I vape here?"

She picked up a lit cigarette from the ash tray on the table. "Won't bother me."

He took a hard hit off the pen and exhaled. "Me and Blu are still in business."

"Wow," she said. "I can't believe you would commit to anything."

"I have my moments," he said. "Anyway, we have this client. She's in entertainment and someone wants her dead. She thinks it's because of some big deal that fell through. Who do I need to talk to?"

"You could have asked me this over the phone," she said.

Crome always suspected he had a thick head. This conversation proved he did. Colette was still harboring some hurt from the past and this meeting wasn't helping. What was the saying? Hell hath no fury...

Thinking fast, he came up with, "I been working a twelve-step. Finally kicked the reds. So I wanted to apologize for being a douche bag to you. You didn't deserve all that."

Her blue eyes took his measure.

And apparently came up short.

"You really haven't changed," she said. "I know all your tells. Apology accepted, but you just made most of that up."

He didn't see a wedding ring, but detectives tended not to wear jewelry so he wasn't sure. He did confirm she had a Glock clipped to her belt underneath a sport coat. Back in the day, she was a crack shot. Much like her looks, he bet she improved her marksmanship with time.

"I was being honest about the reds," he said. "How about after I finish my business here I buy you a steak dinner sometime?"

"How about you keep it in your pants, Romeo?"

It might have been a false positive, but he thought he saw her quench a grin.

"So what have you got for me?"

"Blake Townley," she said. "If there's a deal to screw someone in this town, he's holding the driver."

The first thing Harmony did was call up an old boyfriend. There wasn't a major city in the country she didn't have at least one ex. Lucky for her, the one in LA hadn't turned into a stalker after she'd dumped him. He actually agreed to meet with her.

The last time she'd seen him, he'd been a starving law student. But she knew then he was going places. It was just that she was also going places, just not in the same direction.

The law office where her ex worked took up the top three floors of a downtown high-rise. She walked in wearing an outfit she'd just purchased on Rodeo, telling herself it was a business expense and Blu Carraway Investigations, and Ariel, would be picking up the tab.

And she looked stunning, if she had to say so herself.

Sherman Heywood, the ex, greeted her in the lobby, his eyes taking her measure several times. Two other men in suits almost knocked over a secretary as they gawked.

Sherman gave her a hug and peck on the cheek. "So good to see you, Harmony."

The greeting gave her pause. She didn't expect him to be so handsome in his suit and tie and California tan. And she certainly didn't expect such a warm reception.

"You look great!" she blurted out, and then silently cursed herself.

"Thanks," he said. "You, too."

They stepped back.

She said, "Can we go somewhere and talk? Is now a good time?"

"There's a coffee shop in the lobby," he said. "I've got a break between clients. We can go there."

He led her to the elevators. As they rode down to the ground floor, he said, "I have to confess I've been following your career online."

She grinned. "E-stalking me?"

"Yep."

"Do tell," she said.

"Were you really kidnapped last year?" he asked. "And shot before that?"

She had been both of those things. Her way of dealing with the crap life threw at her was to write about it and post video news segments. Most of her experiences were on record. Most, but not all. Like her romantic life.

Currently she was seeing two men in Charleston. Nothing serious, just dinners and sleepovers mostly. She wasn't sure if the two men knew about each other, but she didn't really care. She made no bones about commitment. It wasn't in the cards for her at the moment.

In answer to his questions, she said, "You are following me, aren't you?"

They walked to the counter and she let him pay for a venti, double shot, no-fat frappucino.

She said, "I'd be in trouble if there was a Starbucks downstairs from my office."

"You have an office?" he said as he carried their drinks to a table in the corner by the windows. "Somehow I pictured you always on the go."

"True," she said. "I have a nook in my apartment where I work. Otherwise, I'm out."

"And your partner, Tess?"

"Yeah?" she asked, not sure what he meant.

"How did you two team up? I mean, you two complement each other well."

She took a sip of her drink. "It was either work together or compete. We thought it was easier to bury the hatchet and conquer Charleston together."

"And you don't seem to mind the danger," he said.

"We've been working with this private investigation firm," she said. "Two really tough guys. They sort of look after us."

"Oh yeah?"

"I'm out here with one of them. We're on a job."

Sherman sipped his blonde decaf. "So you aren't here to marry me?"

"Not today," she said. "But maybe tomorrow."

They laughed, but she thought there might be some sliver of hope in his words. The busy LA traffic passed in front of the window. She couldn't recall seeing so many shiny, nice cars in one endless stream before.

"So am I supposed to be a source or something?" he asked.

"Maybe," she said. "I'm looking for someone who puts big deals together for the top entertainers."

He nodded. "My firm handles a lot of them. Really, it depends on who their agents are. There are a lot of firms in town."

"Which firms bend the rules?"

"Loaded question," he said.

"Okay, which firms have had deals backfire on them?"

"We all have at one time or another."

This wasn't where she wanted to go. "I'm interested in any big entertainment deals that backfired. The seven and eight figure kind."

"Still doesn't narrow it down," he said. "One movie deal alone could be worth a billion dollars. Check out the sci-fi franchises."

"No franchise deals," she said. "I'm interested in the individuals involved. Movies, music, or books."

"That narrows it down a little," he said. "But there are still twenty or so firms along with at least that many agents."

"You make it sound like million dollar deals blow up every day," she said.

He laughed. "They do in this town."

Crome thought Colette had been very helpful. If he had more time, or half a brain, he would have dropped what he was doing and chased after her. But he had a job to do and, by God, the job came first.

He paused before getting in his rental truck, gritted his teeth, and went back inside the coffee shop.

Colette wasn't there anymore.

Relieved, he turned to head back to his ride and found himself looking at Colette.

She smiled. "Forget something?"

"Yeah," he said. "What are you doing later tonight?"

"What did you have in mind?"

Things were looking up.

"Have dinner with me," he said. "Give me chance to make up for being such a piker."

"I'll agree to dinner," she said, "but it'll take more than that to make up for breaking my heart."

"Fair enough," he said.

She stepped up to him. "But I like that you came back."

Crome prided himself on knowing what to do in almost any situation. This was one of the exceptions.

She brushed lint off his leather vest. "My shift ends in a couple hours."

Back in the truck, he called Harmony, who answered with an upbeat, "Hello!"

"You get your ashes hauled or something?" he asked.

"Crudeness," she said. "I'm going with 'no comment'."

"Guy's name we're after is Blake Townley."

There was a pause. Then she said, "Oh, no."

"Oh no what?"

"How sure are you about this?"

He told her about Colette, that she'd always been on the right side of things and was a good cop.

"Oh, no."

"You keep saying that," he said.

"That son of a bitch."

She didn't normally talk like that so Crome kept silent.

"That son of a bitch," she repeated.

He didn't reply.

She said, "You there?"

"I am."

"I think I just got played."

"Meet me at the hotel and we'll figure this out," he said.

Chapter Ten

Charleston, South Carolina

Blu Carraway stood beside Murder and took measure. There were signs of life, and the horse had begun giving soft grunts and snorts which was more than he'd done previously. The bill for the services was already thousands of dollars, but it seemed to be getting results. He rubbed the horse's neck and watched his ears flicker.

With no idea if the three-day-clock Crome had given him was even close, Blu had made several calls to colleagues. Enough of them had agreed to a retainer to be on standby in case the fight came to Carraway Island. With only one road on and off, surrounding marshlands, and only one real approach by boat, his home was as good as or better than most from a defense position. Six well-armed, dedicated, and skilled mercenaries could hold the fort until their adversaries gave up and dropped napalm.

The plan to keep Ariel safe included deception, coercion, and more than a bit of luck. Hopefully Crome and Harmony would be back from California in time to contribute.

Blu would protect his island and his horses to the end. The resolution gave him comfort and peace.

Los Angeles, California

The hotel was five star. Crome sat on a couch in the lavish lobby and people-watched. Much like Sunset Strip, he was not the oddity here either. He began to realize there were people in this city far weirder than he could ever imagine being. In Charleston, he could frighten tourists from the Midwest by as little as a loud cough. In this city, he barely conjured up a nod.

Harmony, in a dress he hadn't seen her wear before, greeted him with a huff.

He gestured toward a celebrity couple standing in the middle of the atrium talking. "Is that—"

"Yes," she huffed again and plopped down next to him. "And on the other side of the room is the entire cast of *Southern Heat*." *Southern Heat* was the latest summer blockbuster, set in Charleston, and loosely based on exploits of their friend Brack Pelton.

"I'm glad they're back here," Crome said. "They were getting on my nerves at home."

"Yeah," she said, "well they're getting on my nerves here, now."

"So who were you referring to on the phone?" he asked.

"Sherman Heywood. He works for Blake Townley and he dodged all my questions and...and..."

Crome sensed a big regret hovering somewhere over Harmony. He didn't pry.

She slapped the couch cushion. "That son of a bitch."

Not caring what signage might be in the area, Crome pulled out his vape pen and offered it to her.

Surprising him, she took it. "How does this thing work?"

He showed her. "The nicotine level's pretty low. It was all they had. Take a hit. It might help."

She pressed the button and inhaled. Her eyes closed and she exhaled a cloud of vapor. When they opened again, their brightness had returned.

With more determination, she said, "We're going to get that son of a bitch."

"That's my girl," he said.

"I'm supposed to meet with him later," she said, getting up. "We've got work to do."

The hotel suite Hope had set up for them was first rate, as far as Crome could tell. He was more of a "mom and pop motor court motel" kind of guy and proud of it. For the most part, this uppity crap got in the way of real life and he preferred to be amongst his peers.

Harmony, on the other hand, relaxed first in the monster-sized bath tub with the water jets and bath salts, and then in the soft cotton robe provided by the hotel, all the while enjoying the view of the city.

Okay, Crome did appreciate a good view, and Harmony in her robe was a spectacular one. So were the city lights below. She sat on her bed and dried her hair with a towel.

He turned to leave. "Lemme know when you're done and dressed." The last thing he needed was to be distracted.

She said, "Hey, Crome."

"Yeah?" he asked, his back to her.

"I never did thank you."

"For what?"

He heard her get off the bed and approach. Then he felt her arms around him from behind. It felt more like the hug of a daughter, or what he suspected one would feel like.

She said, "For saving me and Maureen."

He put his hands over hers, not sure what to say. "You'da done the same for me." Then he thought about how he'd tried to shut all his friends out and find Maureen by himself. "Or maybe not."

She laughed and let him go. "It was iffy there for a spell."

"Get dressed." He walked out of the room.

When the hair dryer started up in her room, he stepped out the main door to the balcony and inhaled vapor, thinking about their next plan. Harmony's contact worked for the man Colette said was the biggest conman in the city, and that was saying something in this town.

Colette. There was still something Crome felt with her after all these years. She was new and fresh, yet brought the familiarity of an old friend which she was. He had to move her past the fact that he'd dumped her all those years ago. It really was for the best. He would not have been good for her in the long run. And probably wasn't good for her now if she was looking for something anywhere near "'til death do us part." In his line of work, that could be next week.

Harmony stepped out on the balcony dressed in a short, black number and heels. "Ready?"

The plan Crome had come up with was aggressive and illegal. But with the timeline Thomas had given them they didn't have many other choices.

He sat in his rental SUV in front of the hotel, waiting for Harmony's date to show up. She'd really proven herself an asset on this trip, even if she felt taken advantage of by her ex. That gave Crome the opportunity to give her some coaching. In this business, he'd learned to use every situation to gain ground. The Army had taught him that. Retreating sucked the enemy in closer. A strategic counter-offensive could cut them off and wipe them out. That was the plan this evening.

Sherman Heywood would soon learn what it was like to jilt someone of Harmony's caliber. The smile on her face when they'd discussed the plan was one Crome hoped she'd never have while thinking about him. He'd created a monster.

Several pretty boys got out of expensive cars with magazine hair and fancy clothes and went inside. Crome had tipped each of the three valets fifty bucks to let him stay parked where he was for as long as it took. So far Crome had been there twenty minutes. Everyone must run late in this town.

A black Lamborghini pulled to the curb and Crome had the

feeling this was their douche bag. The pretty boy who got out, with magazine hair and fancy clothes like the others, tipped the valet apparently enough to have them hold his car at the curb.

Crome just hoped his SUV could keep up.

Courtesy of Blu Carraway Investigations' expansion into the modern era, Crome had access to a tracking device small enough to fit inside a purse and not be noticeable. Harmony had slid the device down to the bottom of her purse. This way Crome could track her using a tablet and GPS. Plus, he was sure he didn't trust her date. During her meeting with him earlier, in addition to a semi-romantic interlude, she'd peppered the guy with questions. It might have tipped him off.

Less than five minutes later, the Lamborghini-driving Peckerwood exited the hotel with Harmony. The valet raised the door to the car for her to enter. Low-slung sports cars and short dresses guaranteed compromising positions. But Harmony situated herself gracefully, as if she'd been born sitting in the lap of luxury. Or at least on the bucket seats of Lamborghinis.

Crome just hoped her temporary Romeo didn't have too much of a lead foot. The tracker would make sure he didn't permanently lose them, but he preferred having a clear line of sight of them at all times.

The Lambo roared away in a cloud of exhaust and tire smoke and Crome gave chase.

The home in the Hollywood hills could only be described one way— a mansion. There was a ton of money in Charleston, but it had nothing on Los Angeles County. The asphalt ended a quarter mile ago and Crome followed on the stone drive from four cars behind the Lambo through the open gate and waited for the people in the vehicles ahead to disembark and the valets to drive their cars away. He followed suit, although his rental truck stood out amongst the four-wheeled overcompensation around him.

Stone also lined the entrance into the home. In front of the door stood a man with a tablet, Crome's first obstacle of the evening.

A quick measure of the situation told Crome he knew the man from back in the day. Their paths had crossed a decade prior when Crome was doing a private security gig with Blu. Mid-forties like himself, this man spent the time since Crome had seen him developing his upper body to near-comical levels.

After a hit of vapor, Crome approached. "How's it hangin', Sammy."

The overdeveloped gorilla looked up from the tablet in his hands. "Mick Crome. You're not on the list."

After a smirk, Crome said, "You got me. I'm not."

Lowering the electronic device, Sammy said, "I'm afraid I can't let you in."

"Of course you can," Crome said.

"Not if I want to keep my job," he said. "They pay me twenty grand to stand here and check names. That's just for one night. I ain't gonna screw up this gravy train."

A line formed behind Crome.

Sammy said, "You gotta leave, Mick. Don't make me do something I don't wanna."

Through his periphery, Crome saw members of the wait staff walking around the side of the humongous structure. "You're right, Sammy. And when you're right, you're right." He put a hand on Sammy's shoulder. "Sorry about this."

Crome walked back in the direction of the valet.

Using the line of people as cover, he ducked around the side of the home, following behind two men dressed in dinner jackets. As easy as pie, he slipped in the service entrance, through the kitchen, and ran into another meat-head.

In a count of less than five seconds, Crome noticed a door to the guard's left, decked the man, opened the door, guided the falling body inside the janitor closet, and shut the door.

He turned to see a Latina woman looking at him.

In Spanish, he said, "I mean you no harm."

She gave him a long look, then said, "I didn't like the way the man treated us anyway."

For some reason, Crome could always relate to people who did the actual work. It was the elitists he had trouble with. He said, "I'm checking on a friend. Is there a way I can see where they are without being seen?"

With a nod, she said, "Follow me."

She led him through the kitchen to a prep area. The other workers gave him strange looks but dismissed him when they saw the woman he was with.

Double doors at the other end of the room had large windows. They gave a view of a short hallway and a large area Crome guessed was some sort of "one-percenter" sitting area. He recognized several A-list actors amongst the crowd of rich and shameless.

And then he saw Harmony with her date. If she was star struck in their presence, Crome couldn't tell. She seemed to be controlling herself quite well. It helped, and Crome had a suspicion she knew this as well, that Harmony was one of the most attractive women in the room. While many of the others had obviously spent a lot of time and money under the knife and with their hair stylists, Harmony had popped out of her mother's womb, kept herself in shape, and learned how to fix her own hair. Unfortunately in this room, authenticity was met with disdain. Crome could sense a mutiny in the sneers of the modified female specimens.

But none of that really mattered after Blake Townley walked in the room with last year's "Best Leading Actress." He wore a horrible blue smoking jacket and apricot ascot. Crome recognized the man from the picture Harmony had shown him back in their suite. He noticed she recognized the villain as well.

Dangling the man over the railing of the back deck that overlooked the valley several hundred feet below might be a fun exercise.

First things first.

To the woman still standing with him, Crome asked, "Who owns this house?"

"That gringo there dressed like a peacock," she said. "He treats us like dirt."

Crome was beginning to think thoughts of marriage to this stranger who'd decided to help him out. "Any chance he has an office I could take a look at?"

A man's voice behind them, in English, said, "I told you to leave, Mick."

Crome turned, ready for blows. "Sammy."

Except Sammy wasn't alone. With him were three other men.

The woman vanished out the double doors. Crome didn't blame her. Sammy said, "Come this way."

"I got a better idea," Crome said. "How about I go through these double doors here and show your boss how bad you screwed up."

He did just that—went right out the doors and walked up to Townley offering a hand.

Harmony opened her eyes wide.

To Townley, who also registered shock, Crome said, "I wanted to introduce myself to the man who could screw people out of millions and sleep at night."

Crome felt himself be lifted in the air and forcibly removed from the room in the wake of Sammy saying, "Sorry Mr. Townley. We'll take care of this."

Chapter Eleven

Two guys muscled Crome through the service door and outside.

Sammy said, "You're gonna pay for embarrassing me like that."

"You were an embarrassment before I showed up, Sassquatch." It was the best Crome could come up with at the moment, what with his arms locked by the meatheads escorting him to his demise.

All Crome needed was a slight ray of hope—a loosened grip on one of his hands, a distracted Sammy, anything.

As they walked him down the path and away from the house, Crome's options faced extinction, especially since behind him was a ledge with a twenty foot drop.

"Stop here," Sammy said.

The meatheads stopped and turned Crome to face his ex-friend.

Cocking a hand back, Sammy said, "This is for messing up my gig."

"Stop!" a voice called from behind them.

It was Townley.

Sammy stood at attention. If Crome had to guess, his old friend didn't know what to do. His boss probably didn't want any blood shed on his property.

"Release him at once," Townley said.

As if regaining his senses, Sammy said, "He's trouble, Mr. Townley."

The meatheads let go of Crome's arms and he dropped to his

feet.

"Obviously," Townley said. "He was in my house at my party without an invitation. We'll go into how that happened later. Right now I want to know why."

Crome rubbed his wrists, feigning soreness. He kept quiet.

Sammy said, "His name is Mick Crome. He's an old acquaintance."

"Is that so, Mr. Crome?" Townley asked. "What brought you to my house?"

"I heard you had a good view," Crome said.

Townley gave him a smile. "I do, but I'm not convinced that's why you're here. I mean at my house." He waved his hand around. "All the houses around here have great views. It's why we bought them."

Crome didn't reply.

Sammy said, "He's from South Carolina."

"Really?" Townley said. "I don't have any business on the other side of the world. This is California. California's where I do my business. So I'm going to ask you one more time, Mr. Crome. Why are you here?"

"You screwed a lot of people over the years," Crome said. "You figure it out."

"And you're here to set the record straight?" he asked, amused.

Crome felt a smile come over his face. "I suggest you get better security than Sammy, especially if you plan on growing your list of enemies."

Townley stepped back. "Get him out of here."

Crome sucker punched the guy to his left and caught the guy to his right with an elbow to the nose.

Sammy tried to draw down on him but Crome stepped into him, grabbed the meathead's wrist and bent his hand in a way God hadn't intended. It snapped like a twig and he dropped the pistol he'd drawn and yelped in pain.

Townley tried to grab the gun that Sammy had dropped but Crome kicked it away.

Sammy got a second wind and charged.

Townley ran back up the path they'd come.

Crome could have tripped the man and sent him over the edge but decided he didn't need a murder beef on top of everything else. Instead, he stepped away from the cliff and used Sammy's momentum to send him crashing into a tree. The giant bounced back but didn't have it in him for a third round.

Crome left them where they were and followed the stone path past the house to his parked rental truck in time to see Townley returning with five more men. Not wanting to stick around any longer, Crome got in the SUV, started the engine, and accelerated out of the drive.

Charleston, South Carolina

Blu watched Tess get dressed. She really was more than he deserved.

She caught him and grinned. "What are you looking at?"

"You."

She slinked across the bed, half clothed, and kissed him. "You like what you see?"

"I do."

They kissed again.

A knock at the door interrupted what was about to turn into something else.

"Um, Blu?"

It was Ariel.

"Everything okay?" he asked.

"I think you need to come outside."

Blu slid off the bed, pulled on his underwear and jeans, and grabbed a clean t-shirt out of a folded basket of laundry. His daughter really was a great addition to the business, and for managing his personal life. She even did his laundry.

He opened the door to find Ariel standing on the other side, her look one of surprise but not fear. She pointed to the front door.

Blu slipped his shirt on. "What is it?"

She kept her finger pointed.

He went to see, sliding his feet into a pair of Birkenstock sandals as he went outside.

Underneath the canopy the vet had set up to provide shade, stood Murder.

But this time the horse was chewing hay from the bale the vet had left, the first he'd eaten since Blu found him on the ground.

Blu pulled his phone out and hit speed dial.

When the vet answered, Blu said, "I need you to get over here."

The saline and medication drips were still connected, giving Murder the hydration and calories he needed to survive. But, if the horse regained his energy, he might try to charge them, or run away and hurt himself. Either way, Blu needed the help and expertise Campbell had to control the situation.

Los Angeles, California

After leaving the crashed party, the next stop Sherman Heywood's Lamborghini made was to a restaurant in North Hollywood.

Crome staked out the pretension trough, his nickname for the place, from a metered spot across the street. If nothing else, Harmony was getting the first class treatment. He toked on his vape pen.

The fight with Sammy, while somewhat refreshing, bothered him. Sammy used to be good at his job. Now he performed exactly how he looked—a dim-witted, middle-aged meathead. His reflexes had dulled. California must have ground his edge down. For whatever reason, sleepy Key West and Charleston had honed Crome's skill set into a precision toolbox.

While the lowcountry beaches could make a better-than-decent Corona commercial, the underbelly of the world Crome lived in forced him to stay sharp.

Through Nikon binoculars that would make a bird watcher drool, Crome kept Harmony and her date in his line of vision. As if reading his mind, Harmony had pointed to a table by the windows when they were being seated. She might be young, but she was a quick study and had learned the importance of self-preservation after working with Blu Carraway Investigations.

The happy couple in the crosshairs clinked wine glasses and toasted something. Crome, sitting in his SUV, munched on a granola bar and drank a Cherry Coke Zero while they dined on five courses. Afterward, the valet brought the Lambo around, opened the door for Harmony, and accepted a lame tip from Sherman.

As the sports car pulled away, Crome watched the valet give them a quick middle finger before he put the binoculars down and gave chase.

A-list party. Five star restaurant. What was next?

It didn't take long to find out. In fact, it only took three blocks before Sherman pulled to a stop at the valet stand of a jazz club. Crome could tell it was a jazz club because that was the name—Jazz Club. He looped around the place and parked in a construction zone half a block over. He and his truck blended in perfectly with the other pickups in the gravel lot.

After a quick glance around to make sure no one working the night shift on the semi-high rise noticed him, he slipped through the chain link fence and found a back entrance into the building. Crome worked the door to so many upscale snob havens that he knew his way around a guest list. Like Blake Townley's shack, there was always a back door. Unlike the house in the hills, this one had a man guarding it.

A couple had just gone through the door when Crome approached.

"How's it goin'?" he asked the startled, overdeveloped Millennial watching the door. Jesus, was everyone on steroids in this town?

"Name?" the kid asked, checking out a tablet.

"What if I told you my name ain't on your list?" Crome asked.

The kid showed he had at least a sense of humor when he said, "I'd say you'd be right."

"Sammy Hart said to come by, check the place out."

"You a friend of Sammy's?" the kid asked, wide eyed. "He got me this job."

If nothing else, Sammy had a lot of friends. He just didn't have any skill left.

"Yeah," Crome said. "He told me his guys had this place covered." Crome nodded.

The kid opened the door. "Tell him Barclay says hi."

Crome walked past and said, "Will do."

The hall, a faded black color with scuff marks on the walls from carts full of supplies moving in and out, T'd into another hall. One direction headed to the kitchen, the other to a set of swinging double doors with windows that opened up to the club.

Crome spotted Harmony sitting with her date, took out his phone, and sent her a text. He watched her glance at her phone, look up at him, and nod.

He nodded back and left, telling Barclay he'd forgotten something in his car.

Chapter Twelve

Charleston, South Carolina

The vet and an assistant poked and prodded at Murder for over an hour. They took more blood samples but were encouraged that the horse showed more signs of life.

Dink and Doofus and the mare Sally had taken to placing the apple treats Ariel fed them in front of Murder. Much to everyone's delight, the black horse picked up one of the apples and ate it.

With things seeming to turn around for the type-A guard horse, Blu showered, put on a fresh pair of jeans and a t-shirt, and left to meet with his lawyer. He still had the murder investigation in Malaysia to deal with.

He wheeled out of his crushed shell drive, across the bridge, and onto the road in front of his property and downloaded an Agent Orange album from his play list. The skate-punk band did a mean version of "Somebody to Love".

Before he got a mile down the road, Andeline called.

Andeline, or Madame Andeline as she'd been known in her previous life, now ran two successful downtown restaurants. A lot of the locals knew her from the old days, and not just because she made a mean bisque. Her clientele moved in the highest circles in the country, and unlike some Hollywood Madames, Andeline's black book was blank on purpose—she protected her clients.

"Hey And," he said.

"You've got the hottest act in the world sleeping in your bed and you don't bring her to me?"

"Tess and I had dinner at your place last week," he said.

"Touché, Mr. Carraway. You earned that one."

"What can I do for you, And?"

"You can stop with the act, bring Ariel by so I can get an autograph, and listen to what I have to say."

"Assuming I know what you're talking about," he said, "if it's so important, why can't you give me what you have right now?"

"Leverage," she said. "It's what makes the world go around."

"Back atcha," he said. "Book me a backroom table for two. One waiter, no tourists."

Andeline had ten years on Blu which put her in her mid-fifties. But that didn't stop her from squealing like a giddy schoolgirl.

Blu had to hold the phone away from his ear until she regained control. "Jesus, And," he said.

"Eight thirty, sharp, Mr. Carraway," she said. "Do or die."

She ended the call.

Before he did anything else, he called Hope and told her the plan.

Hope said, "I'll make sure Ariel is ready and I'll remind you an hour before."

When Hope came on board, she overhauled his makeshift home office, got the rest of his house squared away, and organized his finances. He didn't realize how bad he was at managing his business until she showed him six-month-old invoices he never mailed to past clients to be paid for his services.

He parked behind the law offices of Lester Brogan, housed in the tallest building in the city. Brogan had a pit bull reputation and Blu respected the man even though he used his own private investigators.

Blu rode the elevator to the top floor. It dumped him off in a sea of gray and chrome and glass. He was fifteen minutes early.

The receptionist, a middle-aged woman dressed professionally said, "Can I help you?"

"My name's Blu Carraway. I have an appointment with Mr.

Brogan. I'm early."

"Please have a seat and he will be with you momentarily. Can I get you something to drink?"

"No thanks." He did as she said and sat on a leather chair in the waiting area. Framed pictures hung on the walls of Brogan winning awards or shaking the hands of celebrities. The guy was more than kind of full of himself.

It didn't bother Blu. The man's success had given him confidence. One fed the other. The guy had a reputation for getting results so Blu excused the man's obvious pride even though it was one of the seven deadlies.

Brogan walked out from the back office area past the receptionist and held out a hand. "Good to see you, Blu."

Blu stood and shook the man's hand.

At six-three, Blu stood ten inches taller than the lawyer, but the shorter man had such a huge personality that he would be the center of attention anywhere. His head was shaved and shiny; his Savile Row three-piece suit, silk shirt with cufflinks, Italian shoes, and Breguet Heritage watch exuded wealth and success. So did the Aston Martin in the garage below the building Blu had parked near. He knew it was his lawyer's because Brack Pelton had told him about it.

The man led Blu through a bustling office. According to Blu's research, twenty-five lawyers worked for Brogan. They were the best, brightest, and highest paid in the city. Most other big time lawyers would have a secretary escort potential clients in to meet with them. Brogan had a reputation as a people person. He also had been rumored to make his decisions to take or not take cases based on his initial impression in the waiting area when he greeted them.

Apparently Blu made the first cut since he hadn't been dismissed.

Brogan stopped at a doorway. "Please take a seat. Can I get you something to drink?"

Blu declined and the lawyer stepped in behind him and shut the door.

They took adjacent seats at a large glass conference table.

Brogan began with, "Andeline said you'd be calling me and here you are."

The name drop didn't really surprise Blu. Andeline had a good handle on the pulse of the city. It also let him know they had mutual friends.

Blu said, "As I said over the phone, I might be a murder suspect in another country."

"According to our research, you can't be extradited until things move to an official status," Brogan said.

"And when it does become official?"

Brogan said, "I'm already working on keeping it from becoming so. But I don't work for free and I don't work without a signed piece of paper. Things get messy without either, you understand."

"All too well," Blu said.

"Good. I'll get the contract. All I need from you is twenty-five thousand dollars." He made sure to make eye contact. "That's the friends-and-family retainer. You can thank Andeline."

Blu nodded. "I appreciate your understanding. My banker is ready to transfer the money. All I need is an account number."

"I'll be right back." The stocky man lumbered out of the room.

Los Angeles, California

Crome almost felt dirty, like he was sending Harmony out to sell her body for him. Except after she heard that her Shermanator short-term boyfriend was one of Townley's stooges and had already lied to her, she got real focused on taking the crooked lawyers out. Or rather, setting them up so Crome could. Either way worked for Crome.

What caused him angst at the moment was Harmony guiding Sherman to some make out point like a couple of teenagers. By the time Crome had parked his truck a quarter mile up the road and walked down to the Lambo, her Romeo date had managed to slip the top of her dress off.

Crome rapped on the window and heard her say, "Oh, thank God."

Sherman looked out the window which was partway open. "What the hell?"

"Sorry to bother y'all," Crome said, "but my pickup won't start. You got jumper cables?"

It was a stretch to think the sports car would have them in its tiny trunk, and Sherman probably wouldn't know how to use them anyway. He'd have some executive car service on speed dial.

"Get out of here," Sherman said, almost at a yell.

"You don't have to be rude about it," Crome said. "Either you got the cables or ya don't."

"Beat it."

Crome rapped harder on the door frame, using the rings on his fingers to tap on the metal, surely scratching the paint.

"What the hell?" Sherman said.

He wasn't a small man, and looked like he worked out at the gym.

Crome wasn't worried. He rapped harder.

The door swung up and Sherman leapt out. But Crome was ready and caught Sherman with a solid haymaker across the jaw. The lawyer collapsed beside his sports car.

Harmony slipped her dress back over her shoulder. "Took you long enough."

"It's not as if there's convenient parking, ya know."

The place, overlooking the city, had a multitude of little hideaways, but each slot only held one car and they were spaced fifty feet apart or more. That helped with privacy, whether people were copulating or getting the crap kicked out of them like Sherman was about to.

Crome handed Harmony a bottle of water, lifted the man off the ground, and propped him up on the fender of his car. Then he took the water back and splashed it in Sherman's face. It took two dowsings before the man came to, coughing.

Harmony said, "You lied to me, Sherman. I don't like it when people lie to me."

Sherman looked at her as if trying to focus.

Crome slapped his face a few times. "I'd listen to the lady if I was you, pal."

"Who are you?" he asked.

The biker said, "The guy that's gonna take that set of jumper cables you said you didn't have, connect one end to your battery's terminals and the other end to your nipples."

Harmony stifled a smile.

Sherman blinked.

Crome slapped the man's cheek again. "Are we clear? You want twelve volts up the mammaries? Or do you wanna answer a few questions?"

"This is BS." Sherman attempted to push himself off his car.

Crome pushed him back down and showed his nine millimeter.

The blood drained from Sherman's face as the reality of the situation set in.

"What's it gonna be?" Crome asked. "Answers or the jump start?"

"You can't be serious?"

"He is," Harmony said.

Sherman looked down between his legs at the ground. "What's the question?"

"Your boss hoses people for a living, right?" Crome asked.

The man's head jerked up. "He's a lawyer. It's his job."

"There's screwing and then there's screwing," Crome said. "Something tells me your boss is the dog who likes to hump any leg he can strap onto."

"He's successful if that's what you mean."

Crome turned to Harmony. "You might wanna take a walk. I'd hate for you to see what happens next."

"I want to watch," she said.

To Sherman, Crome said, "Jesus, pal. What'd you do to her?"

Sherman gave them both a sneer. "She's always been easy."

Before Crome could react, Harmony slapped Sherman across the face.

The lawyer tried to stand up as if to return the strike. Crome drove his fist deep into Sherman's stomach, doubling him over.

"Now, where were we?" Crome asked. "Oh, yeah, I remember. Your boss. His problem is he mounts his own clients. He's supposed to be working for them, the bastard."

Sherman held his stomach and grimaced. "Whatever you say. I'm going to call the police and then we'll see who's laughing."

Harmony said, "You think you're getting out of this alive?"

That surprised Crome. Not because he hadn't thought of saying it, or because he wasn't above it given the right circumstances. What got to him was that it came out of Harmony's mouth.

"You're going to kill me?" Sherman asked in disbelief. "All because you suddenly regret our after-lunch interlude?"

"Hell hath no fury," Crome said. "You know the rest."

Sherman spit on the ground.

Harmony said, "Who's Townley's biggest client?"

"Go to hell."

Crome slipped his gun down the back of his jeans, grabbed Sherman's hand and broke two fingers.

The man looked in horror at his disfigured hand.

It was Crome's experience that the initial shock covered the pain for five, four, three, two...

"Ow!" Sherman yelped and gasped and coughed. Then he threw up.

Unfazed, Harmony said, "Who's Townley's biggest client?"

"He'll kill me," Sherman said, holding his injured hand. "Then he'll kill you."

"I'm trembling," Crome said. "Answer the question or I finish with this hand and go to work on the other. And then I take your shoes off and smash your toes with the butt of my gun."

Gagging and coughing, Sherman spit up again but only bile came out. He looked pitiful. Crome wasn't sure he liked how much Harmony enjoyed the man's suffering.

"You've got five seconds," she said.

Sherman shrieked, "Jake Jarnel! Jake Jarnel! His name is Jake Jarnel."

Next to the President of the United States, Jake Jarnel was the most powerful man in America. He worked every angle, legitimate or otherwise. In addition to political aspirations, he ran the largest private military company in the world. And now Crome understood if they were about to go up against Jarnel, this was bigger than anything Blu Carraway Investigations had ever tackled.

Harmony said, "You can call the police if you want. But if we get picked up, I'm going to film a segment that you dropped Jarnel's name, and I have half a million followers. Do you understand?"

Crome almost felt sorry for the young, rich lawyer leaning against the fender of his Lamborghini.

Sherman didn't look at her as he nodded.

As if to add insult to injury, she said, "I want to hear you say it."

Fully defeated, Sherman said, "Yes. I understand."

With that, Crome and Harmony walked to his truck.

Chapter Thirteen

Charleston, South Carolina

At eight thirty, sharp, Blu opened the front door to Andeline's restaurant for Ariel. Andeline met them at the hostess station.

Without saying a word, although it looked to Blu as if all the star struck giddiness built up in Andeline was ready to blow out the top of her head, she led them through a side door to a private room. Behind a curtain awaited a single table with a white tablecloth and candle and two chairs.

After shutting the door behind them all and making sure the curtain was down, Andeline turned into a groupie like everyone else around Ariel seemed to be.

"Oh my God, I love your songs," said the mid-fifties woman to the twenty-seven-year-old. "They are so good."

Ariel put an arm around Andeline's shoulder. "You are so sweet. Thank you so much. And I love your place here."

Andeline bobbed her head up and down. "I'm glad you like it. I had the kitchen prepare a special meal for you both. I hope you enjoy what we have."

"I can't wait," Ariel said, all genuine smiles.

Blu pulled out a chair and the pop star sat. Tonight she wore a tight, silver dinner number that Hope speculated to cost over ten grand. Something about being a Monique Lhuillier, whoever the heck that was. Blu had no idea. Same with the heels—Jimmy Choo.

Blu did know watches, and the Patik Philippe on her wrist was a cool fifty G's.

Again thanks to his daughter, Blu had a linen Boss jacket, silk shirt, lightweight wool Polo trousers and five hundred dollar Italian loafers. She'd also had his vintage 1962 Rolex cleaned and serviced while he was away and it gleamed.

They dined on lobster and filet.

On any other night, this meal in this restaurant would be as much as his shoes. Thankfully Ariel had agreed to autograph whatever Andeline wished. It forced him to contemplate how different her life must be from his when she could pay for anything by simply signing her name to objects.

As they savored the last of their dessert, a raspberry torte, and cups of decaf, Andeline returned to the table. A male waiter followed her carrying a chair. He set the chair at their table and left and Andeline joined them.

"You poor dear," she said, taking Ariel's hand, "I am so sorry for your situation."

"What do you know?" Blu asked.

Still looking at Ariel, she said, "First of all, you could do no better than this gentleman right here with you. He is the best in the business."

"I know he is," Ariel said. "He already saved my life once. And since I got here, I haven't felt this safe in a long time."

Andeline nodded. "Unfortunately, as sizeable as your fame is, my sources say you are a small part of a bigger picture. It's why the hit was placed on you at the club and why Blu is wanted there. Crome and Harmony are on the right path and, from what I found out right before I came in here, just upset the applecart in California."

"Are they okay?" Blu asked, his stomach tightening around the large meal they just consumed.

"That's all I know."

Blu pulled his phone and made a call to Crome and then Harmony. Both went to voicemail.

Los Angeles, California

The trip to the airport, through the TSA checkpoint, and into their first-class seats, was all uneventful. No police stopped them. No Homeland Security. And no canceled tickets.

This time there was no champagne toast. He'd had to call Colette and cancel dinner, which didn't go over well. Although, she brightened up when he suggested she plan a trip to the lowcountry.

Harmony rested her head on his shoulder and fell fast asleep.

Crome wasn't entirely sure what had happened between her and Sherman. But whatever happened, they left the man utterly decimated. His choices had led him to Towley's firm. Instead of assessing the situation, realizing there were bad things transpiring, and running away, Sherman embraced the evil.

He would pay for it. Either Townley would suspect him a traitor, or Sherman would worry he'd come to that conclusion. The young man was better off packing his bags and leaving the state.

Crome rested his head against his seatback, listened to the airplane's blues radio station, and closed his eyes. Soon he, too, was fast asleep.

The next thing either of them knew, the flight attendant was waking them for their arrival into Atlanta.

Charleston, South Carolina

AC/DC's "You Shook Me All Night Long" blared from the stereo in Blu's truck when Crome opened the front door for Harmony. While she got in, he put their luggage in the cargo area, glad to be back on the East coast. He hopped into the backseat, singing along with Brian Johnson, the band's previous front man.

Blu pulled away from the curb, and Crome played air guitar

during the solo.

Harmony said, "You guys are unreal."

In response, they sang, "You shook me all night long!"

"You both wish," she said.

They all laughed as the song ended.

Crome said, "Thanks for that one, partner. I needed a pick-me-up. Now I need a beer."

Harmony said, "I need a vacation."

"We just had one," Crome said.

"You might have," she said.

Blu said, "Murder's eating again."

That changed the tone, and Crome and Harmony wanted to hear the details.

With Crome and Harmony back in the city and safe for the moment, Blu felt himself relax enough to sit beside his ailing horse. Apparently he dozed off because when he awoke he found a woman snuggled up next to him. He was surprised and glad it was Tess. She'd pulled up a chair next to his.

She awoke, kissed him, and said, "Hello."

For someone who prided herself on being all business all the time, Blu found Tess to be affectionate and giving with him. She was exactly what he needed and he thought less and less about their age difference. He also thought less and less about Billie, the woman who had not given him an answer when he'd proposed. He hoped she was doing okay but didn't dwell on the thought. Tess kept his attention because she gave him attention. There were no games.

"Um," she asked, "where's Murder?"

Blu jerked his head around and found the spot Murder had been standing to be vacant.

Instead, the horse stood drinking water from the trough a hundred feet away.

"Well, I'll be." He pulled his phone and called the vet back.

Ariel walked over to them. "If you two love birds are done here, I suggest we head over to that speedy boat of yours, Mr. Blu, and take a trip around the harbor."

It sounded like a swell idea to Blu.

Tess said, "I'll pack a picnic basket."

Ariel said, "I've got one ready to go thanks to your daughter who left and said to call her if you needed anything else."

The three of them, Ariel, Tess and Blu, shot up the Intracoastal Waterway, past the photogenic Battery homes, and up the Cooper River. They passed the new port and the old Navy shipyard and daydreamed about the nice homes lining the river. Blu idled through a no-wake zone and two dolphins joined them. One of them raised his snout above the water right beside Ariel. She held out her hand and he let her give him a gentle pat, the whole scene videoed by Tess for Ariel. It truly was a magical place they lived in.

Blu's phone buzzed in his pocket.

Crome had a hunch things weren't copacetic. It could be the contract on Ariel's head, or the dead bodies in Malaysia people were accusing Blu of murdering, or the fact that this whole thing started when his partner stepped in to do the right thing.

There was just too much money in play here. The millions Ariel cited, whatever Jack Teller had been bribed to drop the ball, the money behind the Asian setup, and the army of lawyers working under Townley just like Sherman. All of them with matching sports cars, a bonus from the boss for keeping their mouths shut while he screwed the rich and famous.

Of course, it could also be the tip from a source that Sammy Hart had arrived in Charleston with three other men. It was only a matter of time before they found Blu's house and Ariel sleeping peacefully inside.

Which was why Crome felt he and Blu needed a plan and why he called Blu, interrupting his boat ride with the girls.

When Blu answered, Crome told him what he knew.

Blu said, "Call in some troops."

"How many you think we need?"

"At least three," he said.

"What about Pelton?"

"Better ask his wife," Blu said. "She might not want him involved."

"Roger that," Crome said. "I suggest you move Ariel to Kincaid's compound. She'll be safe there. At least from Sammy and his men. If Townley gets serious and hires real guns, we could be in trouble."

The call ended.

Blu put his phone in his pocket. "Change of plans."

Ariel said, "They know I'm here."

"I don't think so," he said. "They're ticked off at Crome and are in town for him. I don't want them to find you at my house."

Tess said, "Because they'll come after both of you."

"That's right," Blu said.

"Where am I going to go?" Ariel asked.

"Remember that house I took you to after we got away from the club?" Blu asked. "The family also has a home here. It'll be safe enough from the current set of goons, but I won't lie. If Townley or whoever sends professional killers, we're going to have a problem."

This was the understatement of the year. In this day and age, it was too hard to hide indefinitely. If last year's debacle, the one where Maureen and Harmony had been kidnapped, had taught Blu anything, it was that there were too many ways he and Crome and Ariel could be gotten to.

Chapter Fourteen

From the front seat of his SUV, Blu watched the men exit the hotel. There were four of them. None of them were the best at what they did—Blu and Crome were much better operatives than these guys— but Sammy and his men were determined and they would not let Crome slip by a second time.

The first problem was hardware. The men wouldn't have traveled domestically with their hardware. They would source it locally. There were only a few in Charleston County who would supply their needs with no questions. One of them, a pawn shop owner named Big Al, died during a gunfight in his shop when Blu's daughter got taken from him. That left Jimmy Zoluchi and two others.

Jimmy was the one who tipped off Crome about the visitors. He'd told Sammy to go pound sand and "get his ass out of town before he got capped," his words to Crome's ear. Jimmy represented a dying breed.

Gotta love the local color.

The other two sources supplied the gang-banger trade. There was no honor among them. The new group, mostly Russians out of South Carolina's capital city, Columbia, did not care who they sold to or what they would do with them. The more damage done, the better as far as they were concerned.

Blu had wanted a chance to cross paths with them. Now he'd have it.

Crome called. "Jimmy Z's in if we want him."

"Yeah," Blu said, "but what will we owe him for it?"

Chuckling, Crome said, "That's what I asked. He said it was on the house."

"He wants to rid himself of some competition," Blu said.

"The enemy of my enemy," Crome said.

Blu ended the call.

As expected, Sammy drove to a junkyard on the outskirts of North Charleston. The place was a front for the Russian gang. Across the street was a shopping mall with a roof top that was known to have surveillance cameras pointed at the yard.

Knowing this, Blu called his friend in the Charleston Police Department, Roger Powers.

Powers said, "You want me to see about giving you access to our video on the Red Army?"

The Red Army was the nickname the police had given the Russian mob that had set up shop in their town.

People who immigrated to the US in search of a better life, like Blu's mother who had escaped Castro's Cuba, were not the problem. It was men like these. They were the undigested nuts found in feces and Blu hated them.

"There's a gun deal going down," Blu said. "Either you want to do your job and stop crime or you don't."

"I'm a detective," Powers said. "I solve crimes. I don't stop them."

"You said it." Blu hung up on him.

Of course, he wasn't so naïve as to think the Russians didn't know about the surveillance on them. All he needed was an elevated platform.

The opening guitar riff from Nirvana's "Come As You Are" changed the mood and got his attention. When the repeating verse "I don't have a gun" came up, he thought, "Oh, but I do."

From a water tower five hundred yards away, Blu sighted the junkyard through the scope of his M24 seven-point-six-two millimeter. He had to be really careful when he slipped through the security fence and scaled the ladder with the rifle slung over his back. Charleston learned firsthand the term "Active Shooter" thanks to the church incident in 2015 and the King Street restaurant one in 2017.

There were no innocent people in Blu's crosshairs. Between the Russian gangsters and Sammy's goons, there was plenty of guilt to go around. He watched Sammy speak with the head honcho at the junkyard, a true degenerate named Uri. Both men headed into a steel-sided building while their underlings hung around outside.

A plan had already formulated in his mind, one that would cause some headache and maybe some unintended consequences. As the men exited the building, Sammy spoke with his men, two of whom got in their SUV, backed it up to a loading dock, and opened the hatch.

Two Russians began setting crates on the dock while Sammy's men transferred them to the truck. Blu waited until they'd finished and closed up the hatch. When it looked like all the men were about to get in the truck to leave, Blu fired his first shot.

At a thousand yards, he needed a spotter and was a marginal sniper compared to others in his unit. At five hundred yards, he could give a colonoscopy to a gnat.

The shot knocked the submachine gun out of one of the Russian thug's hands. It took the rest of them a few seconds to react. They all drew their weapons.

The next shot took another gun out of the hands of one of the Red Army.

All the men from both groups in the yard scrambled for cover.

Two fired wildly. Uri shouted at them, waving his hands in the air. Blu sent a slug into the windshield of the car Uri tried to hide behind. He could have parked the round through one of the Russian's pupils.

Three more shots took out the same number of tires of Sammy's SUV.

Blu popped out the clip and slipped a new one in. The first had held standard rounds. The fresh clip had explosive tips. He only needed one more and lobbed a shot into the fuel tank of the disabled truck. It blew up in the most spectacular fashion.

One of the crates must have held ammunition because the men scattered like vampires from sunlight as the fireworks went off.

The setup worked better than Blu had expected it to. He broke down the weapon into three parts, loaded the case, slung it over his shoulder, and double-timed it down the ladder. He slid down the last twenty feet by grabbing the side rails with his gloved hands and controlled his descent.

By the time the explosion hit the afternoon news, Blu was sitting on the upper deck of the Pirate's Cove enjoying a virgin daiquiri.

Crome took a seat next to him.

Paige, the bar's manager, brought the biker a shot and a beer.

He raised the shot glass and Blu tapped it with his. Both laughed and drank.

Paige said, "You guys win the lottery or something?"

Crome handed her the empty shot glass and wiped his mouth with the back of his hand. "You could say that."

They stared at the ocean, not speaking for quite a long time. Brothers in arms for a quarter century, they had grown comfortable with the peace that came immediately after war.

With Ariel squared away at Kincaid's compound, the man more than happy to have the multi-platinum selling artist sitting at his dining room table, Blu felt less encumbered and now free to throw rocks at the hornets nest.

An hour later, Tess and Harmony joined the two men at their table. The sun began to set behind them as they watched pelicans and dolphins feeding on the schools of fish inhabiting the surf.

Blu winked at Tess, who dipped her fingers in her Coke Zero and flicked them at him.

Crome's phone buzzed in his pocket. He answered, listened, and said, "Thanks." He ended the call and turned to Blu. "We got another problem."

*   *   *

The problem was that the Russians were pissed. Since all they had were Sammy and his goons, they took them hostage and had apparently tortured them. No one needed to guess whose names were coming out of their mouths.

Crome didn't care about Sammy or his men. But he did care that the Russians were now heading their way. He didn't even mind when his partner called his cop friend Powers. While the guy had given the smart-aleck answer about his job being to solve crimes and not stop them, he got a small task force together with the intention of busting the Russians once and for all.

They already had all the players on file. Most of them had at least one misdemeanor if not an outright felony on their records. With that and the explosion, it was easy to get a warrant and stage a raid at the junkyard, so they did.

Crome watched from the adjacent rooftop with satisfaction as the police busted down the front gate and were met with resistance. The police returned fire and Crome counted two dead and three wounded Russians. The cost had been two downed officers, but they had their vests on and sustained only superficial wounds.

What they found with their preliminary search of the compound was an arsenal and a substantial amount of prescription pain pills. They'd obviously figured out a way to sneak undeclared weapons and ammunition along with meds through the port. With all the intel that Crome found the police had on this gang, the fact that no one had raided it before was beyond him.

Overall, there were twenty files and twenty heads they were after. When all was said and done, there were fifteen Russians accounted for. Most were locked up, but there were the two full body bags and the three receiving medical attention.

Instead of twenty Russians to handle, Blu and Crome only had to worry about the missing five.

What the police also found were four dead bodies belonging to Sammy and his crew. Crome didn't feel guilty about that, either.

They were in town for the sole purpose of squaring things up with Crome. He thought they got what they deserved.

Blu wasn't particularly thrilled that five Russians, including Uri, had escaped the police raid. It was as if they had an inside track to information. They were retreating at the moment, but in Blu's experience, they usually came back with a really big gun.

He and Crome weren't out of the woods yet. But at least they had a reprieve to focus on Ariel's case again. Something told Blu the answers were in California and Kuala Lumpur, neither of which they could really return to.

They'd have to figure out another way.

And that way appeared fresh off a Boeing triple seven through Atlanta and a smaller puddle jumper into CHS—Charleston International Airport.

Colette eased to a stop alongside Crome's motorcycle on the crushed-shell drive of Blu's island home and got out of her rental car.

With Murder now almost fully recovered, Dink, Doofus and Mustang Sally were unencumbered with the need to take care of their leader and headed toward the new arrival at a fair clip.

To the point that Colette probably thought she was about to get trampled.

Blu whistled and the horses slowed to a walk.

Hope held up a small bundle of carrots. "Give them these." She tossed them twenty feet and Colette caught the bundle.

The horses approached and Colette gave each a carrot and a pat on the nose.

Crome said, "You lost?"

"I thought I was for a moment, there," Colette said.

Blu said, "Well hello, Ms. Colette."

She walked past Crome and kissed Blu right on the lips. "Long time, sailor."

Crome said, "Very funny."

"Divide and conquer," she said, giving him a grin. "Nice place you got here." She slapped a mosquito on her arm.

Crome handed her a bottle of bug repellant. "Welcome to the lowcountry. Better use this."

It didn't help that she wore a tank top, shorts, and sandals, therefore exposing as much skin as possible and still be considered dressed for public. As she sprayed herself down from head to toe, she said, "I heard our friend Sammy caught the bus."

"Stupid mook," Crome said. "He'd still be alive if he'd stayed in California."

"Yeah," she said, "well his handlers didn't anticipate the Russian mob getting involved."

"Where else was he going to buy his guns?" Blu asked.

Examining him through sunglasses, she said, "You're assuming these people have what the rest of us call brains."

Crome took a hit of vapor.

Colette selected a cigarette from a silver case and lit it with a disposable Bic. It was a subtlety, but smokers were less likely to lose their smokes than their lighter. As an ex smoker, Blu knew all too well—hence the replaceable lighter she carried.

"So what are you doing here?" Crome asked.

The biker wasn't entirely annoyed at the fact that Colette had traveled all the way across the country unprompted.

She took a drag on her cigarette and exhaled. "Seems a Sherman Heywood filed charges against two unspecified persons who kidnapped and tortured him."

"No kidding?" Crome said it as more of a question.

"You know him?" she asked.

"You know I do," Crome said. "Harmony had a meeting with him while we were out there."

"Yeah, well he called the police after he was assaulted at a make out place called The Point. When the uniformed officers got to him, he was in shock."

"From what I hear," Crome said, "working for his boss could be hazardous to his health. He should look into that."

"Blake Townley is the reason I'm here, Crome," she said. It came out sounding like she was annoyed.

"He sent you?"

"No he didn't send me," she said. "He's got friends in the highest places, and I'm not just talking California."

Like Jake Jarnel, Blu thought.

"Well," Crome said, sitting in one of the Adirondack chairs on Blu's back deck, "we already got the Russian mafia after us. What's another rich white guy?"

She pointed at him, the cigarette held firmly between her fingers. "This isn't just any rich white guy. Townley has the most powerful men on speed dial."

"And won't they be interested in how he screws his business partners and has people killed."

Most of the rich white men Blu had been in contact with sidestepped quite a few land mines on their way to the top. They'd even eliminated adversaries along the way. Townley was just like the rest of them. Crome didn't understand this, but Blu did.

"So what do you suggest?" Blu asked.

She gave them a stiff smile. "Be ready."

Chapter Fifteen

While she did a decent job of playing hard to get, it didn't seem to Blu, as he filled the horse water trough, that Colette put up that much of a fight before she climbed onto the back of Crome's motorcycle as they headed out for something to eat. Hope finished up her work for the day and also left, thanking him again for letting Ariel pay for a really good air conditioning system for his home which included his office. While the AC was a godsend, he knew it was time to look for a real office again. They had one for quite a long time above a retail shop on King Street. But a new landlord jacked up the rent to a level they couldn't afford. That, along with a decline in business during the Great Recession, meant giving up the prime location to stay afloat. With sufficient cash reserves in the bank again and the closure of the Palmetto Pulse, the local news organization whose past owner, Patricia Voyels, allowed the use of its conference room, they were ready for more space.

As if sensing Blu had some free time, Tess pulled into the drive and parked her convertible Beetle next to his SUV. He watched her get out and walk over to him.

"Hey, you." She kissed him on the lips.

He hooked the hose spout over the edge of the trough and put his arms around her. "Hey, yourself."

Sooner or later, she'd come to her senses, he was sure. But it didn't stop him from enjoying the moment. His ex-wife, Abby, did not share the same unorthodox view of the world. Hope had told him Abby had begun throwing around the term 'cradle robber' on a more frequent basis. It didn't bother him because he didn't leave

Abby for Tess, or anyone else. Abby had graduated as a Registered Nurse and moved to Charlotte as soon as she could and took Hope with her, leaving him with nothing but child support payments. With Hope now over eighteen and Abby now married to her second doctor since divorcing Blu, he really didn't care what his ex-wife said.

He did care about what Hope said, and was relieved when she'd given her father a kiss and said, "It's about time."

"About time for what?" he'd asked.

"Tess had your number as soon as you met her," Hope had said. "I could tell it in the way you answered her questions when she interviewed you that first time. You were smitten."

"I was with Billie at the time."

"Dad, I know you as well as you know yourself. And Billie knew it then, too. That's why she—"

"Okay!" he'd said, a tad louder than he meant. It was just that Billie's silence after he'd asked for her hand in marriage still smarted if he thought about it too long.

Tess said, "Earth to Blu. What are you thinking about?"

He pushed those thoughts back into their box and closed the lid. "There's been a new development. Not only do we have the Russians after us, we also have this tool named Blake Townley and his cronies to worry about."

"The one Crome and Harmony gave the wedgie to in California?" she asked. "Why does he want to come all the way here?"

"Big Kahunas like that don't like getting wedgies," he said. "And they definitely don't want anyone else to think they're weak."

She led him toward the house.

"What do you think you're doing?" he asked.

"Looks like we both have some time to kill," she said, "how about I take your mind off your troubles?"

Who could argue with that?

*   *   *

Crome pulled a chair out for Colette at a table on the upper deck of the Pirate's Cove and watched her look out at the Atlantic Ocean.

"It even smells different," she said.

He signaled Pelton to bring two beers.

When the kid came over, Crome made the introductions.

She shook his hand. "The way Crome spoke about you, I expected someone a lot younger."

Before Pelton could reply, Paige, the bar's manager, walked up to the table. "Don't let the middle-age wrinkles fool you. He might look old, but he acts like a teenager."

Pelton stood behind Crome and he felt the kid's hands on his shoulders. He said, "We both do."

Colette held up her beer. "I'll drink to that."

"Get your hands off me, for God's sake," Crome said, suddenly annoyed.

Pelton kissed him on top of his head. "Love you too, big guy," and walked away.

She laughed.

Crome wanted to get up and pop the kid except he couldn't stay mad at the man who owned the one bar that forgave his ever-growing tab. The kid even carted his drunken butt to his house on Sullivan's Island and dumped him in his spare bed more times than he cared to admit since Maureen had left town.

If he were to think about it, Crome might come to the conclusion that his six-pack-a-day drinking habit had doubled since her departure. But he wasn't about to waste brain cells on that now with Colette sitting next to him. She looked good in her summer wear and he caught her looking at him through her sunglasses.

"What?" he asked.

"I always knew you were a big teddy bear," she said.

He took a swig of beer and swallowed. "What do you mean?"

"You let your friends tease you," she said. "The old Mick Crome would not have allowed that to happen."

"You're lookin' at two-point-oh," he said, raising his bottle.

She tapped hers to his. "I kinda like it."

The truth was he had gone through more than one reboot to get to where he was—probably six or seven if he had to count. The current version drank way too much to avoid thinking about the damage he had done to his friends. Regardless of why she was here, Crome appreciated Colette's company.

"I'm glad you approve," he said. "It ain't easy bein' me."

"I believe you," she said.

A quick search into her past yielded a divorce record and a teenage daughter whose custody Colette shared with her ex. She also had a decent pension with the police department but not much in savings. He'd figure out how to give her the money for her cross-country plane ticket.

"Considerin' the danger you're in for being with me," he said, "I hope you have more than sunscreen in that purse of yours."

"Affirmative," she said. "I never leave home without my Glock."

"Good to know. I suggest we carry extra clips."

She gave him a wink. "Anything for you, tough guy." She picked up her menu.

Crome talked her into letting him order for them. He, of course, chose Pelton's infamous Atomic Burgers. Colette said she liked things spicy. Pelton put enough jalapeños and hot ketchup on them to torch a house.

They ordered two more beers and enjoyed the evening and the acoustic guitar player singing seventies and eighties classic rock.

The Kincaid estate on Kiawah Island stretched across four acres. The billionaire had purchased the land in plots six months into the Great Recession. While many people lost money, most of them the hard-working middle class, the moguls like Kincaid nearly doubled their net worth in the volatile stock markets. Coupled with the foreclosure debacle and real estate collapse, Kincaid got his

22222

compound for fifty cents on the dollar.

It seemed to Blu that Ariel had settled into familiar surroundings. Things like whether or not her guest house was air conditioned were non-issues. The full-time-full-service staff at her beck and call helped improve her disposition, not that she had acted like a spoiled brat roughing it at Blu's and Crome's houses.

Blu found her sprawled out on a lounge chair by the pool which overlooked the Atlantic Ocean, her skin darkening nicely. Beside her was Jennifer who did act like a spoiled brat at times but was good-natured about it, calling herself out while she did it.

With a hand shading her eyes, Ariel looked up at him. "Howdy, Handsome."

"Don't even try it," Jennifer said. "If he ever dumps Tess, he's mine."

Ignoring the sunbathing sirens' teasing, Blu said, "We need to talk."

Ariel tugged the lounge chair next to her a little closer. "Have a seat."

He looked at Jennifer hoping she'd get the hint.

She said, "It's my house. I'm not moving."

Losing round one, Blu sat. "A few problems could be heading our way."

"In addition to ones I already have?" Ariel asked.

"I think they're related, but I'm not sure," he said. "What we have is something bigger than the attack on you."

"What do you mean?"

"The club hit was just the tip of a very large iceberg. Powerful men with more pull than Jennifer's father are in play and me and Crome are now on their radar."

"Nobody's bigger than my daddy," Jennifer said.

He thought she might have even believed it. The man was truly a tycoon, and Blu wondered where his resources ended. This time he might just find out. He said, "Let's hope you're right. Is he home?"

Jennifer took a sip of an iced drink, something pink, smacked her lips, and said, "He'll be back in a few hours. Why not take a dip with us?"

He'd made it a point not to get too close to the pretty, young socialite, even though she sometimes made it difficult. Ever since he'd rescued her from a Mexican Cartel holding her hostage for a big payout from her father, Jennifer had wanted to express her gratitude to him personally. That was a line Blu would not cross. Besides, Blu's reward, aside from a large payout, had been that he and Crome befriended a cartel outcast and were able to move him back into power by wiping out all of his adversaries thanks to the intel he'd provided. It was a win-win as far as Blu was concerned. The cartel wasn't going anywhere so who led it was almost inconsequential in the grand scheme of things.

Blu said, "That's okay. I'll come back later. We need to keep Ms. Ariel out of the public eye until this is resolved."

"I have commitments," the pop star said.

"Do you trust your manager?" he asked.

"Yes."

"Postpone things for at least a week. And under no circumstances are you to say where you are. Do we have an understanding about that?"

Ariel looked like she was about to argue.

Blu said, "I can't protect you at my house any more. These people have taken you in. I do not want the danger around you and me to come here. For their sake, you have to stay hidden."

"I worked so hard to build myself up to this point," she said. "I can't afford to let it slip away."

"It's simple," Blu said. "Either you stay here, hidden. Or you leave Charleston. Those are your two choices."

"Fine," she said. "I'll pack my bags. When do we leave?"

"You don't understand," Blu said. "I'm not coming with you."

Ariel winced as if someone had slapped her. "What do you mean you're not coming with me? Who can I trust?"

"If you don't trust me when I say the best thing for you is to stay hidden for seven days, then you aren't going to trust me on the road. And I certainly can't protect you out there."

Jennifer said, "He's right. My dad's men here are the best, but I won't travel without Blu. I do what he says when he says and I always come home safe. He is the best of the best."

"So he protects you when you travel?"

"He does," Jennifer said. "But I'm not an international superstar. I'm more like a low key diva without the sex video."

Blu hadn't heard Jennifer describe herself that way, and he didn't agree with most of it. She could be a handful when she didn't get her way but she did listen to him without question. The reason she'd gotten captured in the first place was because she had ditched her previous guard and got him killed when he tried to find her. That was when her father, through Andeline, called on Blu. The job had paid a lot of money but it had cost him and Crome quite a lot, more than they would ever care to admit.

Jennifer put her arm on Ariel's shoulder. "I like having you here. I never had a sister and it's been nice sharing things with someone who kind of gets me."

Ariel took a deep breath. "Okay, but I need some things."

"Name it," Blu said.

"A studio. I'm behind on my work. If I can't tour, I can record."

"Done," Blu said, not entirely sure how he was going to do it.

"And I want that trainer, what's his name? Heath? I want him here for two hours a day. I need to be ready to hit the stage when this is over and he is the best I've found in a long time."

"No problem." Again, he'd have to see if Heath was in agreement. It may end up costing her extra to have him change his schedule around.

As if resolving something in her mind, Ariel nodded. "This could work."

Blu clapped his hands. "Good. I'll have Hope make all the arrangements."

His daughter liked a challenge. Setting up a working recording studio in the next twenty-four hours sounded like a good one.

Chapter Sixteen

Blu sat at his kitchen table and cleaned his guns, all the doors and windows in the house closed for the first time ever in the middle of summer thanks to the air conditioning that Ariel paid for. Colette, neck-length blonde curls, California suntan and all, sitting on one of the rockers, had Blu wondering how Crome attracted these women.

His phone buzzed on the table. Blu didn't recognize the number but wiped oil off his hands and pressed the speaker button. "Hello?"

"You really screwed me, Carraway."

"That doesn't narrow it down," Blu said. "Who's this?"

"Jack Teller."

Ariel's ex-head of security.

"You did that all by yourself. What can I do for you?"

"What can you do for me?" He sounded incredulous. "You've done enough. I'm like a leper now. No one wants to work with me."

"I'm sorry to hear that, Jack, but it's not coming from my end."

"Tell Ariel to keep her mouth shut," he said.

"That sounds like a threat," Blu said. "Is that what it is?"

Threats were taken seriously. Especially from disgruntled ex-employees and ones with combat training, whether they were any good at it or not. Blu had learned the hard way to keep people like this on his radar. Teller had been above average at one time which made him more than dangerous enough.

"You take it anyway you want," Teller said. "There are plenty of people who want that tight butt of hers out of the picture. You tell her that from me. All I gotta do is say the right thing to the right person and she's dead."

Before Blu could respond, the call ended.

He needed to find Teller and neutralize this before it got out of hand.

Reassembling his guns helped him figure out a plan. The first call he made, after he finished, put his cleaning kit away, and wiped the oil off his hands, was to Crome.

Crome said, "Teller's a real piece of work. He really threatened Ariel?"

"Yes. Said he was going to start talking. I'm not sure what that means. He might assume she's here but he wouldn't know for sure."

"Except the world knows she flew into town."

Crome was right.

"Except for that," Blu said.

"You know what we gotta do next?" Crome asked.

"Shut him up."

"As much as I want it to be otherwise," Crome said, "we're not in that business. What I was gonna say is we need to find out who he thinks he should talk to about Ariel."

Blu had to admit that his partner had something there.

Snapping him out of his thought, Colette said, "I'd really like to know how all this is linked. So would my boss."

"Are you here on vacation or is this business?" Blu asked. It was a fair question.

"Both," she said. "I decided to take Crome up on his offer of being my personal tour guide. My boss okayed me coming out here. It helped that I bought my own plane ticket."

Later that night, with Tess doing a modeling session with Harmony, a side occupation that fell in their perfect laps, Blu sat next to Crome on the back deck of his Folly Beach rental. Colette slept soundly inside, the jetlag and Crome's sometime insomnia finally catching up with her.

"One of us has to go hunt Jack Teller," Crome said. "You know that, don't you?"

Every time Blu thought he was on the verge of kicking his vape habit, another stressor came around and derailed his progress. First it was Murder, and only God knew what had taken the horse out of commission. Now it was Ariel and the Russians and Townley and Teller. Talk about fighting a war on multiple fronts.

Blu exhaled vapor. "Yes."

"Are we gonna flip a coin or what?"

With a chuckle, Blu said, "We could always send Pelton."

Crome got choked up. "Jesus, Blu. The kid's a natural fit for our agency, but that doesn't mean we should start sending him out on solo missions."

Blu looked at Crome. "So we should send you to accidentally kill Teller?"

"Now, that's not even fair. I only broke two of Sherman's fingers."

"I'm not talking about Sherman."

Sometimes Crome could spiral out of control.

Colette handed Crome another beer. "I could find him."

The past winter, Crome replaced the dry-rotted deck they were sitting on. He'd even sanded and coated the new, stouter floor boards with a thick layer of paint so he could walk across them barefoot. That made it easy for Colette to sneak up into their conversation.

"I appreciate the offer," Crome said, "but I spent half my time in California worrying about Harmony. I don't need to worry about you, too."

She sat in his lap. "You'd worry about me?"

"Damn right I would."

Maybe Crome had changed. The incident with Maureen seemed to have an effect on him. When it was just Blu and his motorcycle in his life, Crome had no worries. With other people in the mix came responsibility. Crome typically ran from responsibility. Blu had a feeling that after this job was over, Crome would head out of town again. Most likely he'd go to Key West,

Florida, and he might not come back at all this time.

The Russians made their move first and it turned out badly.

It started off with a shriek from one of the horses followed by a full throttle gallop from the entire herd around the house. From previous events, Blu recognized this as a warning that there were intruders on their island. The horses could handle one and maybe even two people they didn't like. But more than two caused them to get all riled up and panicky.

He slid his Beretta down the waistband of the pair of jeans he slipped on. Heading for the back door, he grabbed the Mossberg shotgun he had and leaned it against the wall behind the back door beside him.

Over the past winter, Blu had installed motion detection lights around the house. The horses were so smart, they figured out how to move around without tripping them off at night. He wasn't sure if it was out of courtesy or because they didn't like the lights kicking on and impairing their night vision.

Even with the gallop around the house, they did not trip the lights.

Blu pulled his Glock and waited, peering out the windows. The lights kicked on, illuminating three men carrying AR-15's. He dropped all three of them with three sequential head shots.

The front lights tripped on at the same time after another round of galloping horses thundered across the front of the house.

He ran to the front door just as two men turned their rifles on the animals approaching them.

Without time to aim, Blu fired six bad shots. They hit the men before they could shoot any of the animals, but they didn't die from his shots.

Murder, leading the charge, reversed course and trampled over both downed bodies followed by the rest of the herd.

Blu called Crome and told him to get over to his house as quickly as he could.

Then he did a reconnaissance of his island.

Parked a quarter mile down the road were two Range Rovers which meant there could be as many as ten men if they'd crammed in. So far he only knew of five.

He moved in a half-circle pattern from one end of the island toward the other. Behind his shed, he found two men crouching.

Blu said, "Pree-vyět."

The men turned. Blu shot them both from ten feet away. In one of their hands was a device. Blu recognized it as it fell. He turned and ducked behind a palmetto tree and dropped to the ground on some rocks as the IED (improvised explosive device) blew. The volume of shrapnel and explosive gasses and hot air enveloped the area.

When the dust settled, Blu thought he heard the distinctive sounds of a Harley along with automatic gunfire before he passed out.

Blu awoke on a portable gurney underneath the awning that had been used to cover Murder. Dink and Doofus stood nearby just like they had done earlier for their black-coated leader. It was daylight and he squinted.

Sitting up, he felt a hand on his shoulder and Tess moved to stand over him. She kissed him on the top of his head.

It felt really good.

As he moved, an ache set in. Mostly his head, but his shoulder felt tender. He remembered diving onto some rocks behind the tree. The bruising was better than losing a limb, or his head.

"Are the horses okay?" he asked.

She traced his face with her hand. "Yes. All of them are fine. Just spooked."

Dink and Doofus came over, nudged Tess to the side, and put their snouts in Blu's face as if assessing the situation.

He laughed which tweaked his shoulder and caused him to grunt.

Tess handed them each a small apple, along with Sally who joined from the other side.

The horses chomped on the fruit but didn't move.

Murder stood by the water trough, watching everything.

The first people Blu saw, after Tess, were Crome and Brack Pelton, each with pistols holstered and visible.

Then he saw Detective Powers, tall and still fairly lean in khakis and a dark blue polo shirt. His hair was going gray and he wore sunglasses.

Powers, Crome and Brack examined a black crater filled with mangled steel and concrete blocks that Blu could swear used to be the shed that housed his father's old Dodge pickup and tools. The big palmetto behind the shed was also gone from about three feet up.

A paramedic hesitantly approached.

Tess managed to get the horses away from Blu so the medic could check on him.

Crome saw Blu was up and came over to him.

"How're you doin', partner?"

"Peachy," Blu said. "How many were there?"

"You and the horses got seven of them. I came across two more trying to get away. They didn't make it."

"I thought I heard gunfire right before I passed out," Blu said.

"They opened up on me, the dumb commies. Made me drop my bike. That pissed me off."

The fact that they made him damage his motorcycle upset Crome but not the invasion of Blu's island showed how he thought. This was most likely why he couldn't keep a woman for very long.

Before Blu could reply, Crome said, "How're you doing?"

"Better than them, I guess."

Pelton came over. "Jesus, Blu. You might want to think about adding a drawbridge and turrets."

Two years ago, Brack and Blu had to fight off a small army of bad guys on the island. They prevailed, but like today it had been a close call.

The paramedic asked Blu if he wanted to go to the hospital. He declined.

Powers said, "They had modified AR-15's with 250 rounds a minute capability. You and your four-legged friends are lucky."

They were indeed lucky the Russians were so stupid. All the Russians had to do was stand at the bridge and fire a bazooka round into the house. That would have taken care of Blu with minimal effort. The problem, as Blu saw it, was that they wanted payback for the botched arms deal with Sammy. Nine times out of ten, revenge clouded judgment.

Another problem was that they still didn't get all of the original gang of the Red Army. Of the five Russians the police raid didn't account for, Blu, Crome and the horses took care of three of them. There were two left: Uri and his second in command. The problem with this scenario was they had all the money which meant they could buy another army and make another attempt. He didn't tell Powers about Ariel.

But, in the meantime, Blu and Crome found themselves with another pressing problem. Hope had managed to acquire quite a bit of first class recording equipment and have it all delivered to the Kincaid compound. They didn't know how to set it all up, much less understand how it worked.

Since last year, Blu had been encouraging Crome to rebuild a relationship he'd all but destroyed. It was this foresight that allowed him to make a call and save the day.

Phineous Soloman, Charleston's resident photo analyst expert, also had a good handle on electronics. The thirty-year-old might not bathe on a frequent basis, and he might smoke more than a fair bit of ganja, but he understood an opportunity when one was presented to him.

He showed up at the Kincaid compound freshly showered and wearing what looked to Blu like a new set of business casual clothing. Blu emphasized that he would pay five thousand dollars a day for the job, but Phineous had to show up clean and presentable and the kid had complied. Blu had also promised an introduction to someone famous, but he didn't elaborate.

Another contingency for the job had two parts. The first was that Phineous could not leave until the job was done, therefore reducing the risk of word getting out about Ariel's current location. The second part was that he could not post anything about it on social media until given the approval to do so by Blu. Any violation would result in no payment and a visit by the Evil Crome. Evil Crome was Phineous' reference to the time when Crome showed up at the analyst's shop and terrorized him to get information that the kid would have given freely without all the drama. Crome had used Phineous as a pawn to distract Blu but the whole thing had blown up in the biker's face. The biker had been making recompense ever since.

Blu, sore as hell but still alive, escorted Phineous from the grandiose entrance of the Kincaid mansion to the guest house that was being converted into a recording studio. When he introduced the young man to Ariel, Phineous nearly fainted.

He turned to Blu as if asking if this was real.

Blu nodded. "We could really use your help, Phin. Ariel's staying here for a few days and needs to cut some tracks. But this is a secret session, you understand?"

The young man's head moved up and down like a jackhammer. "Absolutely, Mr. Carraway. Glad to help out."

Ariel asked Phineous some questions. Once he got over his initial jitteriness and began to calm down, he actually sounded quite credible. Blu hoped Phineous could do the job, otherwise they were back to being in a pickle.

With that problem resolved, and with Ariel in the care of the professional security team of Adam Kincaid, Blu and Crome could get back to their own problems.

Such as, who the heck wanted her dead, where were the Russians, and where was Blake Townley?

Chapter Seventeen

Tess and Harmony met Blu, Crome, and Colette at the Pirate's Cove for dinner. There were certainly nicer restaurants on the island and in the city, but the four locals felt most comfortable amongst friends.

Blu thought Colette was happy to be around Crome and away from her massive caseload back home.

All of them but Blu got a round of shots to toast the evening.

Since Tess had begun dating Blu, she'd curbed her alcohol intake to one drink to be sociable. Gone were the all night shot marathons with Harmony and Crome. She now spent her evenings with Blu on his island. It worked out better that way for quite a few reasons, one of them being that she had a roommate and Blu didn't.

Brack and his wife, Darcy, joined them for dinner. They all ordered steaks, a new item on the Pirate's Cove menu, and Brack, as usual, picked up the tab. As the evening wore on, the discussion centered on the current situation with Ariel. Who orchestrated the attack? Why did Townley send Sammy and his men to Charleston? Were the Russians getting another team together? What was happening with the murder charge on the other side of the planet? When was Jack Teller going to resurface? And what was Jarnel's involvement?

Unfortunately there were no new answers.

The next morning, Blu set up an early lunch date with Andeline. Her reach extended beyond Charleston, but not all the way to Asia.

What she lacked in international connections, she made up for with local information.

He walked into her downtown restaurant at eleven a.m. and flipped his Wayfarers on top of his head.

Andeline looked him up and down. "I daresay Tess has made a new man of you."

Instead of his usual black t-shirt, jeans and Doc Martens, he wore a navy polo and khakis along with leather loafers that matched his belt, and his father's Rolex.

He kissed her on the cheek. "What are you talking about?"

"For starters," she said, "you have this smile on your face. It appeared when you started seeing her and has only gotten bigger since."

"I thought you were talking about my clothes," he said.

Andeline put her arm in his. "I always said clothes made the man."

He wasn't sure how to take it. Of course, it didn't help that Tess had in fact given him the clothes.

Andeline seated him at a table by the front window and sat across from him. "You know if I had a shot, I'd smother you to death."

He put his hand on hers. "I don't think I'm man enough for a woman like you, And."

She patted his hand away. "Good answer, Mr. Carraway."

A waitress brought a soft drink for Blu and a glass of white wine for Andeline.

They dined on three courses of lowcountry cuisine: she-crab bisque, baked oysters over cheese grits, and devil's food cake.

As he ate, counting the calories, he made a mental note to hit the gym as soon as possible. He hoped he could get there after his food settled and Andeline allowed him to leave.

It was like that with them. She was the city's queen bee and men flocked to her for many different reasons. If Blu didn't know better, he'd think she was back to running a high end escort service similar to the one she got busted for five years ago.

As they finished the last of their meal and pushed the plates away, she said. "I'm hearing whispers."

"Like what?"

"More like subtle inquiries about any new celebrities in town."

So far, they had managed to keep a lid on Ariel's whereabouts but it was only a matter of time now. And the postings of her commercial flight to the city would not help.

"Has Ariel's name come up?" he asked.

"Yes," she said, sipping a cup of coffee. "But so far, since no one else in town has seen her, I think it's assumed she's somewhere else."

"According to one of Crome's sources," Blu said, "we're about out of time."

"Then I guess you better get busy," she said.

"Thanks for lunch," he said, standing. "I'm not sure why you couldn't have given me this over the phone."

She stood. "I just like having a handsome male around."

He kissed her cheek. "Why don't you borrow Brack's dog?"

She laughed. "Don't think I haven't tried. That dog melts my heart every time I see him."

Like every other woman.

"If things go south," Blu said, "get out of town."

"I've never run from anything in my life," she said. It was the truth. Even when she got busted for running a brothel, she stayed and fought it. Thanks to Blu's skill as an investigator and poor work on the prosecution's part, the charges were dropped.

"Still," he said. "I don't want anyone getting hurt because they're friends of mine."

"You want a clear conscience," she said. "Well, I'm not going to give you one. You need to fix this before that happens."

It wasn't what he wanted to hear, but she was right. His friends had already sacrificed a lot for him and for Crome. It was unfair to keep putting them in harm's way.

* * *

After an intense workout at the gym with Roger, who asked repeatedly where Heath was, Blu showered and got back to work. He'd told Roger the partial truth that Heath was on a special assignment for Blu's investigation agency but assured him he was not in any real danger. The whole truth was he was being well paid to train Ariel. She wanted him at her beck and call and that cost money. Heath agreed because it wasn't permanent and he needed the cash. By Roger asking Blu where he was, it was obvious Heath hadn't told his friend much.

As he drove away, Blu resisted the urge to vape and instead chewed on Nicorette.

The Bluetooth in his truck picked up a call and he hit the answer button.

Hope said, "Hey, Dad."

"What's up?"

"You got a strange call from someone named Jack Teller."

Warning bells went off. "Oh yeah?'

"He said, 'Tell your old man I made the call.'"

"Okay, thanks."

After he hung up with Hope, Blu dialed Crome.

"Our time just ran out."

Crome said, "What's the plan, boss?"

When a tough decision had to be made, Blu was the boss. Every other time, like when dividing the money, they were equal partners. Such was being in business with Mick Crome.

Blu said, "We need to find out who's going to come at us and when."

Even if Blu thought Crome was an annoying business partner, he had one heck of a list of sources from all over the world. It was how they'd found out Sammy was coming to town. And now it would have to be the way they found out what was next.

In the meantime, they had to circle the wagons. That meant making sure their friends understood the dangers coming their way.

They called everyone to a meeting at the Pirate's Cove.

Tess already knew about it. So did Harmony because she was close to Tess.

Brack and Darcy Pelton sat at a table in their bar and listened as Blu revealed everything.

When he was done, Paige, the bar's manager, said, "So that's why we had to be hush-hush. I can't believe Ariel has a contract out on her."

"Believe it," Crome said. "And now so do we."

"What are you going to do?" Darcy asked.

Before Blu could answer, Brack said, "You're going to move Ariel, aren't you?"

"No," Blu answered. "She's safer there than anywhere else I can think of."

Crome said, "We can control everything if she stays in the city. And Kincaid's guards are the real deal."

"Why do they hire Blu when the daughter travels?" Darcy asked.

Harmony said, "Because she has a crush on him."

Tess said, "That's not funny."

With a grin, Harmony said. "Just kidding, I think. But who knows, she probably does. The real reason is because Blu is very good at that part of the business."

"Yes he is," Crome said.

"So now that we're done polishing his medals," Brack said, "you want to answer my wife's question: What are you going to do?"

"We're going to find out how they're going to come at us and then we're going to stop them."

The call came in later that afternoon. Blu got the message from Crome, bought a plane ticket, and was gone that night, through

Atlanta, and on the tarmac of LAS, the Las Vegas international airport, eight hours later but only five with the time change.

A call to Jimmy Zoluchi, Blu's mobbed up source from a long way back, got him an under-the-table firearm contact since he didn't pack any heat in his carry-on.

Blu drove his rental Tahoe to a parking lot of an abandoned big box store outside of town, the temperature a cool hundred degrees as dusk settled.

It wasn't long before a Porsche SUV with dark-tinted windows pulled up next to him.

Blu got out of his truck. This was the most dangerous moment of the trip. The people in the Porsche could rightly assume he was unarmed. If they were playing for the other team, Blu was dead.

Two men got out of the Porsche.

Both were dark-skinned like Blu who stood leaning against his rental truck.

"Mr. Carraway?" asked one of them, a sharp dressed man about thirty with a thick head of hair, sunglasses, and a silk shirt and linen pants. He'd been the passenger.

Blu said, "Mr. X."

It also unnerved Blu that the man knew his name whereas he didn't know theirs. The only saving grace was Jimmy Z. If this turned into a setup, Jimmy would have the wrath of Crome to deal with. Blu assumed that was understood and the only reason he agreed to these conditions.

The young man smiled and waved him to the back of the Porsche.

The tailgate automatically raised and inside the cargo area were several black cases. Blu noted that no one was in the backseat of the luxury SUV which meant it was just the three of them.

Blu had already provided Jimmy with a list of what he wanted while he was in town. Pointing to the cases, he asked, "May I?"

"Of course."

Mr. X's associate was less polished but looked tough. As tall as Blu, the man had a strong build. Blu suspected he'd be a formidable opponent if things took a turn for the worst. The successful arms dealers had gotten smarter and Blu guessed that while it was just the three of them in the lot, Mr. X probably had a small army nearby to take care of any problems.

Blu picked up the first case, a small one that housed a new Ruger EC9 nine millimeter. He'd wanted to try it out since he'd read about it, checked the action, found it empty, and put it back in the case. The next case had what everyone either loved or hated, an AR-15. Because every other joker seemed to carry one, Blu felt the need to have a model, a Smith & Wesson M&P Sport II, at his disposal. He didn't know what Teller would do and decided to be safe rather than sorry.

The last case, the largest of the three, had an M24 sniper rifle. Because he had left his at home, Blu wanted one close by. Even if he never used it, he somehow felt better with one in his possession.

He put the rifle back in the case. "I'll take them."

"Excellent choices, Mr. Carraway," Mr. X said. "I like a customer who knows his weapons."

Blu took out an envelope. Inside was the agreed upon five thousand dollars. He went to hand the money to Mr. X.

The young man declined. "It has already been taken care of."

"I'm sorry?" Blu asked, readying himself for an attack.

"This is courtesy of Mr. Zoluchi," the man said. "He wanted me to tell you that since the Red Army left town his business has had an uptick."

Blu eased his rental truck's key fob out of his pocket and pressed the button to open the tailgate. While Mr. X and his guard watched, Blu transferred the three cases from the Porsche to his truck.

"Where's the best place to get ammunition?" Blu asked.

Mr. X smiled.

His guard opened up the rear passenger side door of the Porsche. Lined on the back seat were boxes of bullets and empty clips for all three guns. Blu loaded them into the back of his truck as well.

When he was finished, he turned to shake Mr. X's hand and found him and his guard already in their truck. The engine barked to life and they sped away.

While he trusted Jimmy Z well enough to meet his arms source, he wasn't convinced the man was trustworthy. In the backseat of his rental SUV were similar cases to the one's housing the weapons in his trunk. He transferred the weapons to the cases he brought and left the empty ones the weapons had come in on the ground next to his truck. It was too easy these days to plant tracking devices.

The boxes of shells would be harder to transfer so he took a slight risk. It didn't matter. The bullets would be loaded into the clips and the packaging discarded as soon as he made it back to the city and his hotel room. He didn't care if Jimmy knew where he stayed. He just didn't want the gangster to know the places he planned to visit.

Charleston, South Carolina

Crome was climbing the walls. Blu had insisted on going alone and he didn't like that one bit. Crome hoped it wasn't some macho thing where Blu felt like he had to face Teller man to man. Hollywood glamorized the move, but it was really stupid to give up a tactical advantage. No one trained in combat ever did it willingly.

Colette sat up in bed behind him and rubbed his shoulders. She'd done her best to distract him, but now that they were finished his mind was back to wandering.

Kissing his back, she said, "Don't worry. Blu is the best there is."

He turned to look at her. "Thanks a lot."

Smiling playfully, she said, "You know what I mean."

"Do I?"

She kissed him on the lips and he watched her walk into the

bathroom.

When all of this was over, he was heading out of town, maybe for good this time. Key West and massive amounts of alcohol called to him.

Chapter Eighteen

After the shooting incident in Vegas during that country music concert, it was harder to sneak weapons into hotel rooms, but not impossible. A golf bag didn't have to carry clubs. It could carry a multitude of odd shaped objects. Blu bought one from a large sporting goods store, emptied it out, and shoved both rifle cases inside it. They barely fit.

He also bought three colorful duffel bags for the ammo and clips. With his weapons hidden, he checked into his hotel. The valet loaded a cart with his luggage and wheeled it in for him. A bellhop guided him to his suite, unloaded the cart, and accepted a twenty dollar tip on his way out the door.

Blu called Crome, who seemed both happier and grumpier than usual. Colette must have thrown him for a loop when she showed up. The old biker wasn't used to being chased, especially by the same woman twice.

She was a good one. The problem with Mick Crome was his destructive lifestyle. If Blu looked any harder, he'd realize his own lifestyle wasn't much better, so he shifted his train of thought to another topic: Jack Teller

It made sense that he'd hole up in cities known for debauchery.

Over the phone, Crome said, "You get the guns?"

"Jimmy hooked me up at no cost."

"Ha," Crome said. "There was a cost, alright. Those damn Russians. He's got more business than he knows what to do with. You got what? Three guns? He's going to make a ton of money all because of us."

"Still," Blu said, "you can't get busted for buying arms illegally if you don't have to buy them."

"True enough," Crome said.

"How's Colette?" Blu asked, hoping to rattle him again.

"Um, she's good."

"Well that's nice. You check on Ariel?"

"Every couple of hours," Crome said. "I call Phin and he gives me an update. The poor kid's smitten. If she gives him credit for the mixing, we might have just given him his first Grammy."

If it happened, they'd need another photo analyst because the kid would be gone.

"One more thing," Crome said. "You got a special delivery heading your way. Should be there any moment."

Blu didn't like the sound of that.

There was a knock at the door.

With his phone to his ear, Blu peered through the eyehole. It was Harmony.

Crome continued, "Don't worry. Tess is okay with it."

"You don't say." Blu opened the door.

Harmony gave him a big grin.

Blu handed her the phone. "Tell him you made it."

The reason for sending Harmony was two-fold, as Blu listened to her explanation. If it were Tess, he might be distracted and make decisions not in the best interest of the job, and Harmony was better at manipulation.

Blu couldn't argue with either point, except that he'd still worry about Harmony like he would any of his friends. In this manner, she didn't rank lower than Tess. It would have been better if they had all discussed the plan together. He thought he was going to be able to work solo. Now, he had the strawberry blonde bombshell to handle and that could be a fulltime job all by itself.

Harmony smiled at him. "You didn't think we were going to let you come out here all by yourself, did you?"

"What's this 'we' stuff?" he asked. "Last time I checked, my name was on my business card. And your name is not on my employee list."

She put her hands on his shoulders. "Listen, Sugar. You are the best thing to happen to Tess in a long time. I want to make sure you come back to her in one piece. Therefore, I volunteered to come out here myself. It took quite a bit of convincing, but she relented. Crome, on the other hand, was ecstatic from the get-go."

Of course the biker would be. He seemed to enjoy setting Blu up.

There wasn't much he could do about the situation since it was already here. He said, "So what's your plan?"

"Easy," she said. "I'm the diversion."

It was nice to see someone completely at ease with who they were. Too bad she was too mature for Crome. They'd make a good pair.

Blu and Harmony ordered room service and worked out the plan. Thanks to Andeline and her connections, Blu learned that Teller liked a certain type of service and there were a limited number of choices for it, even in Vegas. For an extra ten thousand dollars, and a promise of anonymity, Blu would have the information on Teller's next appointment.

Unlike in California where Harmony was on point with Sherman, she would not show up at Teller's door to perform the service. Blu would not allow this to happen, no matter how much she tried to convince him otherwise.

The service Jack Teller requested was violent in nature and the women were paid quite a bit of money for quite a bit of pain.

Blu had learned through Colette that a few of Teller's girls had turned up dead.

He reluctantly pulled out his vape pen, another reason not to quit today already in front of him, stepped out onto the balcony overlooking the pool below, and sucked in a lungful of dry Vegas air as he looked through his binoculars.

Harmony came out and stood beside him. "Checking out the women at the pool?" She took the pen out of his hand, inhaled, and blew out a stream of vapor.

"Very funny." He lowered the binoculars. "I can see Crome and I have not been a good influence on you."

"I used to smoke in college," she said, "and the trip to California was not a good one for me."

"What about it?"

"I let myself get manipulated," she said.

"I heard Crome broke the guy's fingers."

She smiled. "He did, but I was madder at myself than anything else. I got taken in by Sherman's charm and good looks."

It seemed Harmony got a small taste of her own medicine, although Blu would not mention it to her at the moment.

She said, "You're thinking I got what I deserved, aren't you?"

He took the pen from her hand and vaped.

"Nothing to say?" she asked. "I'll take that as a confirmation."

"What you do," Blu said, "you do to get closer to the truth. There's chivalry in that. What he did to you was use you to get something that only benefited himself."

She reached for the pen. "That's an interesting way to look at it."

Watching her take another hit, Blu thought she might actually make a good addition to his agency. Of course, she'd need to have more self defense and weapons training. But he had a hunch whoever's side she fought for had a tremendous tactical advantage.

Before he could formulate his thoughts into words, his phone buzzed in his pocket.

Charleston, South Carolina

Crome did not really think it was a good idea when Harmony

proposed to be Blu's backup in Vegas. But he'd learned that arguing with her or trying to convince her otherwise didn't work either. So, he talked with Tess and they came away with a plan: Let her go. Derailing Blu's plans would be unfortunate, but they both felt he was the most pragmatic man they knew so Harmony wouldn't be in much danger. It was the "much" in that last sentence that caused Crome concern. She didn't exactly blend in.

But he had enough to do in South Carolina to keep himself busy. While Colette sat on the back deck of the Pirate's Cove and did online research, he took a ride to Myrtle Beach. His underworld source there was Bert Dorman.

Dorman ran a bar on the outskirts of town that catered to those living on the fringes of decent society and those that had jumped off the deep end. With long hair held back by a do-rag, handlebar mustache, black t-shirt advertising some topless bar in Chicago, ripped jeans and boots, Dorman was a twenty-year older Crome.

The older biker stood behind his makeshift bar that had been assembled by welding several shipping containers together underneath some old live oaks on an unwanted piece of property outside of town. When he saw Crome, he limped over to him.

Crome shook his hand. "What the hell?"

Dorman smiled. "I dropped my bike last week. Could'a been a lot worse."

It was every rider's worst nightmare. Crome understood only too well. He'd dropped his when the pikers with machine guns drew down on him on the attack at Blu's island.

"You break anything?" Crome asked.

"Just my pride," Dorman said. "You wanna beer?"

"You bet."

There were three other men at the bar. Crome recognized them. Two pushed pain pills while the third recently got released from prison where he'd served time for armed robbery. Crome wasn't worried. He'd had a run in with one of the pushers back when he was on reds, but it had been a long time ago.

He and Dorman sat at the bar while the bartender, a tatted up, long-legged, black-haired woman with dark skin and tight shorts poured the drinks. Her tied up t-shirt distracted Crome and he almost forgot what he was there for.

At Dorman's nod, the vixen poured Crome a twenty-two ounce Budweiser and sat it on a coaster in front of him.

Crome said, "Can I buy you a drink?"

The bartender leaned forward and gave him a smile that could stop a train. "Mr. Dorman told me to watch out for you."

"Looks like you can take care of yourself, you ask me," Crome said.

Dorman said, "No one asked you."

Apparently he was still pissed he lost Maureen. After Crome rescued her from the same kidnapper who'd taken Harmony, Maureen decided to move away and not tell anyone where she was going. Crome understood her anger at him. She didn't deserve it, but there wasn't anything he could do about it now.

The bartender left them and refilled a glass of beer for one of the pushers.

Crome said, "Jesus, Bert. I'm just trying to be social."

"Bein' social is sayin' 'howdy' and 'thank you, Ma'am'. You wasn't bein' social. You was bein' an asshole. Only everyone else but you knows it."

If Crome didn't need some information, he might have thrown it back at Dorman. But now wasn't the time. There'd be another, and he'd knock the old man on his keister.

For now, he lifted his glass, raised it to Dorman, and took a long pull. Setting the glass on the coaster resting on the steel plate that made up the bar's surface, he asked, "So what have you heard?"

"About you and Blu? Not much."

"What about in the business?"

"I'm always hearin' things," Dorman said.

The old man was testing him. Trying to see what he was after and what dots he could connect. There was no way Crome was getting out of here without giving him something. The trick was to give him pieces of a puzzle he couldn't put together.

"Who're the big players?" Crome asked, keeping his eyes on his beer and his expression flat.

Dorman shifted on his stool toward Crome. "You lookin' to relocate?"

"Maybe."

"Well," Dorman said, his face lit up, "hog my hooter."

If his old riding partner hadn't turned into such an arrogant ass, Crome might have felt guilty about lying to him. A lesson he learned the hard way, and relearned last year when he went around trying to burn every bridge he ever had, was that he could win the battles and lose the war. Dorman might think he's sitting on top of Old Smoky but he was just one arrest away from going down for good.

Crome asked, "Who's paying?"

Dorman laughed. "Everyone's payin'. It's an operative's market." He took out a pack of Marlboros and lit one up. "The question's more about morality inasmuch as you have any. Stories I heard, you sold your mother five times over and would do it again if the price was right."

Crome eyed him. His first instinct was to pummel the old man to death. But his own middle age had brought him wisdom. His hard-earned intuition told him Dorman was pushing him into doing something stupid.

He said, "I been known to bend a rule or two."

"That's an understatement," Dorman said, exhaling smoke. "So what are you after here?"

"Employment."

"You already got that. Thanks to your partner, you two are the class act of the business. And that's in spite of you. Everybody knows nobody gets the drop on Blu Carraway when he's on the job."

"What about me?" Crome asked, but knew as soon as it left his mouth it was a mistake.

"Maureen would still be here if you hadn't pissed her off."

There it was. The old man did still blame him for Maureen. If Crome were honest with himself, he'd lay most of the blame at his own feet as well. But he was sick and tired of everyone else doing it for him.

Most of him wanted to get up and leave, but he still needed what Dorman had so he stayed. He looked into his beer again. "You're probably right."

"Now that we have that clear," the old man said, "what are you really looking for? The only reason you ran back to Blu was because you screwed up in Miami and needed to get out of town."

To Crome's knowledge, nobody knew what happened in Miami that caused him to get out of town and on the road when he ran into two idiots talking about Blu two years ago. Crome had been away for three years making serious money working for the mob. And then came Miami. A mobster's twenty-five-year-old son was buying and selling children and Crome broke his neck when he caught him in the act. He set it up to look like a suicide. It was anything but. The young man would still be terrorizing and raping children if Crome hadn't stopped him.

Wanting to know what Dorman referred to because nobody knew the truth, as far as Crome could tell, he asked, "What are you talking about?"

"That tadpole that hung himself. Word is he was your responsibility."

"My job was to make sure no one else got to him. What he did to himself was on him."

Dorman stubbed out his smoke. "His daddy never bought the suicide story."

The daddy was a bigger degenerate than the son. The apple didn't fall far from the tree.

Crome said, "I did my job. Nobody got to junior but himself."

It was a true statement if not entirely the truth.

With a nod that caused Crome to wonder if Dorman knew something or was fishing, the old biker said, "They still blamed you, though. Didn't they?"

"I didn't stick around to find out," Crome said.

"So why the questions about the business?" he asked.

"I just wanna know if a group is trying to consolidate is all," Crome said.

Dorman seemed to think about that for a moment. "I'm sure there's always someone trying to do that. Word is Blu has an exclusive with Kincaid. His own security team would prefer to have the whole thing, but the daughter won't have it. She only wants Blu when she travels."

Crome didn't know about the exclusive. But, knowing Blu the way he did, he figured his partner signed the contract. It's easy money but came with strings. And it explained why Blu dropped what he was doing and headed out of town every time he got a call. Contractually, he had to.

Dorman did not answer his question, and Crome got the impression he was holding back. He looked at his old mentor. "You got a piece of the action?"

The tell was so faint only someone who knew the curmudgeon for as long as Crome did could pick up on it. But it was there, he was certain of it. A faraway look in his eyes, like having to go into himself to keep from revealing anything. Crome saw it for less than a second. The old man was keeping his cards close.

It meant there was money at play, a lot of it if Dorman was ready to throw Crome to the wolves. Or maybe they had drifted apart enough that selling each other out didn't seem that far a stretch any more.

Crome excused himself and went to the restroom, another container divided in the center by a sheet rocked wall. Each side was supposed to be gender specific, but in this day and age and when things were really busy at the bar, it was every man and woman for themselves. Crome used the side designated for men and relieved himself. One look at the sink and he realized his hands would be cleaner if he didn't wash them here. He took out a business card, wrote a note on the back of it, and, on his way back to Dorman, stopped and handed the card to the stunning bartender.

"What's this?" she asked.

"A business proposition," he said. "What does it look like?"

She read the note and then looked at him, fanning herself with the card.

He waited for her response.

With absolutely no subtlety, she held up a hand with five fingers.

Crome couldn't be sure what she was willing to give up for what he assumed were five hundred dollars but it was worth the risk. On the back of the card was where he'd be spending the night. He returned to his seat beside Dorman.

The old biker said, "She's not gonna tell you anything."

"She's too new." Crome slammed the rest of his beer and set the glass on the bar. "It ain't her words I'm interested in."

The bartender came over and refilled his glass, giving him a wink as she went to serve another of the degenerate patrons.

With a sigh, Dorman said, "There is talk about some larger group trying to take over. I'm not sure why or who's behind it. But they're getting some of the players we know."

"Was Sammy Hart part of it?"

"I heard that, "Dorman said. "I also heard he bought the farm. Something about a run in with the Red Army?"

"I heard that, too."

"Of course," Dorman said, looking directly at Crome, "I also heard you and your partner set him up. I'd say his crew thinks that, too, but they all managed to perish along with him."

"Tough break," Crome said, not really meaning it.

"You and your partner are causing trouble for some people," he said.

"No one's approached us about joining anything," Crome said.

"No one is going to. You guys go rogue too many times. I'm not for sure, but I bet they think they can't control you. And that makes you a liability."

A new Dodge Challenger rumbled into the parking lot. Seeing

as how the entire bar seating area was pretty much outdoors, it wasn't hard to notice. It was one of the endearing things about the place and the reason why most of the barflies came from the fringes of society—the layout made it hard as hell to sneak up on anyone.

Two men got out of the new muscle car. With one glance, Crome took in their measure and readied himself for violence. They walked with a military influence. The Army had taught him self-confidence and the Rangers taught him self-awareness. Unlike everyone else at Bert's Bar, these guys had a purpose and Crome suspected it had something to do with him.

They took two stools at a raised table across the way from where Crome and Dorman sat.

Crome said, "Friends of yours?"

"Never seen them before."

While Dorman might be telling the truth, Crome thought the man knew who they were. He asked, "What are they doing here?"

"Drinking, I suppose," Dorman said. "Like everyone else."

Crome leaned in. "If they cross my path again outside of this place, I'm going to take care of them and then I'm coming back here. We clear?"

Dorman gave a sideways glance to the men and then to Crome. "I can't help what goes on outside of my bar."

"No one else knows I'm here," Crome said. Even Blu. And, thanks to someone slipping a tracker on his bike last year without him knowing it, he swept his Harley almost daily and had done so before he left Charleston two hours ago.

"If they're here for you, someone else must know."

Crome got up. "You been holding out on me since I showed up. I'm not sure what for, but I can guess. See you around, Bert." He walked to his bike, fired it off, and sprayed gravel as he roared down the unpaved road to the highway.

Chapter Nineteen

Las Vegas, Nevada

The call came from Jack Teller. Blu answered while standing on the balcony of his top-floor suite with Harmony vaping by his side.

Teller said, "I heard you were in Vegas."

"Good news travels fast." Using the binoculars, Blu peered over the pool and into a room across the hotel compound. Teller stood on his own balcony with two naked young women. They looked at Ariel's ex head of security in complete fear. If they were legal-aged Blu would eat his P.I. license.

Blu handed the binoculars to Harmony.

"Don't worry," Teller said. "I'm going to handle you personally."

She looked through the specs, whispered, "What a pig," and then said, "I hope you give him everything he deserves."

Into the phone and in answer to Teller's question, Blu said, "Mighty generous of you. But I think I prefer you watching over your shoulder."

"Yeah, right," Teller said.

Blu said, "In your hotel room, I left you a present in the fridge." He ended the call, snatched the binoculars from Harmony, and watched Teller turn and head inside. Blu saw the man stare at a black refrigerator as if contemplating whether Blu was serious, and if he was, if there was a bomb ready to blow when he opened the door.

As if coming to a conclusion that it was a ploy, Teller jerked open the door. Nothing happened and he didn't find anything because Blu didn't leave anything. The reaction he wanted, and got from Teller, was to get him scared, and then make him feel relieved that Blu hadn't been in his room and was just yanking his chain. He wanted Teller to not believe Blu could be good enough to have found out where he was staying, sneak into his room, and plant something.

Teller smiled to himself, shook his head, and closed the door. He turned to his guests.

Blu realized that Harmony wasn't beside him anymore. He heard her talking in the room behind him.

She said, "I saw a man enter room four-one-three with two young girls. They did not look old enough to be doing what they were going in there to do."

On one hand, Blu was mad because what she was doing might spook Teller. On the other, it was the right thing to do.

Myrtle Beach, South Carolina

The two men in the Challenger did not follow Crome as he headed into the tourist district of the coastal town that used to be sleepy forty years ago. Myrtle Beach was a lot of things, but calm wasn't one of them anymore especially in the heat of the summer season.

His modified Harley Davidson rumbled as he idled down the main drag lined with neon and people trying to get away from the reality of their normal lives.

He had a few hours to kill before dark so he found a spot on a side street and walked to a local oyster bar. A two-top table opened up at the bay window by the street and he sucked down a dozen raw oysters and a few beers as he people-watched. For once, he wasn't drowning in his beer for some screw up of his own doing. He'd served his penance and gotten on with his life, and it surprised him that he'd stuck it out with Blu this long. Normally he ran from monotony.

With his appetite satiated, he rode out to the campgrounds, picked a spot, and set up camp. Unlike a hotel room where he always felt trapped, sleeping under the stars gave him an edge. Someone would have to be real quiet to sneak up on him. With his payment for the campsite in cash, there was no electronic record of him being anywhere.

He cleaned up in the showers, changing into a fresh set of clothes he had in the saddle bags, and opened up his sleep roll on the ground next to his bike.

As he stretched out, he thought about Colette. He wished she was here with him. Of course, they'd need a tent.

He began to doze off.

It felt like he'd only been out for a few minutes when a sound woke him up. He slid the nine millimeter Glock out from under his mat and raised it.

A female voice whispered, "It's me."

In the darkness, he spotted her silhouette against the moonlight. He was pretty certain it was the bartender from Bert's.

He said, "Pull up a sleeping bag."

She sat down next to him on the ground. "You really know how to impress a girl, don't you?"

"I haven't had many complaints," he said.

"First things first," she said. "My five hundred."

He pulled a money clip out of the front pocket of his jeans and handed her five crisp hundred dollar bills.

"Were you followed?" he asked.

"I don't think so."

"The guys in the Challenger?"

She stretched out next to him. "They stuck around and talked to Bert. I punched out at my normal time and took off toward my house."

"Whattaya got that's worth five hundred?" he asked.

"Whattaya think?" She kissed him.

He let her but didn't take it any further at the moment. "I agree about that, but I was looking for something a little less physical."

"I'm not sure I understand."

"Information," he said. "Dorman's trying to get the drop on me. I want to know what his plans are."

She kissed him again. "And you think I know?"

This close, she smelled of perfume, sweat, and bar wash. He liked it. She also had a faint musky scent that he recognized. It was desire.

He was in trouble.

She said, "Can't we talk about it later?'

Normally, when things were going this good, something was wrong, as if he were in the middle of a set up. Probably the one he was asking her about. She'd betrayed him.

He hadn't let go of his gun.

When he saw the first figure approach, he raised his Glock and fired.

The blast caused her to shriek away.

A voice said, "Dammit!"

Crome shoved the bartender down and spun around to catch the other assailant.

A gun blast went off and Crome felt the heat of the bullet as it whizzed by his head.

He returned fire and caught the man in the chest, dropping him to his knees before he keeled forward.

The woman shrieked again and tried to tackle Crome.

The timing couldn't have been more terrible for her.

The first man Crome had shot fired his weapon at Crome. It hit her in the back.

She grunted and died in his arms as Crome shot the man again. The second shot hit home and he fell to the ground.

A police siren wailed in the distance.

The police came and tried to shut the campground down. But aside from families on a budget, the other people who camped here lived on the fringes like Crome. They would not want to be questioned by any authorities because a simple background check could lead them back to jail. Most of them vanished into the woods.

Crome really didn't want to stick around either, but slugs from his registered Glock were in the two men. He wouldn't get far and would get locked up anyway.

He'd tried to save the woman, but she was gone. It was a pity, really. Dorman would have to answer for her as well as the other two, and Crome would not ask his questions nicely the next time.

If Dorman wasn't dead already because he'd botched up the job of taking out Crome, the old biker would wish he were. Crome felt that as soon as word got out that the ambush failed, Dorman's days were numbered. Whether he punched the old man's ticket or someone else did.

Las Vegas, Nevada

After watching Teller's party get interrupted by the police, who hauled him off in handcuffs, Blu and Harmony went to work. Harmony, along with Hope back in Charleston, internet-sleuthed while Blu managed the boots-on-the-ground aspect.

While Harmony stayed in the suite in front of her laptop, Blu left to run down a source Jimmy Z had given him. It appeared as if Jimmy's gratitude extended beyond the guns. Blu was appreciative but apprehensive. He would not be indebted to the local mob for anything.

He rode the elevator down to the lobby, didn't get the sense that someone was watching him, and made his way to the valet. Of course, there were so many people around that it wouldn't be easy to separate the professionals from the people-watchers. Chimes and beeps from the game machines drowned out the conversations.

The valet brought his truck around and he sped away. And that's when he spotted the tail. The trick was to tip their hand. By speeding away, their only choices were to try and follow or let him get away. With professionals, it was always better to let them get away and pick them up later. Tipping a hand only let them know someone was following. It gave them a chance to be ready and to create an ambush.

The tail was another SUV and it cut off two cars as it pulled out after Blu.

Knowing he had a tail told him two things: Someone was interested in him and someone knew which hotel he stayed in. The second was easy because he'd registered under his own name. The first was the intriguing part. With Teller in lockup, verified by Harmony with a few well-placed phone calls, the tail either worked for him or someone else, and the someone else could be a long list.

As he contemplated this driving up the strip, his phone rang. He used the truck's Bluetooth to answer.

"Yo," he said.

Crome said, "Dorman's dirty."

"Tell me something new."

"He sent two men and a woman after me. They're all dead."

"What?" Blu slammed on the brakes to avoid rear-ending the cars stopped in front of him. He needed to pay more attention to his driving.

"I killed the men; one of them shot the woman. I'm in lockup."

Blu said, "You call the lawyer yet?"

"No," he said. "This is my one phone call."

"I'll take care of it. You at the Myrtle Beach P.D.?"

"Yep."

"Help's on the way."

"Good. All they got in here right now are drunks."

"You got that right," Blu said.

"Very funny, partner," he said. "How're you makin' it with Harmony?"

Blu thought there was a slight tone of jealousy in Crome's voice.

"Apparently better than you did," he said. "She hasn't gone out with another guy since we've been here."

"Ouch."

"If you're in jail," Blu said, "who's watching things?"

"Pelton."

"You better hope he doesn't shoot anyone, Crome, or we'll be in more trouble."

"He ain't gonna shoot anyone that don't deserve it."

"That's encouraging," Blu said. "BOLO for Brogan."

"Roger that."

The call ended.

Blu called Lester Brogan. The lawyer promised to handle it at his usual rate of a thousand an hour without another retainer.

With Crome in jail and Pelton keeping an eye out for Hope and Tess, Blu had to make sure he didn't get locked up like his partner. There were too many angles to cover as it was.

It was time to lighten the load.

On the outskirts of the city, he pulled into a gas station to fill up the tank. The tail passed by. Whoever was in it made a lazy U-turn and waited at a curb. They either wanted to get noticed or were not professionals.

Blu finished pumping gas, took his receipt, and went inside the convenience store. He bought a bottle of water and a granola bar, and exited out the other door. A paint store was next to the gas station and he cut across the parking lot, jay-walked across the street, and knocked on the window of the tail.

It was Colette.

She buzzed down the window. "It took you long enough."

"Your tailing skills leave a lot to be desired," he said.

She gave him a smile. "You wouldn't spot me if I didn't want you to."

"Crome's in jail," he said.

It wiped the smile off her face.

Chapter Twenty

"What do you mean Crome's in jail," she said.

"You should have been watching him," Blu said. It was a hot, dry evening. Typical Vegas.

"He took off on me," she said. "I didn't know what else to do so I came out here."

"How'd you find me?" he asked.

"Credit card trace," she said.

He looked over at his rental SUV. "We should drop one of the trucks."

"There's a Wal-Mart down the road," She said. "Follow me there."

He backed away from her truck and she sped off.

He had to double-time it back to his SUV and accelerate hard out of the gas station to catch up.

Sitting in the passenger seat of Colette's SUV, he asked, "What the hell are you really doing here?"

"Truth be told, I was bored. I can't believe Mick ditched me."

He gave her a long look.

Keeping her eyes on the road, she said, "I know, I know. It's how he is."

"He's been my friend for over twenty years," Blu said. "The guy's a walking train wreck in aviator shades."

His phone buzzed. It was Harmony. He answered with, "What did you find?"

"Teller got the girls from a service that runs them out of a house in the suburbs." She rattled off an address.

"Good job," he said.

Harmony said, "You're thinking you could use a gal like me on your team, aren't you?"

It was exactly what he'd been thinking. "Why do you say that?"

"You've been getting that look in your eye," she said. "I know men. It's not the one I normally get."

"Thanks for the intel," he said. "I'll be in touch. By the way, Colette's in town. We're on the job now."

Harmony said, "Just remember, I've already been shot and kidnapped. I can handle just about anything."

She ended the call.

Blu thought, "This girl is one big bag of mixed nuts." But she was as tough as they came and could get places he and Crome never dreamed of and it sounded like she was interested in a job.

The problem was the pay would not be that great and the medical benefits were nonexistent. The compensation was in the chase.

Colette said, "Where to, Boss?"

He loaded the address Harmony had given him into the truck's GPS. "Follow the arrow."

"Roger that." She lit a cigarette.

Blu pointed to the nonsmoking stickers throughout the interior.

"Don't worry," she said, "I'll just bill you for the cleaning fee."

Everyone was a comedian these days.

She turned on the radio. George Strait's "Run" began to play.

As he pulled out his vape pen, he said, "I didn't figure an LA girl for a country music fan." He cracked the window, vaped, and tapped his fingers on the window sill.

"I was born in Kentucky," she said. "You forget?"

"Yep."

"Your partner remembered."

It was Crome's gift. He could be caught stealing from Fort

Knox and talk his way out of it. Most women bought his act, at least
for the short term. The problem with a murder charge was it was
harder to skate on. Even with Brogan representing him.

"You should marry him, then."

She laughed. "My mom mighta raised a floozy, but she made
sure she raised a smart one."

"You said it."

Back in the day, when Blu could have just about any woman he
wanted, Colette bypassed his charm and went right for Crome. She
hadn't changed in twenty years.

"So," she said, "you and Tess, huh?"

"Yep."

She said, "Hey, I followed a man who dumped me twenty years
ago across the country. There's nothing I can say except 'best
wishes'."

It was Blu's turn to laugh.

A black SUV pulled up next to them on Colette's side. The
window rolled down.

Blu leaned over, grabbed the wheel, and rammed the other
truck just as the passenger raised a machine gun above the
sightline.

The shots went mostly wide. The black truck careened into the
median and flipped over.

"Slow down," Blu said.

Colette didn't respond.

Her eyes were open. Blood trickled down her cheek.

Blu put it in neutral and engaged the emergency brake.

The truck eased to a stop as he guided it to the side of the road.

He felt for a pulse. There wasn't one. In the rearview mirror,
he caught the sight of a figure approaching. He pulled the Ruger,
opened the door, aimed, and dropped the man holding the machine
gun and walking toward the truck with two shots.

A hundred feet away, another man scrambled out of the
overturned SUV which was on fire. He barely made it through the
window, a pistol in his hand, and Blu hit him with a headshot.

Blu waited as the truck burned. Either there were others inside or there weren't. They would die trying to get out or burn alive. Blu didn't care.

He didn't have to wait long. The gas tank blew up and the truck was engulfed in flames.

Blu ran back to Colette's SUV, dialing 911.

Myrtle Beach, South Carolina

Crome took the news, but tried not to process it. Colette was dead. He held the phone to his ear as he rode in the front seat of a Mercedes belonging to a lawyer who worked for Brogan.

Times like this all he saw was a bunch of dead bodies. All that mattered was making sure they were the right ones. Someone had sent the gunmen after her and Blu and that someone would not make it.

He ended the call with Harmony, not saying anything and cutting her off from whatever she was trying to tell him next.

The lawyer dropped him at police impound so he could pick up his motorcycle. Two hundred dollars and four new scratches on the deep lacquer finish later and he was on his way. The scratches alone would have sent him over the edge, but seemed inconsequential at the moment.

He rode back to Charleston and went straight to the Kincaid compound to have another talk with Ariel.

The security detail let him through the front gate and he was escorted to the makeshift studio. He waited patiently while she finished laying down vocals against a slow, pulsating rhythm for a song that he was positive would go to number one. Even hearing it only for the first time just then. The woman had some serious talent and Phineous wielded the electronics like a pro.

The beat ended and she grinned.

Phineous took one look at Crome and did not grin. He got up

from his chair and cut the distance between Crome and Ariel.

"I've seen that look before, Mick," the photo analyst said. "Whatever you got stored up inside you better leave it before you talk to her."

The lanky man had grown a serious backbone in the last year. Crome could have killed him with one hand and both of them knew it. Still, the younger man held his ground.

Crome said, "You sure you wanna do this?"

"Are you?"

Taking a two second breath in followed by a four second exhale, Crome said, "Tell her I'll meet her by the pool. Alone. You don't hafta worry, Kid. I'm only here to talk."

Before Phineous could reply, Crome walked out and made his way to the large Olympic-sized pool that overlooked the Atlantic Ocean.

Jennifer Kincaid lay sprawled out on a lounge chair, asleep in the mid-morning sun. The princess of Charleston didn't have a care in the world, and meanwhile people were dying. Such was the life of the privileged.

Crome walked past her, his boots clomping lightly on the concrete but not loud enough to wake the sleeping beauty. At a table shaded by an umbrella, he quietly pulled out a chair and sat. While he waited, he sucked on vapor and calmed himself down.

Ariel approached with caution, her bare feet padding on the concrete. She wore a light-colored tank top that exposed white bra straps and short khaki shorts showing off tanned legs.

Crome watched her but didn't get up. Now wasn't the time for chivalry.

"What's wrong?" She asked. "Is Blu okay?"

"Colette's dead."

She put a hand to her mouth, her eyes as bright and as wide as two full moons.

"Blu's in jail," he continued. "Capped two men and let two others burn to death."

She blinked.

He said, "They deserved what they got, the bastards."

"I heard you also were attacked," she said.

"Yeah. I got set up by an old friend. I didn't trust him anyway, but it would take a lot of money for him to turn on me like that."

"This is all my fault."

Crome set his vape pen on the table. "You know, I wanted to come over here and blame this all on you. Lay every dead body at your feet."

She slumped in her chair, the weight of the world on her shoulders.

"But the truth is," he continued, "this is bigger than you, if you can believe that."

Her eyes met his. "What's that supposed to mean?"

"You got a serious case of 'Imma-star-itis'," he said, "but this is about one or two evil men in the middle of a power grab. You're just a pawn like the rest of us."

With a long sigh, she asked, "What do we do now?"

He stood. "You don't want to know."

"Yes I do," she said. "This started with me. I'm in this whether you like it or not. I may not be able to put up a good fight, but I can help."

She had a point. The term 'bait' came to mind.

He said, "You sure you want in?"

"Whatever it takes," she said. "Colette died because of this thing that started with me. I'll never go another day without remembering her. Whoever did this is going to pay."

"Blu capped the guys who killed her," Crome said. "That's already done."

"Someone sent them, though. Right?"

Smart girl. "Yes."

"Then that's who I want."

In a court of law, this would go down as 'conspiracy to commit murder' and it was punishable in South Carolina by up to twenty-five years in jail. Crome had a feeling that Ariel had lawyers nastier than even Brogan who could get her out of murdering the

President, if she needed. Privilege came in many forms, but was always backed by money.

Bert Dorman smoked a cigarette alone at his bar. Everyone in the underworld including his usual patrons had heard that the old biker tried to set Crome up for a fall and failed. These were people that had an uncanny survival instinct. They knew that Crome would come after Dorman and might not be too concerned about leaving civilian casualties.

All this was going on in Crome's head as he idled to a stop next to Dorman's shiny F150. He dropped the kickstand, leaned the bike over, and took a seat next to his old friend.

On the bar beside Dorman's ashtray was a small metal bucket filled with ice and longneck bottles. The old man lifted one of the bottles out, twisted the top off, and set it in front of Crome. He threw the top over the bar and into a trash can.

Crome took a long pull of the beer, turned, and shot two men who'd tried to sneak up from behind. He swung his pistol back around but Dorman had a revolver pointed at him.

The old man said, "I'm sorry it has to go down like this."

"Me, too," Crome said, eyeing his friend.

"It's been nice knowing you, Mick."

"You, too, Bert."

The blast of the discharged firearm echoed in the trees.

Las Vegas, Nevada

Two drunkards in the holding cell who were similar in stature to Heath and Roger tried to make a game of picking a fight with Blu. It was the last mistake of the evening they'd made, the first few being whatever they'd done to get thrown in jail.

Blu, not looking for a fight but relishing in the opportunity, had used it to work off some of the anger he had from Colette's death.

The men, both with huge, ripped chests, thought strength made up for brains and skill in combat. It only worked in first-strike situations and long battles. But in a crowded jail cell, Blu saw them coming.

They had no chance.

Afterward they lay on the ground, broken and bleeding. Blu claimed one of the few bunks for himself and fell soundly asleep.

No one came near him. No one wanted the same beating the two body builders had received.

Chapter Twenty-One

Myrtle Beach, South Carolina

Crome watched Dorman as blood trickled to the ground at their feet. The revolver was on the bar between them, the sounds from the gunfire still echoing in his ears.

Brack Pelton said, "I'm calling for an ambulance." He'd shot Dorman in the shoulder blade.

Crome said, "They'll take a while."

"And the police."

Pelton had a contact with the locals. And Crome knew Dorman had the bar rigged up with cameras. It would show enough for a good lawyer to use to keep the kid out of jail.

Crome drank from his beer.

Pelton should have aimed for the heart. Or the head. Either way, Dorman would be dead instead of dying so slowly that the ambulance would make it in time to save the bastard.

That's exactly what happened.

Crome finished off the beers on ice in the bucket while the ambulance hauled away the old biker. The police came, including Pelton's friend, Detective Williams.

They tried to ask questions but only received one-word answers.

Crome wasn't happy Dorman had lived, but he wasn't real upset either.

A couple hours later, someone, not Brack or Crome, snuck into the I.C.U. room where Dorman lay recovering from having the bullet removed and gave his I.V. a hot shot. The old biker died peacefully in his sleep.

Las Vegas, Nevada

Blu faced the judge the next morning and was released without any charges. There wasn't enough evidence to prove it wasn't self defense. The fact that Colette was killed by machine gun spray from one of the men from the black SUV and that the footage from traffic cameras verified Blu's story were enough.

Harmony met Blu at the courthouse. They took a cab back to the hotel where Blu washed the jail funk off his skin and changed clothes.

She sat on the couch, hugging a pillow. "Crome confronted Bert Dorman."

Crome was a lot of things, but he wasn't stupid. Blu asked, "Alone?"

"He took Brack with him. Dorman had two guys and Crome shot them. Brack shot Dorman."

"Uh-oh."

"Dorman didn't die there. Someone got to him in the hospital."

"What a mess."

She said, "It means Dorman knew something someone didn't want him talking about."

"You hungry?" Blu asked as he picked up the phone.

"Yogurt."

Blu ordered room service, a yogurt parfait for Harmony and an American breakfast for himself along with juice and a carafe of coffee.

It came within fifteen minutes.

Harmony answered the door and signed the charges to the room.

They ate in the peace and quiet of their suite while outside the chaos that was everyday Vegas chugged along.

Colette was just doing what she felt was right. She didn't need to die. Not like that.

Mourning ended with the morning. Blu felt exposed since they'd arrived. He wasn't sure why they weren't attacked on the way back from the courthouse or why they'd been left alone in their room.

But he couldn't let them be sitting ducks any longer. He called the head of hotel security and made arrangements.

The hotel had options others did not. Most of its patrons preferred making a grand entrance—the shiny limousine pulling to the curb, the valet opening the door, the beauty exiting the car first followed by the peckerwood high-baller. All timed and choreographed and practiced the world over.

There were others who preferred privacy. Private entrance, private elevator ride, private table. They came and went with no one the wiser. Blu was interested in the second option. They needed to leave the hotel without being seen.

For enough money, the hotel would accommodate most anything. With the expenses agreed upon, the hotel security staff made it happen. They even arranged for another rental vehicle, a Silverado pickup, to be waiting.

Blu set the satellite radio to the eighties channel and Harmony promptly changed it to modern pop. He didn't argue. His taste in music was mostly the older stuff, but he didn't mind branching out.

From memory, he loaded the same address Harmony had given him the day before, when Colette was shot. This time, he drove and Harmony rode shotgun. He used the time to have a frank discussion with his new potential candidate.

Harmony had dated at least one member of the S.W.A.T. team over the past year and had received some decent training on the proper use of firearms. It would be Blu and Crome's job to teach her the improper use of them. Which didn't mean juggling loaded weapons with the safeties off. It meant that sometimes guns were used strictly for intimidation, sometimes they were used for blunt force trauma, and sometimes they were used to shoot first.

He'd already picked up where Biff or Blane or Baxter— whoever the sorry SWAT sap was she'd dumped after she'd gotten what she wanted out of him—had left off. She was responsible for what came out of the muzzle. There were innocents all over the place. Living with killing someone who didn't deserve it was a life sentence. That and they couldn't get verbal information from a dead body.

Common sense type stuff.

She ate it up.

Charleston, South Carolina

Crome was all messed up from Colette's death and the betrayal of his friend of more than twenty years. All this for what? Was the money really the reason?

The short answer was yes.

Pelton said, "You okay?"

They sat in chairs on the back deck of Crome's Folly Beach rental overlooking the Atlantic.

"I never thought I'd ever have a place with a view like this," he said.

"It's the best place on earth," Pelton said. "Except for the bugs."

"True, that."

"If I'm overstepping, let me know," Pelton said. "But I can't believe whoever is behind this would risk killing a cop." Meaning Colette.

Crome had been wondering the same thing. He took a drag from his vape pen and exhaled. "Either they shot her by accident or she knew something. Like Dorman."

"We're next, you know."

"I'm not so sure," Crome said. "It seems like they're more interested in cleaning up loose ends."

"Well, I'm sleeping with one eye open until this is finished."

Crome wondered if Pelton slept with one eye open anyway, but didn't say it. Between the kid and his wife, they had made quite a splash in the city. He was convinced there were plenty of ticked-off people who'd prefer if they weren't around. He asked, "What could they know?"

"I suppose that's what we have to figure out."

From the stairs, a female voice said, "I think I might have found out something."

Both men turned. It was Tess.

What had Blu done to deserve this one?

Las Vegas, Nevada

The house was in a nondescript subdivision in the North Las Vegas suburbs—homes in the two to three hundred thousand dollar range. Large plate glass windows, yellow paint, single story. A luxury SUV and sedan were parked in the drive.

From the front seat of their rental pickup parked at a curb, Blu said, "Looks pretty normal, doesn't it?"

Harmony said, "I grew up in a neighborhood like this. When I was ten, my neighbor was charged with pedophilia."

Blu looked at her.

"He liked boys. Otherwise, I would have for sure been one of his victims." She said it matter of fact. "I vowed that day to pay more attention to the world around me."

"Is that why you got into investigative journalism?"

"That and I can be narcissistic."

"I don't buy that for a moment," he said. "You care about others. Narcissists don't. Crome is more of one than you'll ever be."

She leaned over and kissed his cheek. "Thank you for that."

A dark-skinned man exited the house, got in the sedan, and backed out of the drive.

"Should I stay or should I go?" Blu asked.

"That's one of your oldies songs, isn't it?"

It was still a tough pill to swallow that eighties music was now oldies. Through gritted teeth because he didn't expect the age shot, "Yes it is."

"Touchy, touchy," she said. "You better lighten up if you want to chase younger women."

"Double ouch."

"Relax," she said. "Tess is happier than I've seen her in a long time. She needs someone like you. Stable, honest, not a hound dog like Crome."

"I don't mess on the carpet, either," he said.

"There's that, too," she said. "I say follow him. The house isn't going anywhere."

How could someone so young put things in perspective like that?

He started the truck and, when the sedan turned the corner, followed at a distance. This job had tentacles in Malaysia, California, Las Vegas, and, because Ariel was currently there, Charleston.

It seemed to cover the entertainment industry, private security, and now maybe human trafficking given how much it kept showing up.

But at least he wasn't bored.

"You checking your six?" Harmony asked.

She really had been spending too much time with him and Crome. He checked the rearview and memorized the vehicle makes and colors. He'd check again in a few minutes.

He said, "Thanks."

Here like the rest of America, the pickup blended in better than just about anything else on the road. He'd think about getting one for surveillance and maybe have different magnetic contractor signs for the doors.

The driver of the sedan drove into town and pulled in at one of the major hotels. He had the valet park his car and walked inside. Blu did a quick pull up to the curb. Harmony jumped out and fast-walked inside to find the target while Blu dealt with the valet.

By the time one of the young men in the red vests got to him, Harmony and their target were long gone. Blu did not like being separated from her, not after everything that had happened.

His phone buzzed in his pocket.

Harmony said, "Miss me yet?"

So much it hurt, he thought. "Where are you?"

"On my way up to my room."

"You're on the elevator?"

"See you soon," She hung up.

While it was the only way they could find out where he was going, he didn't like the situation. But all he could do was find the elevators and wait for her to call back.

He watched the crowd, felt someone watching him, and spotted Uri and two of his goons.

Blu called Harmony. "Get the hell out of there. Meet you at the valet."

"But..."

"Now. It's a setup."

"Roger that."

He walked directly at the Russians, who seemed to not know what to do as he closed the distance.

Using a waiter as cover, Blu ducked down a row of slot machines ten feet away from them, zigzagged, and took a side exit outside.

He handed the valet his ticket.

The guy said, "Man, I just parked it."

Blu handed him a twenty. "I'll give you another one if you get it to me in two minutes."

"Done."

The next sixty seconds were the longest he'd experienced in a while. Harmony had still not exited, although it might have taken her some time to get an elevator going down.

Three things happened at once.

Uri and his two goons came out the same door Blu had.

Harmony came out the main doors.

And their truck showed up.

Blu yelled, "Get the truck and give him a twenty," as he dropped the first of the two goons with a solid haymaker.

The second goon did not go down so easy. He ducked and Blu missed him and took a hit to the ribs. It nearly winded him.

He used the seconds he'd lost while getting hit to drive an uppercut into the man's jaw and felt bone and teeth dislocate. The man's head jerked back and he went down.

Uri, five feet away, pulled out a pistol.

Blu did not wait for him to get it all the way out of its holster. He jumped into the bed of the truck.

Harmony floored the accelerator.

The back window took two hits along with the tailgate.

Chapter Twenty-Two

Charleston, South Carolina

Crome watched Blu's girlfriend walk toward them, pull out a chair, and sit.

Tess selected a beer from a cooler by Crome's feet, popped the top, and took a long swig.

"We're waiting," Crome said, annoyed at the semi-display of drama. Tess enjoyed toying like this.

She set the beer on the rail and faced them. "Colette moonlighted as a volunteer who worked with sex-traffic victims."

"She was a good person," Crome said. "So what?"

"So you think she came all the way out here just for you?"

Since last year when Crome lost his mind and went AWOL after Maureen got nabbed, he'd been getting attitude from both Tess and Harmony. Although, lately, Harmony had been cutting him some slack.

"You wanna lose the 'tude, Blondie?"

She gave him a grin. "No. Not for you."

"Okay, fine. Why else did she come out here?"

"She told me she always loved you."

There was no let-up with this one. He didn't know what to say. He'd dumped Colette because at the time he wasn't ready to settle down and she was. He was at his best riding free with no strings attached. Any commitment other than his Harley felt like a noose around his neck.

"I thought you said she didn't come out here just for me?"

"She knew you let her go for her benefit," Tess said. "You know, Mick, you do have good qualities even if you're always trying to prove otherwise."

Pelton laughed.

Crome almost killed him.

Tess continued. "The more I learn about Colette, the more I want to kill those who took her out. I can't prove she was the target, but there were only two people in the car and they shot her."

"Yeah, but they would have killed Blu if he hadn't got them all first."

"All I'm saying is, like last year, we don't know what's going on yet. But Blu was tracking Teller through his taste for S&M. Colette knew the business intimately. She could probably dime every major player west of the Mississippi."

"She was a good cop," Crome said, sighing.

"What about Dorman?"

"He had connections to all the local thugs. Since your partner killed Skull two years ago, a cottage industry of specialists formed in South Carolina. Dorman had the local muscle all locked up."

"How does the Red Army fit in?"

"They were a new breed trying to offer a one-stop-shop. You and your partner did everyone else a favor when you took them out. That's why Jimmy Z can't be anything but helpful. Dorman, while he benefited, probably knew you two weren't in it for the money and sooner or later he'd have to deal with your partner's morals."

"You said that like I don't have any."

She gave him a look that said, "Do you really want me to say it?"

"Fair enough," he said, acknowledging she was right.

Pelton laughed again. "Don't sweat it, big guy. You're still my hero."

The kid was really asking for a beating. "You're not my type."

"Too masculine for you?"

"Naw," Crome said. "Too tan."

They all laughed, a nice vacation from the sadness of Colette's passing.

Las Vegas, Nevada

Through the broken back window, Blu told Harmony where they needed to go. It was a run down casino on the fringes of sin city run by a friend. No valet. No flashy lights. No prime rib buffet.

This place catered to those who were either not welcome in the big hotels anymore or couldn't afford them.

Anywhere else, a pickup truck riddled with bullets would stand out. Here, the holes might be seen as badges of honor. Harmony parked the truck in an open slot away from the main drag and got out. Blu hopped down from the bed and felt the pain in his back from the hard landing when he'd jumped in. They walked inside, sharing hits on Blu's vape pen to calm their nerves.

They were greeted by an older version of Jimmy Zoluchi, grayish hair, larger paunch, but the same eyes. He introduced himself as Jerry. He was Jimmy's brother.

"Any friend of Jimmy's is a friend of mine," he said.

He first kissed Harmony's hand and then shook Blu's. Then he guided them behind a reception area consisting of clean but worn-out couches and a more worn-out woman behind the desk with long, pink fingernails, bottle-dyed hair, and heavy makeup. She smoked a Virginia Slim behind a sign that said "Thank you for not smoking".

The office was clean and also worn out. It resembled Jimmy's office at the used car dealership where Blu purchased his SUV.

"By the looks of your truck," Jerry said, "I'd say the rumors are true that you ran into Uri."

Blu sat carefully in one of the visitor's chairs. His back continued to protest, but it was loosening up.

Harmony said, "You're Jimmy's brother, aren't you?"

Blu hadn't told her.

"Guilty," he said. "Thanks to you all, we're expanding our business in Charleston again."

He smiled at them.

"What?" Blu asked.

"You still haven't gotten Uri."

"I didn't realize that was what you were paying me for," Blu said. "Oh, wait a minute. You're not paying me."

"Might as well be," Jerry said. "We got you the guns and told you where Teller was."

Harmony opened her palms. "Like you said, your business is growing thanks to Blu. What more do you want?"

"Uri taken care of."

Blu looked around. "Why don't you take care of him with your own guys?"

"Can't do that," Jerry said.

"Why not?" Harmony asked.

"Because," Blu said, finally getting it, "they really can't."

"Well," Harmony said, "I can see that based on what talent you have here."

Blu almost laughed, but he didn't want to add insult to injury. Harmony had tagged Jerry pretty good with that one.

Unfazed, Jerry smiled.

"What I mean," Blu said, keeping his composure, "is that Jerry can't be seen outright trying to take Uri out. There must be some other business we don't know about between the factions."

"That's a good way to put it," Jerry said. "But if you continue on your path, I won't have to worry about it."

"What if they find out you're helping us?" Harmony asked.

Jerry smiled matter-of-factly. "Then we'll have to take care of it."

Meaning they'll have to take care of him and Harmony and they won't use the local thugs Harmony picked up on that weren't worth spit. They'll bring in hired guns, professionals. Men as good as or better than Blu and Crome. And they'll do it for a large sum of money so success is guaranteed.

"We're discrete," Blu said. "Although they could track us here."

"I doubt it," Jerry said. "Uri only had time to get the two men you found with him and you took care of them. He's scrambling to find more as we speak. Which he will. This place breeds desperate men, but, as you pointed out, Ms. Childs, sometimes not the best."

Blu said, "I need my guns and we need a new place to hide out."

"And another vehicle," Harmony said.

Jerry said, "Done. And I need something from you."

"What's that?" Blu asked.

"My daughter and ex-wife want to go to Mexico. I want you to watch over them."

"Deal," said Harmony.

Blu looked at her. Maybe asking her to join the team wasn't the best idea. Especially if she thought she'd be calling the shots.

Jerry had them taken to what used to be a decent suite. He said he had nicer individual rooms, but Blu liked to be able to keep an eye on Harmony as well as be able to have the space to plan.

Charleston, South Carolina

Crome asked, "So what's left for us to do here?"

"Protect Ariel," Tess said.

"We have that covered right now, but if the pros come to town, we'll have to move her out."

"What would that look like?" she asked.

The sun was dropping behind them and they all loaded up with bug spray to repel the mosquitoes and no-see-ums.

Crome explained his thoughts.

Pelton and Tess listened, and then Brack said, "That's okay. I might have an alternative that doesn't require sneaking her out of the state where we lose the home court advantage."

"What's that?"

"You know my pastor friend?" he asked.

They both nodded.

"When Darcy got shot, he and his congregation escorted her out of the hospital. No one hunting Ariel is going to check North Charleston. At least the section of town I have in mind."

"You don't mind putting innocent people in danger?" Tess asked.

It was a fair question.

"These are people who, through experience, have a canny way of getting things done in spite of their situation."

"How does that help us?"

Pelton said, "Where else are you going to find an entire community working together like that around here?"

Crome caught on to what he was trying to say. "We'd have to pay a ton of money, bring in a dozen skilled guys to even come close. And we couldn't do it quietly."

"Still," Tess said, "I don't feel right about it. These are innocent people we're putting at risk. You want to ask a neighborhood of African Americans to risk their lives for one rich white girl?"

"I already did, once," Pelton said. "Brother Thomas took it as a personal challenge."

While Tess ordered pizza, Crome called Blu and learned that he and Harmony had a run in with Uri and had barely gotten away. And that they were now guests of Jerry Zoluchi.

He explained Pelton's plan.

Surprisingly, Blu liked it. "He did that for Darcy a few years ago. You meet Brother Thomas? No way would I want to come up against that guy."

Crome chuckled. "Yeah, I guess you're right about that."

They talked about a few more details and then ended the call.

The pizza came and Tess, Brack, and Crome ate in silence, their minds running through the plans.

Chapter Twenty-Three

Las Vegas, Nevada

Blu got off the phone with Crome thinking Brack Pelton had something with his idea. If war came to Charleston over Ariel, the Church of Redemption would be her saving grace and it might save her award-winning derriere in the process.

He told Harmony what Crome had said.

She said, "That's pretty good."

"I know, right?"

"What does Brother Thomas say?"

"Are you kidding?" Blu said. "He's going to eat this up, machine guns or not. Besides, the whole church congregation will pitch in. We'll have eyes and ears all over their community."

"Money can do strange things, you know?" she said.

He knew what she meant. If Ariel's enemies came to town and started throwing a lot of money around for information, someone might sell her out for a couple of bucks.

"We'll have to risk it," he said. "This is the only way I see stashing her someplace safe without a paper trail."

"Why not just leave her at the Kincaids?" she asked.

"Because, while it's defensible, it's also a known target. North Charleston is a mid-sized town. I prefer guerrilla warfare to defending a position."

She gave him a smirk. "I should have guessed that. So, what are we still doing here?"

"We have to deal with Teller and Uri."

"Do we have to?" she asked.

"If we don't deal with them, they will deal with us. I refuse to look over my shoulder."

She pulled the comforter and top sheet down and sat on the bed. "I hope they sprayed for bed bugs."

"Me too," he said.

She scooted over and patted the seat beside her.

Not sure where this was going, he tilted his head as if to ask her intention.

"I'm not going to try anything," she said. "Jeeze, Blu. You're a hunk and all but you're Tess' man. I got my own problems."

He sat.

She rested her head on his shoulder, said, "I need a nap," and fell asleep.

He closed his eyes for what he thought was a minute.

When he opened them up again, the clock had spun ahead four hours.

Harmony rubbed her eyes. She crawled over him and began stretching.

He didn't feel right watching her contortions, slid off the other side of the bed and did fifty burpees.

The knock at the door gave Blu hope that maybe some more food was being delivered.

Instead, it was Jerry. He said, "We've got some bad news."

Colette was dead and both Uri and Teller were after them. What could be worse?

Blu waved him in.

Harmony came out of her room wearing a short robe, holding a toothbrush, and distracting them both.

Jerry regained his composure quickly, looked at Blu, and said, "Jack Teller is dead."

"No great loss," Blu said. Apparently someone was taking care of their problems for them.

"He was found in your hotel room. We went to retrieve your weapons and luggage and found his body there."

Okay, that was some bad news.

Harmony asked, "How'd he die?"

"Shot, but we don't think it was by any of your guns. You'd hid them well and they appeared to be undisturbed. We retrieved them along with your luggage."

"Where's the body now?" Blu asked, really hoping he didn't get the answer he thought was coming.

"We took care of it."

The last thing Blu needed was to be indebted to the Zoluchi brothers.

"We think Uri did it," Jerry continued. "He's trying to set you up."

A small voice in the back of Blu's head told him Jerry wasn't giving him the whole story or had changed a few details. Either way, if Teller was dead, they could focus their attention on Uri and his new team.

"What do you suggest we do now?" Blu asked, not really needing advice. His mind raced for its own conclusion. He had it before Jerry answered.

Jerry said, "We don't know where Uri's hiding exactly. But this is Vegas. The town is always full of international guests."

"Who's here from Uri's motherland?"

"Boris Treko. That's the other bit of bad news. He's Uri's boss and he's not happy Uri got bested by you."

"Why doesn't he take that up with Uri?" Blu asked, not trying to be funny.

"Oh, he is. And then he's going to want to take it up with you. They don't like any signs of weakness."

Harmony brushed her teeth, but Blu could tell her mind was going a mile a minute. She stopped, removed the toothbrush, and pointed it at them. "So we know where Uri's staying now."

"I would bet he's with Treko," Jerry said.

She continued, "Why don't we send them a welcoming gift?"

"Like flowers?" Blu asked.

She twirled the toothbrush around and put her free hand on her hip. "Something like that."

Blu thought Jerry was getting rattled. No makeup, barely wearing anything, hair down, Harmony could stop a 747. Some washed-up, middle-aged gangster like Jerry was putty in her hands.

Without knowing exactly what Harmony's plan was, Blu decided to give her a lot of room to operate. She wasn't the type to throw him under the bus, but she was the type to let Jerry self destruct if it served her will. Blu said, "Where do we start?"

To Blu, she said, "Get dressed." She spun around, the robe ends hiking up hypnotically, revealing a bit more flesh.

Jerry stood there, captivated and speechless.

Blu gave him a moment to compose himself again, and then said, "How about we all meet in your office in fifteen minutes."

Nodding and still not talking, Jerry left the room.

There was no more debate. Harmony Childs would have to work for Blu Carraway Investigations. Otherwise, her superpowers might end up being used against him. She'd have Crome for breakfast any time she wanted.

After he finished a quick shower and shave, Blu called Crome while he dressed, turning on the phone's speaker.

"We're going after the Red Army."

"I thought we did that already," Crome replied.

"They've got reinforcements here in Vegas. Harmony's working on a plan to take them out. It could blow up in our faces, but nobody said this would be easy."

From behind him, Harmony said, "Thanks for the confidence."

"Is that the radioactive blonde?" Crome asked. "How's it going, Legs?"

"You talk pretty bold from two thousand miles away," she said. "Wait till I get home."

"On pins and needles," Crome said. "So what's this plan of yours?"

Before she could say anything, Blu said, "Hold on."

He turned on the text function and typed out. "Room could be bugged."

She read it and he sent it to Crome.

Crome's reply was to switch to text.

She typed out her plan.

Blu was impressed.

After twenty seconds of silence, Crome texted back. "I'm glad you're on our side, kiddo. But, I'd leave Jerry out completely. Feed him something else."

"Roger that," was her reply.

Charleston, South Carolina

All Crome could think about, and say, was, "If Blu doesn't hire her, he's an idiot."

Tess said, "I agree."

If she didn't come to work for them, they'd have to consider capping her. No one who looked like her and thought like her should ever be given the chance to sit across the table for the other team.

Pelton said, "I thought I was devious."

"When this busts open," Crome said, "Ariel should already be gone from the Kincaids."

Standing, Pelton said, "I'll get to work on Brother Thomas. You two figure out how we're going to get her there without anyone noticing."

Crome and Tess watched him walk down the steps. After a few seconds, the sound of a tuned V-8 motor rumbled to life and roared away.

Crome said, "I'm surprised you don't mind your sister being in

Vegas with your boyfriend."

Her cheeks reddened but she kept her words in check. "I trust them."

"Right," Crome said. "If it's one thing I know, it's that Blu has a way with the ladies."

"You know, Crome," she said. "You can still be a complete ass when you want to be."

He inhaled vapor. "I know. I'm just yankin' your chain."

"Why?"

"At first I was afraid that Harmony in close proximity and unchaperoned with Blu would be a disaster for all parties. Now I'm more concerned that there's nothing to worry about."

"Why is that a bad thing?" she asked.

"Because while he has a way with the ladies," Crome said, "he hasn't had good luck picking the right ones."

She stood. "What are you saying?"

"Don't get me wrong, Tess," he said. "I think you're great. But there is a slight challenge with you two, you have to admit."

She sat again. "I know. But it feels right. He treats me better than anyone else ever has." She sighed. "I'm really falling hard for him."

"Just don't hurt him," Crome said. "Can you promise me that?"

Chapter Twenty-Four

Las Vegas, Nevada

Blu marveled once again at Harmony's plan. Who else could think up a way to knock the Russians out while also dropping a bomb on a human trafficking ring? And all in one shot, to boot.

But first they had to deal with Jerry, who wouldn't appreciate getting played.

Typing out scenarios on her laptop to avoid talking in case the room was bugged, Blu and Harmony fleshed out the details.

What seemed to work the best entailed getting some local intelligence, which could be dangerous depending on how many eyes and ears the Russians had been able to round up.

The first thing they needed to do was snow Jerry. If he was anything like his brother, he would not be an easy mark.

A knock at the door interrupted their plans.

As if knowing they had him on their minds and in their texts, Jerry smiled when Blu opened the door.

"Everything okay?" he asked, stealing a glance into the room.

"Sure," Blu said. "Come on in."

Jerry did not hesitate.

Harmony sat facing a laptop. Instead of the hotel's wifi, they had been using her phone as a hot spot. For all they knew, Jerry could be monitoring everything. As far as Blu could tell, from a thorough look around the room, there were no cameras. But the pros knew how to hide them. He bet Jerry knew how to get it done.

Also, recording the activities of the rooms might give him an edge, like now. Hopefully Blu and Harmony had covered their tracks well enough.

Harmony said, "It's nice not to have to worry about someone sneaking up on us, at least for the short while we've been here. Thanks so much for that."

"My pleasure," Jerry said. "Anything else you need help with?"

"There is something," Blu said. He motioned for Jerry to take a seat.

Jerry sat opposite Harmony, probably strategic from a gawking perspective, while Blu sat next to her. He'd always preferred up close and personal to across the room and creepy.

Jerry looked at Harmony. "Name it."

Taking her cue, she said, "We think it might be helpful to know who the Russians are cozy with in town. The locals."

Nodding, Jerry said, "I can help you with that."

"And," she continued, "we'd like to know who Jack Teller was friendly with."

"I can get that, too."

"Finally," Blu said, "we'll need to split up."

"You mean you two?" he asked.

"Yes," Harmony said. "Do you have some good people you can pair us up with?"

Jerry didn't answer right away. And his face went blank for three seconds. It was as clear of a tell as Blu thought he would get from the man. It meant that he hadn't been expecting that last request, but it was obvious he'd thought of the first two.

"Sure," Jerry said. "I can do that. Any preferences?"

"Brunettes," Harmony said. "Both of them."

"Man and a woman?" Jerry asked.

"Two women," Harmony said. "Smart and funny."

Jerry nodded again, slower than before, a small, sly grin crawling across his face. "Of course."

"They need to take the attention off of us," Blu said. "At least me." He jerked a thumb Harmony's way. "Good luck finding one who could do that for her."

"Thanks for that, Handsome," Harmony said.

He felt his cheeks flush. It was his tell and he knew Jerry caught it because the stubby man laughed.

"I've got just the girls for this. I think you'll be quite pleased." He stood. "Anything else?"

"Can you send up some food?" Blu asked.

Jerry walked to the door. "Right away." He opened it. A bellhop stood next to a luggage rack.

"Here are your bags and weapons."

The bellhop wheeled the cart in and unloaded it.

Blu tried to tip him but he waved it off.

Jerry said, "Umberto doesn't take tips from my special guests."

In Spanish, Blu said, "Thank you, my friend. May you always be at peace."

"And you as well," Umberto replied. He wheeled the cart out.

Jerry said, "Adios," and left the room, closing the door behind him.

Blu walked over to Harmony's computer.

She switched the screen view to the word document they'd been using as their communication board.

He typed, "Two women?"

"You liked that, didn't you?"

"Jerry sure did."

"The pig."

"I guess I should say thanks for not ordering me a stud."

She laughed and said aloud, "Time to get ready."

Within twenty minutes, Umberto returned with another cart. This one had a three course meal of salads, perfectly-done, medium rare filets with potatoes, and cheesecake for desert. As darkness blanketed the city, they ate by candle light, two friends having a nice, peaceful meal, both of them knowing they might not have another. Also included was a bottle of wine of which Harmony had a glass.

Blu sipped Perrier.

Charleston, South Carolina

Pelton hitched up a catering trailer to his Ram pickup truck and drove to the Kincaid residence with Paige and two waitresses. Crome and Tess rode in the covered bed on a mattress under empty boxes.

After serving food to the Kincaid family, all the house staff, and the security detail, they packed up everything and left. Ariel rode in the bed on the mattress underneath the fake boxes with Crome and Tess.

Pelton dropped Paige and the waitresses off at the Pirate's Cove along with the trailer and drove to his house on Sullivan's Island.

Brother Thomas and two women from his congregation arrived at the Pelton home. The pastor pulled his car underneath the house into the garage area next to the pickup. The precious cargo was offloaded from the bed of the truck and into the trunk of Brother Thomas' Volvo.

Crome followed the car at a distance on his motorcycle.

Halfway to the Church of Redemption, he pulled off and Tess picked up the tail.

The car made it all the way into North Charleston with no issues. At the church, Brother Thomas pulled through a large door into a warehouse behind the church. Ariel was helped out of the car and escorted to an apartment Brother Thomas had set up for visiting clergy.

Overall, the plan went off without a hitch as far as Crome could tell. He was quite pleased with everyone. It was boring and predictable and overdone, and it had worked exactly as they intended. The Army had taught him that overkill, if an option, worked quite effectively.

Las Vegas, Nevada

The women that Jerry set Blu and Harmony up with were not what Blu had expected. Instead of two young, bubbly escorts, the pair that showed up were in their mid-to-late thirties, tall, beautiful, and intelligent. Blu got the feeling they were escorts, but for more mature clientele. They were perfect for this job. Harmony seemed to take a liking to one of them right away. The tanned woman's name was Kendra.

The other escort had Middle Eastern features and was named Mona.

Both wore cocktail dresses as stunning as Harmony's sequined number.

The three women toasted the evening by finishing off the bottle of wine from dinner.

Jerry showed up again to make sure everything, meaning the escorts, was to their liking. He also had a sheet of paper with potential lists of the characters the Russians and Teller might have connections with.

The escorts gave Jerry hugs and cheek kisses. He bid them all a good evening. What Jerry hopefully didn't suspect was the reason for Kendra and Mona. They were a great decoy. The Russians and Teller's friends would have their people looking for a tall, dark-skinned man with short hair and a strawberry blonde model. The escorts allowed them to go out into public because they messed with the BOLO description of the couple.

Their other benefit was to ease Jerry's mind. He struck Blu as the type who would have them shadowed anyway. So why not use it to their advantage. Kendra and Mona would be instructed to keep Jerry abreast of their whereabouts.

Charleston, South Carolina

"You place the order?" Crome asked.

Tess gave him a "Who do you think I am?" look.

He couldn't help himself. His nerves were getting the best of him. He hated being in Charleston and not in Vegas where the action was. This must have been what the command center felt like during the Gulf War.

"Why don't you vape or something?" she asked.

He realized he was hovering over her while she sent Harmony a text. Outside of Blu's house, he caught sight of Murder the miracle horse. The black stallion stood strong among his peers. Whatever had knocked him on his butt seemed to have passed. They all stood by the water trough in the small field across from the house. Crome picked up his vape pen and took a drag.

Tess joined him on the porch, spraying herself with a layer of bug repellant. "All we can do now is wait."

Chapter Twenty-Five

Las Vegas, Nevada

Blu stopped the vehicle Jerry had provided him and Mona, a repurposed decade-old Cadillac Escalade, in front of the valet at the high-end restaurant, got out, walked around, and escorted his date inside.

He wore a nice Italian suit and they were seated at a semi-private table off to the side but with a good view of the inside of the restaurant. Blu liked to know who came and went. It was part of his tradecraft and it had saved his life on more than one occasion.

Mona seemed at ease with a complete stranger. She ordered a glass of red wine and after the waitress left, said, "So, why don't you tell me a little about yourself."

"What would you like to know?"

"Whatever you want to tell me," she said. "Maybe how you came by the name 'Blu'. Is that real or a nickname?"

"My mom," he said. "She liked to be different."

"Mine, too," she said.

Her wine and his club soda came.

"Toast," she said. "To whatever the hell Jerry wants you to do for him."

So she thought he was working for Jerry. That was a twist of the truth.

"Back at you," he said.

She laughed. "He didn't tell me you were funny." After a sip, she set the glass on the table. "I think we both know why I'm here. I'm not sure why you are."

"Me either," he said and meant it.

"Clearly you don't need help finding a date," she said.

"I appreciate that," he said. "And clearly neither do you."

"One of the perks of my job is the dates come to me," she said.

"They would anyway," he said.

She leaned over, kissed his cheek and rubbed the lipstick mark off. "Thanks for that."

"Truth is you're here because I need people to be looking at you and not me."

"Honey," she said, "the ladies are all looking at you."

"Not all of them," he said. "Besides, chances are the ones I need to fool are men. And most of them are looking right past me."

"Well let's drink to their demise," she said.

He said, "I like the way you think."

They clinked glasses again.

A white man in a suit entered the restaurant. He had a medium build with a slight bulge under his left arm, and he did a quick survey of the place as he was seated at a table in a corner. Blu immediately did not like him. He was alone, packed a gun, and looked like he knew how to use it.

Mona said, "What's the matter?"

"See that guy over there," Blu said, not hiding his interest in the stranger.

"Never seen him before."

"Are there others here you have seen?"

She gave him one of those smiles women gave to men who said something stupid. "Of course, but I can't tell you who. We have rules."

"Understood." He didn't anticipate there being the possibility of some of the men already knowing she was an escort. It was a mistake, but not the biggest one of the moment. That award went to not suspecting the two women at the table next to them as trouble.

Because they both pulled pistols with suppressors out of their handbags and aimed.

Blu lifted the table up as Mona began to scream.

He threw it at the women and yanked Mona by the arm as he drew the nine millimeter Ruger.

The women ducked out of the way of the flying table and tried to follow.

Blu pushed Mona around a corner, pulled the trigger four times, and saw the women fall in a spray of blood. The man he'd suspected was already out of his seat and firing at him.

He backed around the corner, found Mona crouched down, picked her up, and kicked open the back door of the restaurant, gun drawn.

The alley behind the building was empty, but the man following would be coming out next.

Blu pushed Mona aside, aimed, and didn't fire as a woman stumbled out.

The man had sent a decoy through the door first, some innocent.

When Blu didn't fire, the man must have thought it was safe.

He peeked his head out and Blu drilled four holes through the cracked door, nailing the man with each shot as the bullets perforated the wood.

No one else came out.

Blu picked up Mona. She could barely walk. Apparently Jerry did not warn her there could be gunfire. That detail was on the old gangster. Blu's job right now was to keep her alive.

Around the corner, they flagged down a cab. He pushed a quivering Mona into the backseat, shut the door, and handed the cabbie a hundred dollar bill through an open window, telling him to take her back to Jerry's hotel as fast as he could.

When the cab took off, he called Harmony.

She answered with, "What's up, Doc?"

He walked the opposite direction of where the cab headed. "It was an ambush. I'm coming to you. If they don't know where you are, they will soon enough."

"Roger that," she said, all business now.

Charleston, South Carolina

Crome answered Blu's call. "They found you, huh?"

"Now what's that supposed to mean?" Blu asked.

It sure was fun to yank his partner's chain. "Oh, I don't know. How about the fact that you ain't exactly Frankenstein's Igor? And I bet the date they set you up with was hotter than them guns they gave you."

"Got me there, Crome. This is just an FYI call."

"Oh yeah," he said. "Well FY my I. Call me back when everything's finished."

"Stay in contact with Harmony," Blu said. "I'm on my way to her now."

"Just because your cover's blown doesn't mean hers is."

"Really?" Blu said.

And Crome knew he'd just said the dumbest thing he could have. Harmony would stand out anywhere with anyone. If they found Blu so quickly, and they had eyes in every major restaurant, hotel and casino in the city, then they'd have Harmony in the cross-hairs already.

"You're right," Crome said. "I'm on it. Get to her as fast as you can."

"Out." He ended the call.

Las Vegas, Nevada

Blu could not run because there were too many tourists walking on the sidewalk in front of him and he could not flag a cab because the traffic was too thick and he'd make it on foot faster.

It gave him time to think about what had happened in the restaurant. The way the women had drawn on him, it was almost as if they'd been signaled to do so. The man, Blu's original suspect, had only jumped in after they'd gone down. It was not the best plan, but probably the best whoever was behind it could come up with on short notice. The two women were a nice touch. He wished he'd thought of that. But unfortunately, Harmony thought of it first. He just didn't think to apply her logic to what the Russians might do, which ended up forcing him to shoot them.

There would be video footage of the incident, he was sure. Vegas might be sin city, but there was too much money at stake not to take precaution. The restaurant had some connection to the Russians which was why Blu wanted to go there in the first place. He liked rattling cages.

Unfortunately, he'd almost gotten Mona shot. There was no getting around that.

When he got to the club Harmony and Kendra were supposed to be dancing in, he sent her a text.

She replied, "Come inside."

"Get out of there. Now."

There was no reply. The next minute was longer than he wanted it to be. He tried to keep his mind clear of doubt as the seconds ticked by. Vaping did not help.

Was she okay? Did they find her? Do they have her? Was this a set up?

There were many questions and no answers.

And then two gorgeous women exited the club, arm in arm—Kendra and Harmony.

Blu hailed a cab. "Can I give you ladies a lift?"

A taxi pulled to the curb and the three of them piled in.

Harmony said, "What the hell, Blu? I thought we were supposed to be drawing them out?"

He said, "Whoever is interested in us doesn't care what we know or are doing. The three I ran into drew down and were not shooting to miss on purpose."

Kendra said, "You got shot at? Where's Mona?"

"She's okay. I put her in a cab back to Jerry's hotel, which is where we're taking you."

Harmony said, "What did you tell Crome?"

"Why?"

"He's been sending me texts that sound like he's reading them from Valentine's Day heart candy—Be mine, I'm all yours, LUV you, My Valentine."

"You been replying?" he asked.

She looked up from her phone. "Yes."

"It worked. I told him to stay in contact with you. He always was a little unorthodox."

Blu's phone buzzed. It was Crome.

"Yo," the biker said. "Time to skedaddle. Hope booked your return trip. Your flight leaves in two hours."

"Roger that." Blu ended the call. "Anything back at the room you're partial to?" he asked Harmony.

"Why?"

"Well, we can drop by and pick it up or we can leave it all and head to the airport. Personally, I'd rather we be on our merry way."

"I guess that's it, then," Harmony said.

Kendra said, "What about me?"

"You ride with us to the airport and then you tell Jerry we went home."

Chapter Twenty-Six

Charleston, South Carolina, Church of Redemption

Ariel looked around at the basic accommodations of the apartment: popcorn ceiling, white walls with framed pictures of Jesus, and dull brown carpeting. Reflecting on her life, she decided to think about making some major changes. She loved her work, it defined her. Having to hide out was terrible.

Someone knocked at the door and she answered it.

Brother Thomas entered the room with his imposing figure and a huge smile on his face. "Sorry to bother you, Ms. Ariel. You got everything you need?"

What a sweetheart!

"I do, thank you so much," she said. "Please have a seat if you want."

He sat on the couch.

She joined him.

"Always glad to help one of God's children, mm-hmm," he said.

She looked down and then met his eyes. "I'm not sure I'm on that list, but it's nice to hear you say it."

"Of course you are," he said. "He lookin' out for you like He do all of us."

Sitting back, she sank into the old, soft couch. "I think back to that first night when Blu saved me. That was one hell—I mean heck—of a coincidence."

"You say that like you don't believe in coincidences."

"I don't," she said.

He smiled. "Now you gettin' it, mm-hmm."

Harmony rested her head on Blu's shoulder as he scrolled through the news on her iPad. They were traveling at five hundred miles an hour through the night. Everything turned out as planned and they were not suspects in Teller's murder as far as Blu could tell. However, not all of what happened in Vegas this time stayed there. It made the national news and the shootout in the restaurant had been completely overshadowed by the other events.

The largest human trafficking bust in the city rocked the country. Its impact on the Vegas underworld was catastrophic. A random tip led police to a hotel suite where Russian diplomats had been staying. A gunfight ensued and all of the foreign guests along with a man identified as Uri Kuchev had perished. Ten underaged young women had also been in the room. Two died in the gunfight. The other eight led the police to a house in the suburbs where twenty more young women resided along with five adults.

Information was scarce, but it appeared as if the home was a satellite of a larger international organization. More evidence was being investigated, so the article Blu read advised to check back for updates.

With just a few phone calls, Harmony's plan had succeeded in taking out two of their enemies and made the world a better place. Local organizations were in the process of rescuing the remaining victims of the ring.

Blu only wished he'd been there to see the Russians attempt to open fire on the S.W.A.T. team that raided their room.

Jerry Zoluchi might suspect Blu and Harmony's involvement, but he would never be able to prove anything. After all, they were across town with two of his escorts who could vouch for their every move.

* * *

What they hadn't been able to get closure on was Ariel's situation. After touchdown in Charlotte and a four-hour drive to Charleston, Blu spent time among the horses.

To his surprise, Murder allowed him to approach and even took an apple out of his hand.

Dink and Doofus nuzzled Blu and even gave him kisses. Same with Mustang Sally. Murder wouldn't stoop to anything resembling affection, but allowing Blu the chance to get close was a breakthrough in itself.

His daughter Hope, fearless as always, joined her father. She carried the garden hose and proceeded to fill the water trough. It had rained overnight but not enough to replenish what had been consumed.

She said, "Glad you made it home safe, Dad."

"Me, too. Everything okay here while I was gone?"

"Not really," she said. "Crome's taking Colette's death hard."

"I don't blame him," he said. "What about the other thing?"

"All taken care of," she said. "Good reports so far."

Since Vegas, Blu had become paranoid about eavesdroppers. It was the day and age of drones and high powered microphones and it all meant privacy was a distant memory. So much so that Blu had called Brack Pelton to see who his wife used to debug her family's business offices.

He was glad Ariel had settled into her new temporary home. Chances were good the low-income side of North Charleston did not resemble what she'd become accustomed to.

Blu finished with the horses, took a shower, dressed in linen slacks, sandals, and a linen shirt, and picked up Tess at her apartment. They had dinner at Andeline's restaurant and had drinks at a rooftop bar.

Standing at the railing overlooking the Cooper River, she asked, "Miss me?"

He put his arm around her. "Of course. Miss me?"

She rested her head on his shoulder. "Yes."

"It's different, isn't it?"

"If you mean different than my other relationships, I'll say yes. You are a strange man, Blu Carraway."

"And you are a strange woman. This shouldn't be working as well as it is."

With a sigh, she said, "I know. I mean, I actually trust you. I don't trust anyone. Not like that."

He kissed the top of her head. "There's too much to lose."

"I'm glad you think so."

They stayed like that for a while before going back to her apartment.

The call came in early in the morning. It was Brother Thomas.

Blu coughed to clear his throat. "Yes?"

"Mr. Carraway?"

"Call me Blu, Brother."

"Um, okay. It might be nothin' but one of my parishioners said a strange car been spotted around. We been keeping track and this one cruised by a couple times."

"Did they get a make, model, and plate?"

"Of course." He said it as if the question didn't need to be asked and rattled off the information.

They ended the call and Blu had his DMV contact, Gladys, run down the plate. She got back with him at nine with an address. It was registered to someone local. Blu and Crome decided to do some reconnaissance on the residence.

They did not like what they found.

Blu and Crome parked across the street of the modest two-story in West Ashley. From the front seat of the Xterra, Blu watched Jimmy Zoluchi exit the house.

Crome said, "This is all kinds of wrong."

"Yep."

His partner sucked on vapor and exhaled. It trailed out of his cracked window.

Blu said, "If your cloud gives us away, I'm going to kick your ass after the shootout."

"Fair enough," Crome said.

Blu didn't think his threat had deterred anything.

Another inhale and exhale of vapor.

He was right. Crome couldn't care less.

Jimmy walked to his classic Monte Carlo, got in, and left.

The residence belonged to a man named Anthony Dreg. Andeline didn't have anything on him. Neither did Tess or Harmony. All they knew was the guy's age, thirty, his height, five-eleven, his eye color, brown, and his weight, one-ninety. And he didn't wear corrective lenses.

"Looks like Jimmy found him at the pound."

Jimmy Z. did not hire low rent muscle, meaning this guy must have some skills. Tess and Harmony were looking into it.

The concern was how close Dreg had gotten to Ariel. Either Brother Thomas had a leak in his congregation or Jimmy Z. was smarter than Blu had given him credit for.

Blu said, "He's working both sides."

"Yep." Crome took another drag and exhaled.

"What are you thinking?"

After rotating his head and stretching his neck, the biker put away his vape pen. "The movie *The Godfather*: Keep your friends close but your enemies closer."

"Let's pay Jimmy a visit. Let him know how much we appreciate his help in Vegas."

They worked out a plan on how to handle Jimmy while they sat on Dreg's place.

Dreg never left his residence in the first eight hours Crome staked it out with Blu.

One thing about Blu was his focus.

Crome preferred action. He liked always moving forward, or sideways. It didn't matter. What mattered was motion, progress. Not sitting on his butt for a third of a day.

They got a call from Harmony and decided enough was enough for the time being.

As Blu wheeled the SUV around a cul-de-sac at the end of the road and headed back, a man stepped out of Dreg's house, got in the SUV in the drive, and backed out.

"See that?" Crome asked, although it was obvious Blu had.

"On it," Blu said.

They drove casually out of the subdivision, Dreg behind them. At the exit, Blu turned right and Dreg made a left.

Crome kept Dreg in his sight as Blu wheeled into a gas station, got them turned around, and accelerated in pursuit. "Five cars up on the left."

"Got him."

While he kept his mind clear and focused, Crome took his vape pen out. He handed it to Blu who took a hit and handed it back.

"Jesus, Crome!"

"What?"

"How much nicotine's in that?"

Chuckling, Crome said, "Wussy," and took a hit. Last year, when Maureen was taken, he'd spec'd the nicotine level at the max his vape shop would sell. Now, it was about half that but still quite a bit higher than what Blu used.

Blu shook his head as if trying to dislodge something stuck in his ear.

"Pay attention or you'll lose him," Crome said.

"I'm on it." His partner sounded annoyed.

Getting one over on Blu made Crome's day. The guy had yet to learn not to be so trusting.

They watched the grey SUV take a left and head into the city.

"What's the plan?" Crome asked.

"We need to figure out Jimmy Z.'s connection. I want to learn more about Dreg."

Thinking it was about this time that they normally divided to conquer, he made the suggestion.

"Take it easy," Blu said. "The only other piece of intel we got right now is Jimmy. Until we figure out what role Dreg plays, there isn't anything else to check on."

Blu was right, Crome was just antsy. And thirsty. Bottled water wasn't cutting it.

They got somewhat of an answer after Dreg parked at a meter on King Street. Blu pulled over at a bus stop and Crome hopped out.

Free at last, Crome paced Dreg from across the street. Since he'd never come across the man before, Crome didn't worry about being seen. Dreg wouldn't know he was a threat.

The man walked into a sports bar. Crome gave him a few minutes and then followed him in.

Since it was happy hour, the place was kicking. Crome went to the bar and ordered a twenty-two ounce draft. Using the beer as his reason for being there, he scanned the room, found Dreg sitting at a table with Sherman Heywood, and called Harmony.

"Your boyfriend's in town."

Crome knew his bedside manner sucked.

"Which one?" Harmony asked.

He also knew she would get riled up.

"The Shermanator."

She didn't reply right away.

"You there, princess?"

"Very funny."

"Which part?" he asked.

"You're serious? Sherman's here?"

"Having a drink with one Anthony Dreg as we speak." He took a long pull on his beer.

If Sherman saw him, there'd be a problem. But he didn't think getting up off the barstool and walking away was the right thing to do, either. Crome did his best to blend in with the other patrons around the bar.

Harmony said, "Kill them both."

"Not yet," he said. "They're closer to Ariel than we'd like. We need to find out where this all goes."

"What do you want me to do?"

"Let me see you in your underwear again."

"And after that? I don't have all day to wait for the Viagra to take affect."

She'd definitely been around him and Blu too long. He respected her that much more. "Very funny. You're probably right; I wouldn't want to have to stand in line anyway."

"Touché, Mr. Crome."

His phone buzzed, indicating an incoming message. It was Blu.

"Hold on," he said to Harmony and typed out what he'd found.

Blu answered with, "Kill them. JK."

"Already did," Crome replied. He didn't elaborate. Speaking to Harmony, he said, "Blu's getting anxious. I'm going to finish my beer and tag out. Let him sit on the two Peckerwoods while I go outside."

"Because it's all about you, Crome."

"Of course it is," he ended the call.

Blu met him at the door. "Truck's two blocks up."

Crome walked out. He had his own set of keys to Blu's truck if he needed them.

Chapter Twenty-Seven

Blu found Dreg and the other man exactly where Crome said they'd be. He ordered a sweet tea from the bar.

A woman in office wear—silk blouse, tight skirt and heels—holding a glass of red wine bumped into him, saying, "Excuse me."

"No problem," he said.

"You come here often?" she asked, then giggled.

Auburn hair, green eyes, freckles over a suntan. Naturally pretty, but not drop dead. It worked for her, and for him. She could be mid-to-late thirties. But she was no Tess.

"That's supposed to be my line," he said, giving her a smile.

"Sorry."

"What's your name?" he asked, glancing at the men who were still talking.

She finished her drink and signaled the bartender to repour. "Blythe."

"There's one for the books," Blu said.

"Oh yeah? What's your name?"

Her wine came. Blu gave the bartender a twenty.

"Thanks," she said. "I'm waiting."

"Blu Carraway."

"Blue? Like the color?"

He said, "No E. My mom's a little eccentric."

Most of the patrons were twenty-somethings. The older ones had gotten smart and stayed out of bars. Except for him. And Blythe.

She said, "It suits you."

Sherman and Dreg were still talking.

"What do you do for a living?" Blu asked.

"Paralegal," she said. "As soon as I finish law school, I'm hanging out my own shingle."

"Good for you." The world really needed more lawyers.

"So what do you do?" she asked.

"Private Investigator." Blu caught Dreg getting more animated.

"Really?" Blythe said. "Wait a minute. I've heard of you. My firm hates you."

"I'm guessing the verdict didn't go your way." If the firm was on the other side of the aisle from the one he worked for, they would definitely hate him.

"Something like that. It cost our client a lot of money."

"We can't all be winners," he said.

She raised her wine and they clinked glasses.

Dreg got up and stormed out.

Blu stood. "Nice to meet you, but I gotta run."

She said, "What do you want with Tony Dreg?"

He stopped and looked at her. "Excuse me?"

"You've had one eye on him the whole time," she said, tracing his cheek with her fingers. "But I'm flattered I had the other one."

Using the walkie talkie app on his phone, he said, "Dreg's coming out. Stay on him. I'll catch up in a minute."

Blythe grinned at him. "You're dying to ask me a question."

"A few, actually."

"Good," she said.

"You're with Blake Townley, aren't you?"

Another grin.

Sherman Heywood walked up. The fingers on his right hand were taped up from when Crome had broken them. "Your partner is a dead man."

The young man had made quite a few mistakes in his approach to the situation. The largest error was his thinking that he could intimidate Blu. The second was that he didn't think Blu would kick him in the balls in public.

That was exactly what happened as Blu stood and gave the young man a quick hit to the genitals.

Sherman went down, curled up in a fetal position, his hands on his groin.

The people around them gave Sherman room to recover, but otherwise didn't really seem fazed.

Blu said, "You want to get out of here?"

Because the bouncers were on their way.

"Um, sure," she said, grabbing her purse from the bar.

They headed for the door.

"Wait a minute, Carraway," said a strained voice from behind them.

Blu didn't pay attention as he exited.

The bouncer, a guy Blu had done some physical training with, met them at the door and nodded. "Nice kick."

"I thought so," Blu said.

"Get out of here before I lose my job."

"You got it," Blu said.

He took Blythe's hand and they walked up King Street. This screamed set up, but he wasn't too worried. He had his nine millimeter tucked down the waistband of his jeans underneath his t-shirt.

As they walked, Blythe, letting him lead her, asked, "Where do you think this is going to end?"

They threaded in and out of the tourist pedestrian traffic on the brick side walk past high-end retail stores. His SUV was ahead.

"Not for me to say," he said.

His phone buzzed and he pulled it out. Crome had tried to contact him using the app, saying, "I'm on foot. Dreg's getting in his truck. Pick me up."

Into the phone, Blu said, "On my way." He stopped at his SUV. "Well, Ms. Blythe, if that's your name. You have a choice. I can leave you here or you can come with us. Try anything and I'll shoot you."

She gave him an appreciative nod. "I believe you."

They both got in after he pressed the unlock button. He started the truck, put it in gear, waited for a gap in traffic, and accelerated toward Crome.

Leave it to Blu Carraway to pick up a woman in the middle of a surveillance job. But he had to admit, this one was quite a looker. Not Blu's normal model choice, this one was more of the 'girl next door' persuasion.

Crome got in the back seat and they picked out Dreg's truck five vehicles ahead.

"This is Blythe," Blu said.

"Pleasure to meet you," Crome said, shaking her hand.

"Before you get any ideas," Blu said, "she knows the Shermanator."

"No kidding?" Crome asked.

Blythe said, "Your partner kicked him in the balls."

"She's with Townley," Blu said.

Crome leaned forward so he could talk to them better. "Jeez, Blu. You must really like this one."

"She picked me up," he said.

Crome chuckled. "Not exactly a ringing endorsement. I mean that plus the Townley connection means she's not particular."

"Don't forget," Blu said. "She's probably got a mic on us and her piece-of-work boss is listening in as we speak."

"Hey, Blake," Crome said. "Tell your momma I said hi. We had a thing while I was in California embarrassing you and beating the crap out of your Heywood puke."

"Are you guys for real?" Blythe asked.

"You're riding in the car with us, aren't you?" Crome took out his vape pen and offered it to her.

Before Blu could warn her, she took a hit and flinched.

Now that was funny. It made him laugh harder.

She shook her head as if to clear any cobwebs out.

Blu said, "My partner likes things in self-destructive amounts. That includes alcohol, violence, and nicotine."

"Don't forget women," Crome said, taking the vape pen back and sucking in a lungful.

"How could I?" Blu asked.

"Your files say you're both forty-six years old," she said. "I find that hard to believe."

"Too mature for ya?" Crome asked, pointing his vape pen at her.

She turned around to face him. "I do prefer younger men."

"I'm in love," Crome said.

"Keep it in your pants, Romeo," Blu said.

Dreg headed toward North Charleston.

"Guess where he's going?" Blythe asked.

"The mountains," Blu said.

"Try again."

Crome pulled out his nine millimeter and pressed the barrel to the side of Blythe's head. "I don't like guessing games."

Everything about her seemed to tighten up. Either she wasn't used to danger or she'd underestimated them. Probably the latter.

"You better tell him," Blu said. "I don't want to have to clean brains out of my truck again."

Crome cocked the hammer back.

She flinched.

The chamber was loaded, as usual. The safety was off.

One wrong move and Blu would have to really clean brains out of his truck. Although this would be the first time, not another like he'd led her to believe.

"Ariel," she said. "We're after Ariel."

"Who?" Crome said.

"Yeah, right," she said. "You guys know exactly who I'm talking about."

"What we know," Blu said, "is more than we're going to let on. If we catch you lying, I'll swerve and hit a bump and Crome's piece goes off. And I'll have to get another truck."

"If you kill me, you get the electric chair," she said.

"Only if they find the body," Crome said.

"You mean like they did in Miami?" she retorted.

Crome hadn't told Blu the whole story. Some things were better left unsaid. "More like Kuwait. We leave your body to rot just like Hussein did to his soldiers. You hear that, Townley, your prime piece of tail here gets picked clean by the local fauna. You want that?"

Blu said, "We got company."

Crome turned, saw a mid-sized sedan gain on them. He pulled a second gun, one he had stuck down the back waistband of his jeans, and aimed it out the back window, tracking the car as it approached and still keeping the other pistol to Blythe's head. The car pulled out to pass and almost got even with them. When a man with a shotgun aimed at them from the passenger seat, Crome shot out the back passenger window behind Blu.

Blythe screamed.

The man with a shotgun who'd lowered the car's passenger window slumped over.

Blu swerved toward the car.

The driver reacted poorly, swerved away to avoid getting hit, and ended up ramming into a large delivery truck in the middle turning lane.

Dreg seemed to recognize he had company and sped up.

Blu kept him in sight, although they'd managed to lose a few car lengths.

"Where's he going?" Crome asked.

"I don't know now," she said. "He knows you're back here."

"Where was he going?" Blu asked.

"We got a tip that Ariel was at some church in North Charleston. He's trying to figure out which one."

"Who's your local contact?" Crome asked.

"We don't have one."

Crome pulled the trigger. The window behind Blythe blew out. There wasn't anyone beside them when he did it.

She convulsed in her seat.

"I told you not to lie," Crome said. "Last chance. Who's your local contact?"

"Some low-end mob guy," she said, hyperventilating.

Crome said, "Get yourself together. You croak and we go back and work on Sherman. You wouldn't want us to do that, would ya?"

She shook her head.

"Good," Crome said. "You got a name for this local mob guy."

She didn't reply right away.

He put the gun to her head and cocked the hammer back again.

"Zoluchi," she said. "Jimmy Zoluchi."

"What's his interest in all this?" Blu asked.

"Ten million dollars."

Crome felt his eyes bug out of his head. "Ten million?"

"Ten million dollars," she repeated. "Just like I said." She took a deep breath. "Just like I said."

He didn't say it, but Crome knew he was going to have to take a run at Jimmy now, too. It wouldn't be pretty.

Blu said, "Don't shoot out any more of my windows."

Chapter Twenty-Eight

This had gotten way out of hand. That's what Blu was thinking as he pulled to a curb, ending the tail on Dreg.

Blythe gave him a pathetic, wide-eyed stare.

He said, "Get out."

She opened the door.

"If we see you in Charleston again, you don't want to know what we'll do."

Stepping onto the sidewalk, she slammed the door.

Blu accelerated away. "She could report us."

Crome said, "Somethin' tells me she ain't gonna do anything."

That was something to think about. "You think she was a plant?"

"Yep," Crome said. "Sent here to do exactly what she did. Give us Jimmy's name."

It made sense. If people weren't happy about the outcome so far, and they knew he and Crome were the cause of all the problems, they'd work on unraveling things. Jimmy Z. might not know he was being played. "We need to see Jimmy."

"Is just what I was thinking," Crome said.

Blu pulled into a do-it-yourself car wash with a vacuum system and they cleaned up as much of the glass as they could.

Both back windows would have to be replaced.

Next, he called Jimmy and when he answered the call, Blu said, "You're such a patsy."

"What the hell?"

"What were you doing with Dreg?"

"Who?" Jimmy said.

"The house in West Ashley? What were you doing there?"

"How do you know about that?"

"Answer the question, Jimmy," Blu said, "or Crome and I are going to pay you a visit you won't like."

"You threatening me now, Carraway? After all I did for you?"

"Listen Jimmy, someone tried to pull a shotgun on me and Crome and when we squeezed hard guess whose name squirted out?"

There was a pause. Then Jimmy said, "I got a call from some guy who offered me twice retail for my Monte Carlo. He tells me to bring it by to make sure. I go to his house and he tells me he's not interested so I leave."

"You sure this is the truth?" Blu asked. "Think real hard, Jimmy. I mean real hard, before you answer me."

"I don't have to say squat to you, Blu. We go back a long ways. I don't have to put up with this. You better learn who your friends are."

"Jimmy," Blu said in the calmest voice he could muster. "I told you the truth. Someone dropped your name. Said you were working on a ten million dollar payoff if you help get rid of me and Crome."

"People are always trying to set me up," Jimmy said. "I don't pay much attention."

"Yeah," Blu said, "well we tracked these same people across the country. LA. Las Vegas. And your name pops out after you help us. What does that tell you?"

Another pause. This time he didn't reply.

"That's right," Blu said. "It says they want us fighting with you. And whoever wins, it doesn't matter because they want all of us gone. This way they only have to do half the work. They're banking on us doing the other half."

"Lemme call you back, Blu."

"My truck's compromised. What do you have on your lot you'll let go of?"

"Everything's for sale," Jimmy said.

"I'm not paying twice retail."

"Don't I know it. Come by. I think I got something for you."

The call ended.

Crome said, "How'd he sound?"

"I'm not sure he's telling me the whole truth," Blu said. "But I don't think he's involved in setting us up."

"We should'a held onto that Blythe chick," Crome said.

"And risked a kidnapping charge? No thanks. She was just a messenger."

Jimmy Z. had a two-year-old Grand Cherokee SRT with low miles that he wanted to offload. It was black and mean with a monster motor, big brakes, and steam roller tires. Blu fell in love with it immediately.

Riding shotgun on the test drive and holding on for dear life, Crome said, "If you don't buy it, I'm gonna."

Back at the car lot, Blu and Crome went to Jimmy's office.

The mobster said, "I didn't have nothing to do with that hit. I saw it on the news, although they're looking for a black Xterra, by the way."

"Prove you didn't." Blu gave him a dollar number including a trade on his truck.

"Jesus, Blu," Jimmy said. "We're friends, but we ain't that close."

Crome said, "We took care of Uri for you and this is how we're treated?"

Jimmy opened his hands as if in surrender. "I like you guys, but I gotta run a business here that doesn't include selling cars at a loss."

Blu looked out the window at an F-150. It was in good shape, less than ten years old, and also black. He'd lost his work truck in the explosion. "What's your best price on the Jeep and that Ford out there? Two in one deal."

"Now you're talking," Jimmy said. He gave a number that was

not out of the ballpark.

Blu countered with something less.

Jimmy hemmed and hawed and threw another one back, more than Blu's but less than the first.

"You give me a long warranty and maintenance in writing and you got a deal," Blu said.

They shook hands.

Crome said, "Now, Jimmy, tell me what you were really doing with Dreg."

Jimmy sat back in his chair. His flat-topped hair stuck straight up on his head an inch. His arms were tanned and his gold watch glistened in the fluorescent lighting. "He said he had information on some rock star named C. Said you'd be interested in it. I went out there and all he said was she was in town. I told him to go pound sand and I left."

"You realize going out there to meet him pretty much told him she was here."

The mobster looked down as if in shame. "I didn't know anything. I got played."

"Wanna get even?" Crome asked.

With a smile, Jimmy's disposition brightened considerably.

Blu said, "We need all you can find on a redhead named Blythe. She might be connected to Blake Townley out of LA but I'm not sure."

"If she's in town, I'll find her," he said. "She the reason you got two shot out windows?"

"No," Blu said. "Crome's the reason I got two shot out windows. The idiots with the shotgun who kissed the delivery truck caused one. Blythe not talking caused the other. My freaking ears are still ringing."

"It worked on both counts, didn't it?" Crome asked.

Jimmy's secretary came in with some papers. Blu signed them and became the proud owner of two new-to-him vehicles. It must be Jimmy's plan to sell Blu a vehicle every couple of years. The Xterra was a nice truck, but it wasn't particularly fast and would now be a liability since there was a BOLO on it. The time was right to trade, even though all his cop friends knew he'd been driving a black one.

In fact, as he drove back to his island home in the SRT with Crome following in the Ford, Powers called.

"We're looking for a truck like yours. Care to comment?"

Blu wasn't ready to fess up yet. "What are you talking about?"

"Your truck. There's a be-on-the-lookout on it."

"My tag or just a black SUV."

Powers wasn't stupid. Blu was stalling and his friend knew it.

"Gee, Blu. I'm calling everyone I know with a black Nissan SUV and you just happen to be first on my list."

"Well, whatever it was, it isn't me."

"Did I say you were the first?" Powers asked. "I meant to say you were the only one on my list."

"That makes me feel better," Blu said. "I'd hate to think you were two-timing me or something."

Powers said, "Why don't you pull over and let's talk?"

Blu checked his rearview mirror. Sure enough, behind Crome was an unmarked Charger.

That meant Powers was sitting on Jimmy's place.

"How about I buy you lunch?" Blu asked.

"Only if your partner in the pickup joins us."

"Fair enough."

Blu called Crome.

"Is that Powers behind me?" Crome asked.

"He wants to have a meeting," Blu said.

"The cheap bastard wants us to buy him lunch, doesn't he?"

Any time Crome used the word "us" when referring to paying for anything, it usually meant Blu.

"Something like that."

Blu's house was south of the city. They were too far away from their Pirate's Cove standby so they went to Folly Beach. While he would have liked to try the food at Pelton's Kiawah Island Bar and Grill which was even further south, it would have taken Powers too far out of his jurisdiction for lunch. He'd stop by Blu's island periodically to visit, but he didn't make a habit of it. There was too much for him to do in Charleston.

This was probably why he was pissed off and wanting this impromptu meeting. He didn't need more work and anytime Blu's name came up, no matter where in the county, Powers got the call.

They parked the vehicles at a public lot and Powers looked over Blu's new purchase through his sunglasses. He wore similar attire from the last time Blu had seen him, khakis and a burnt orange polo.

"Jimmy sold you this?" he asked, referring to the Grand Cherokee SRT.

"Yep."

"You run the VIN to make sure it wasn't hot?"

Typical Powers. Everything was black and white. Either you were a good guy or a bad guy. Except Blu and Crome were sometimes both. Blu wasn't sure where he fell in Powers' opinion, but he felt confident Crome definitely fell into the bad category.

"No," Blu said. "But feel free to. I'm sure Jimmy's not stupid enough to sell me a stolen vehicle, knowing how much blowback he would get if I got busted."

"Touchy, touchy," Powers said, giving him a smile.

The detective walked around the truck. "Tires are going to cost you four-hundred apiece. And forget about gas mileage."

"I didn't know you worked for one of those consumer magazines," Crome said. "You get a new job?"

Ignoring him, Powers said, "It goes like stink, doesn't it?"

Crome said, "That's for sure."

"Spending Ariel's money already, huh?"

Both Blu and Crome kept their poker faces on, but the detective should not have known her connection to them.

"What are you talking about?" Blu asked.

"Ariel, the pop star. Word is she's one of your clients."

No one said anything. It wasn't that Blu wanted to hide his connection to Ariel from Powers. It was that people in the detective's world were talking about it.

Blu said, "Before we eat, let's get something straight. You ever had a client of mine you didn't know about get dropped into your everyday conversation like that before?"

"Not like this," Powers said. "That's why I tracked you down."

"Could have just called," Crome said.

"Where's the fun in that?"

Blu had to laugh. It was something Crome would have said and Powers threw it right at him.

With a smirk and an exhale of vapor, Crome said, "Let's eat."

They walked into the restaurant and ordered she-crab soup and pimento cheese sandwiches.

While they sipped iced tea awaiting their food, Blu said, "Something's bothering you."

"Damn right it is," Powers said. "There are those cops who are the real deal and I'd trust them with my daughter's life. And then there are those who I wouldn't ask for change for a dollar. The comments are coming from the latter bunch. It's like someone's putting feelers out. Of course they came to me and of course I didn't know squat because I didn't until now."

Blu nodded.

The detective asked, "This have something to do with the Red Army?"

"Indirectly."

"Don't be so long-winded, Blu."

Crome hiked an arm over the back of his chair. "What my partner's tryin' not to say is we ain't sure what's going on yet. We got something that's connected to Vegas and Los Angeles and Kuala Lumpur and our pop star friend and we don't know what it is."

"How come there are so many in your line of work after you?" Powers asked. "It's like the business is eating itself or something."

Blu hadn't thought about it that way, but it wasn't an inaccurate statement. There seemed to be some puppet master pulling the strings.

The food came and they ate in silence, Blu thinking about their next play. He had to get Ariel out of North Charleston since they were now looking for her there.

Powers finished first, stacked his soup bowl on his sandwich plate, and pushed them away. "I want to do some checking on this."

"You want to bust Jimmy and are going to use us to do it," Crome said.

"That's not true," Powers said. "I don't want another blood bath like what you two set up at the Red Army camp. We're still finding pieces of Uri's crew in the rafters."

That detail seemed to make Crome smile.

"Don't you appreciate Jimmy's way of doing things more than those Russian thugs?" Blu asked.

"On a sliding scale, sure," Powers said. "But Jimmy really isn't any better for Charleston. He's just less bad."

"True, but it's reality. Not some philosophical debate."

"My job is to solve crime and determine guilt," Powers said. "Your job is to work for your clients. We're never going to be on the same plane."

Chapter Twenty-Nine

What Blu needed was a break in the investigation. Dreg seemed to be it. With his new surveillance wheels, he sat on the man's house again, this time with Tess.

His phone buzzed. It was Harmony.

"Sherman's checked in at the Palmetto Inn." She sounded absolutely giddy.

They, meaning Blu Carraway Investigations, had a connection at the hotel. Blu had a feeling Sherman was going to really regret coming into town. Whatever Crome and Harmony had done to him in California would pale in comparison to what was coming.

Dreg walked to his car.

Tess said, "Here we go." She booted up her iPad. Four hours earlier, a friend of hers that worked for the DEA had moonlighted for Blu Carraway Investigations by planting a tracker on Dreg's car. They'd used the same guy last year to plant one on Crome's bike. He did it in thirty seconds but it took Crome two days to find the device. The man was good. Plus he worked cheap—read "free." He had a crush on Harmony and she was smart enough to be flirty but non-committal. If she decided she needed to know how to place tracking devices or bugs that were virtually impossible to find, it would be the guy's lucky day. At least for as long as it took to train her. From Blu's experience, Harmony was a quick study.

Young MC's "Bust a Move" started up on the eighties station.

Blu tapped his fingers on the steering wheel. Tess nodded her head to the beat. He rolled his hand toward her and she caught the wave and finished it up. They laughed and he found himself even more smitten with her.

Dreg apparently failed to see Blu's new four-door missile of a truck or at least thought it wasn't something to worry about. Instead, he rolled with traffic.

"I'm not sure I like where this is going," Blu said, realizing their target headed toward North Charleston. While there were plenty of other reasons to go there, the fact that Ariel was there gave him cause for concern. He did not need a shootout at Brother Thomas' church or for any of the congregation to get hurt.

Blu pulled into a gas station and topped off the tank with premium. The truck drove like an angry grizzly bear. There was not much on the road that could outrun it, even many of the high-end sports cars and especially on Charleston's mediocre-at-best roads. The one downfall was the fuel economy. However it was a small tradeoff for so much power. In three years, he'd moved up from a barely running Land Cruiser to his Xterra, which was nearly new and had working AC, and now this thing. There was no way he could go back to a lower end model.

Even the stereo kicked and now, as he pulled out of the gas station, "Beat It" rocked out of the high-end speakers.

These songs were older than Tess, but she didn't seem to mind. Of course, her calling them oldies would be something he'd have to overlook.

At about the time Eddie Van Halen's guitar solo wailed in the famous Michael Jackson song, Blu and Tess caught up with Dreg. He'd stopped at a family-style restaurant and was already inside.

Blu called in an order of two BLT's with mustard instead of mayo along with two ice teas and sent Tess in to get them and check out why Dreg was there.

Ten minutes later, she came outside with a bag and two drinks in a tray. He reached over and opened the door for her.

She handed him the drinks and climbed in with the bag.

"Our boy's with a young guy. I snapped a pic." She pulled her phone out of the back pocket of her shorts and showed him. He momentarily got distracted by her toned legs.

"What?" She smiled, catching him looking.

His face reddened.

She kissed him. "I'm glad you look at me that way. But we've got to concentrate right now."

Said the novice to the pro-PI.

He really needed to get his head back in the game. Taking the phone from her, he enlarged the picture on Dreg's lunch date.

She said, "It's Sherman, isn't it?"

"Yep. The guy's like syphilis," he said. "You can't get rid of him."

"We don't want to get rid of him just yet, do we?" she asked. "He's got to take us to Townley."

Right again.

He opened the bag, got out a wrapped sandwich, unfolded the wax paper on one end, and took a bite. The last time he'd eaten was a while ago and his blood sugar had begun to wane.

Tess also ate.

He drank down half the cup of tea. Apparently he'd been thirsty as well.

As she munched, Tess called Harmony.

"Guess where your boyfriend is?"

"Which one?"

Blu laughed—typical Harmony.

"The one you want to string up," Tess said.

"Sherman? He's eating lunch at a place off Dorchester Road."

"You know that because?" Blu asked.

"You had Neil put a tracker on his car."

"Well good golly Ms. Molly," Blu said. "It appears we all ended up at the same place."

"Maybe you two did," Harmony said. "I'm sitting here with Crome."

"We got the better deal," Blu said.

"Tell me about it," Harmony said. "He's checking out my underwear collection."

In the background, they heard Crome say, "You should see

some of the stuff she's got."

"I have," Tess said. "Victoria's Secret would be jealous."

This was not a visual Blu needed at the moment.

"Where else has Sherman been?" he asked.

"The Palmetto Inn."

Crome said, "I got Juanita on it already."

To Tess, Blu said, "He does a good job multitasking."

Harmony said, "I agree. It would be nice if he were working on two things associated with the job instead of my drawers."

The biker said, "Where's the fun in that?"

This had to be some form of employer sexual harassment. It was a good thing she wasn't officially on the payroll yet.

Maybe hiring her would be a bad idea after all.

As if reading his mind, Harmony said, "I can handle Mr. Crome here. What I can't handle is myself anywhere in the vicinity of Sherman Heywood. See to it that he meets his demise or I will."

"Tell you what?" Blu said. "You pick up Dreg and we'll follow Sherman. Otherwise Dreg might get suspicious."

"Deal."

Crome, while having the time of his life annoying Harmony, had been working on what their plan needed to be.

If Harmony got a hold of Sherman again, the young man would not live to tell his friends about it. Blu could handle the pressure of the job as long as he could keep Ariel safe. As soon as she was directly threatened again, the rulebook he lived by would go out the window and people would die. That's where Crome knew he came in.

Fighting in the Middle East was boring as hell up until the enemy engaged and then it was anything but. Crome's kill ratio was double the next man's. And the next man was Blu. Together they made a dangerous pair.

While it was tempting to take off after this job, and Crome hadn't ruled it out, he wasn't going to leave until they finished.

Then he'd go somewhere alone and mourn Colette's death and what could have been a good time with her by drowning in margaritas and senoritas south of the border.

What they needed to do right now was figure out the play and then rewrite the rules. It started with Blake Townley but was being executed by Sherman and Dreg. Obviously Townley did not have much in the way of leadership or he would have left his plan in better hands.

The next move became crystal clear to him. They needed to take out one of the players and see what happened next.

He called Blu and said as much.

Surprisingly, his partner did not disagree. He'd come to a similar conclusion.

Crome's thoughts echoed Blu's own. So much that it scared him. Was he turning into his renegade partner? Blu hoped not. He couldn't see himself taking off for three years to drown in alcohol and cheap women like Crome was planning. If nothing else, he still had a sense of responsibility.

Which was why he needed to be clear on what he meant by "taking out one of the players."

On the phone, Crome said, "Which one?"

"First answer a question. What's this look like to you?" Blu asked.

"What do you mean?"

Blu could sense a sliver of irritation creeping into Crome's tough-guy image.

"For this exercise, let's say it's Dreg. What does "taking him out" mean to you?"

"Busting a cap in his ass," Crome said, nonchalantly.

Of course it did.

"Did you have something else in mind, Blu? I'd surely love to hear it."

He did. "Yep. I prefer the way we handled Sammy and the

Russians."

"There's no time for that."

"Sure there is," Blu said.

"I'm waiting," Crome said.

"Remember Blythe?"

After a pause, Crome said, "Yes."

"I called Juanita. She asked her friends and they think they found her."

"We can't kidnap her again," Crome said. "That's already a felony if she decides to press charges."

Blu couldn't decide if it was more surprising that Crome wasn't out the door with a round chambered and ready for action or actually trying to talk him out of the plan.

"We don't have to kidnap her," Blu said. "All we have to do is make her feel like she's in danger."

"She'll call either Dreg or Sherman and one of them will come running," Crome said. "I like it so far, but then what."

This was the tricky part. "We let Jimmy Z. know what's going on."

"Jimmy?" Crome asked. "What do we expect him to do?"

"He's got another syndicate running an operation on his turf," Blu said. "You think Townley called Jimmy to let him know?"

"Jimmy'll want a cut of their action," Crome said. "Or he'll send them packing."

"And while he's busy with two of the three operatives we know about, we sit on the third and see what happens next."

"My plan's cleaner," Crome said.

"No," Blu said. "It looks easier, but the back end is messier. You'll be facing a murder charge. With my plan, you sit back and drink beer and vape on a stakeout."

"I'm tired of that," Crome said.

Anyone else and Blu would question their sanity. Anyone but Crome.

After a few seconds of silence, Crome said. "Okay, okay. If I have to. Who's gonna call Jimmy?"

*   *   *

The plan as Crome saw it had one major flaw. No one got taken out permanently. Sometimes dropping the right person sent a message. Sometimes the message was received and the planned outcome was achieved, and sometimes WWIII erupted.

He couldn't honestly say which way this scenario would go. In that respect, Blu's plan made the most sense. It carried the least amount of risk for them, but it was so boring.

At about the same time a note was slipped under Blythe's door, Jimmy Z. got an anonymous call from a burner phone describing Blythe, Dreg, and Sherman and who they were connected with. He might suspect Blu, but people were always feeding him information. It would be up to him to recognize the opportunity. Jimmy wasn't stupid. He wouldn't have lasted as long as he had in the business if he were. He also wasn't impulsive, except when it came to sleeping with his wife's sister last year. That got him in a lot of hot water.

This time, Jimmy reacted in the manner in which they'd anticipated.

Sherman showed up to Blythe's hotel room and then five minutes later, four of Jimmy's goons paid them a visit.

Guns might have been used, but no shots were fired.

Blythe and Sherman would spend the next few hours answering questions from an interrogator not accustomed to following the rules of decency. Much like Crome.

While all that was going on, Crome sat in the F-150, vaping and drinking coffee because beer would not have been good at the moment for a lot of reasons.

Dreg did not disappoint with his reaction to Blythe and Sherman being taken.

He first tried to check out Blythe's hotel room. Somehow word had gotten back to him that she might be in trouble.

When he didn't get anywhere with that, he made a phone call to California from the driver's seat in his car. Crome knew this because Tess' friend who'd planted the tracker also managed to slip a bug inside the car. Crome had a love-hate thing for the DEA agent. He loved the man's skills, but hated that he'd used them to plant a tracker on his own bike. It took him two days to find the thing. Blu had distracted him for no more than half a minute and that's all the time the guy had to plant it. Thirty seconds and it took Crome two days.

Crome listened to Dreg make his call.

"Mr. Townley? We might have a problem."

Crome wished he could hear the other side of the conversation, but listening to Dreg grovel was almost enough.

"Yes, sir. Sherman called me and said Carrie received a threat and was freaking out. Thirty minutes later I get a call telling me Carrie and Sherman have been abducted."

A pause.

"No sir, I don't know by whom yet."

Another pause.

"Yes sir. I agree I should have been the one to check on Carrie but you told me to be ready to move on Carraway."

An audible sigh.

"Yes sir. I agree. This probably is Carraway. I—"

"No sir, I don't think that's a good idea."

"Well, you're paying me to tell you these things sir. Your words."

"Yes, sir, I will continue to look for them until you get here."

"Yes, sir."

"See you soon."

It sounded like the call ended.

Crome said, "Hot damn."

He called Blu.

Chapter Thirty

"I don't think he's going to fly commercial," Blu said, thinking this might be a good opportunity. After all, he and Crome now had the home court advantage.

He had the call on the truck's Bluetooth.

"And he ain't comin' alone," Crome said.

"True, that," said Blu.

In fact, the mogul will probably try to hire the S.W.A.T. team. This would require some finesse, otherwise they might get shot.

Listening to the phone conversation, Tess said, "They know what Harmony and Crome look like. They might not know what we look like."

"They probably got pictures," Crome said. "What do we do about Ariel?"

"Nothing," Blu said. "Brother Thomas has got her stashed up tight. Only a few of us know exactly where she is."

"Even Harmony and I don't know," Tess said.

"Probably for the best," Crome replied, trying to get her riled up.

"Yet you guys are going to need us to bail you out. It's only a matter of time."

Crome said, "We like to work people to their strengths at Blu Carraway Investigations."

"Very funny, Crome," she said. "Imagine how much better we'd be if we were involved in the planning."

"What do you think this is?" the biker asked.

It was a poignant question. He and Blu didn't hold traditional meetings. This phone conversation was about as structured as it got with them.

"A cluster," she said.

"Now that we have that settled," Blu said. "Who's tracking Townley?"

"Harmony's on it," Tess said. "I already texted her."

"Glad somebody's thinking," said Crome. "I don't wanna be the only one."

"Don't worry, Mick," she said. "We'll make sure the wind doesn't blow out your candle."

"He-he," Crome snorted.

Blu said, "Back to the challenge at hand—"

Tess said, "My man's so official sounding, ain't he?"

"He's got my vote," Crome said.

"I think," Blu said, ignoring their failed attempts at sarcasm, "that we need some additional resources."

"Pelton and Powers?" Crome asked.

"For starters. We also might need Jimmy."

"You mean for more than he's already doing?" Crome asked.

"He doesn't know he's helping us out right now," Blu said. "And I don't plan on telling him."

"The enemy of my enemy," Tess said.

"That never gets old," Crome said. "Call the P's. I got some checking of my own."

That could mean a whole lot of things, most of which were in the gray area and quite possibly illegal.

Blu and Tess showed up at Pelton's bar. The place seemed to get cleaner every time they visited. Twenty years ago, the place was a dump. Now, it won "Best Beach Bar" awards and, mostly, had the backing of the town council as long as there weren't any more gunfights. To Pelton's credit, there hadn't been one in three years. The kid was on a roll.

Pelton's dog Shelby, the lady-killer, greeted Tess. As if under a trance, she lowered her derriere to the floor and gave the dog a proper greeting.

Paige, the bar's manager, waived at them. Unlike the old days when there was no dress code for employees, she wore a polo shirt with the bar's cigar-smoking Jolly Roger flag embroidered over her heart along with khaki shorts.

Blu walked around his girlfriend and her new love interest and took a stool at the bar.

"You're here to take my ex-boss away again, aren't you?" Paige asked.

"Yep," he said. "Wait a minute, what do you mean ex-boss?"

A voice behind him said, "I sold controlling interest."

It was Brack Pelton. The guy had a perpetual tan and his shaggy mane had been tamed. He also wore similar uniform shirt and shorts although he had a green shirt to Paige's hot pink.

Blu thought his selling his share was probably a big step, but he didn't know what to say.

Paige filled the void. "He found his calling and it isn't pouring drinks."

Pelton and his wife had more money than anyone deserved. Certainly more money than they could spend in a lifetime. Blu would bet, and he could easily find out, that Pelton gave Paige the deal of the century.

"I was planning on coming by your island for a chat," Pelton said. "You saved me the trip."

"You wanna work for me?" Blu asked.

"On a contract basis," he said. "Assuming that's okay with you."

It was more than okay. The kid had driving and combat skills and he worked cheap—nearly free.

"Your wife okay with this?"

A female voice on Blu's blind side said, "Not really, but what choice do I have?"

It was Darcy Pelton.

"Is anyone else going to sneak up on me or is this the whole gang?" Blu asked.

"It's just that it's so easy," Darcy said, smiling.

Brack's wife, a dead ringer for a younger Elizabeth Shue, did not have on the bar's uniform. Instead, she wore business casual in the form of a blouse, skirt, and flats. Her curly blonde hair was held up with one of those clip things.

"I suppose," Blu said, "you could always tell your husband to pick more grownup friends."

Darcy gave him a stiff smile. "That would only encourage him more."

To Pelton, Blu said, "There's a hell storm coming in from California. I'm not sure how big but it's going to be bad."

"Count me in," he said.

Blu gave Darcy a weak smile. "I was afraid he'd say that."

She gave her husband a kiss. "Try to be home for dinner."

All the men in the room watched her walk out the front door.

"Working with me," Blu said, "is not going to be healthy for much of anything in your life."

"Who else is gonna do it?" Pelton asked.

The list was short, but there were a few that would still work with him and Crome. Which reminded him, he had to call Powers.

Crome made a call to one of his sources. This one had no direct knowledge of anything going on in Charleston, but knew everything going on in the private security realm.

"How's it going, Baxter?" Crome asked.

"Not bad, Mick."

"You're not gonna ask me how I'm doin'?"

"I already know," the source said. "Bad."

"What do you know?"

"You and your Anglo-Cuban partner peed in the wrong bowl of cereal. I've never seen so much consternation in all my days in this business."

"What's coming our way?"

"The whole enchilada."

"Meaning?"

The man cleared his throat. "Most of the free agents joined Jake Jarnel and they are pissed about Sammy."

Jake Jarnel, the piece of work trying to consolidate private security.

"Sammy?" Crome asked. "The guy was a tool."

"No argument here," he said. "But he was one of them and you aren't."

"You make it sound like a cult."

"That's a good way to look at it. Another way is they're now muscle for something bigger than they were before."

"Thanks, Baxter."

"Stay cool, Crome. Don't lose your head on this one. There are a few watching to see what happens."

"Sounds like we could use some help."

"Don't expect any on the front end. If Jarnel wins, they don't want to be on his bad side."

Politics. Apparently there were bootlickers in the muscle trade as well.

Crome and Harmony showed up at the Pirate's Cove. Blu still felt a tinge of surprise that his partner still stuck around. It couldn't last much longer.

The six of them, Brack and Darcy, Blu and Tess, and Crome and Harmony, sat at a big table on the lower back deck. Paige closed off the area to the tourists, calling it a private party, and served them personally. It was another precaution.

They ate platters of atomic burgers, hand-dipped onion rings, fresh-cut fries, and fried dill pickles. Blu would have to work out extra hard at the gym to make up for such a large ingestion of grease but it was worth it.

Tess said, "So we have an army of trained killers funded by one of the top thousand richest people in the world after us. And

Townley's in the mix as well? He must owe Jarnel or be an investor."

"That about sums it up," Crome said.

Darcy said, "I've been tracking Townley's money. He's leaving an easy trail to follow."

"Probably a set-up," Blu said. "But you know that, already. Don't you?"

"I suspected as much so I mined data on the companies he owns. Turns out he's been buying them himself below cost."

"What does that have to do with us?" Crome asked.

"Not you guys," she said.

"Ariel," Blu said. "He tried to hose her out of several million. She caught on and told him to go pound sand."

"So that's why he's upset?" Darcy asked.

"What did Colette find out about him?" Tess asked.

"I called her partner," Crome said.

Everyone at the table looked at him.

Blu said, "That was thoughtful of you."

"Save it," Crome said. "She told me she had some stuff on Townley."

"And?" Tess asked.

"And she's on her way here as we speak."

The group was silent.

Harmony asked, "And you were going to tell us this when?"

"I figured I'd work it into the conversation at some point and that's what I did."

"Not very well, you ask me," Pelton said.

"Nobody asked you, Jarhead," Crome said.

The younger man smiled.

Blu said, "You met her before?"

"Nope."

"And you don't think this could also be a setup?"

Crome took out his vape pen and winked at Pelton. "It's worth it, you ask me."

"When does she arrive?" Blu asked. "And where are we going

to stash her? If Townley finds out, she's in trouble."

"No more than we are," Crome said. "She can stay with me."

That would not be a good idea for either Colette's partner or Crome, Blu thought. "She can stay with Tess."

"Or me," Harmony said. "I owe her that much."

Darcy and Brack agreed to pick up Colette's partner. It kept some distance between her and the rest of them. As far as Blu could tell, the Peltons were not Townley's nor Jarnel's target.

At least not yet.

After Pelton joined Blu's merry men of mayhem in Charleston, all bets were off.

With that going on, Blu drove Crome to the shooting range. He really liked the new Ruger he shot in Vegas and wanted to show Crome. It was half the price of the Glocks Crome used and was made in the USA. The reason the cost was important was because in their business, they tended to be rough on firearms.

The place they went to shoot, Blu's favorite range, was the same place Crome had taken Ariel. Plug It And Stuff It had been around a long time.

They walked in and were greeted by ten-year-old Lucy with a, "Hi, Uncle Brack. Hi, Uncle Crome."

"Hey Sweetie Pie," Crome said.

The biker loved to kill people, yet with this young girl Crome was docile as a kitten.

He went up to her and she let him kiss her hand.

Blu handed her a dollar bill. She pocketed the money and giggled.

Crome pulled out a five. "Cheapskate."

Lucy jumped down off her stool and danced around the shop.

Pops said, "Where's Ariel?"

"Working on her music," Crome said.

The old man seemed disappointed but said, "You lugs look like you're up to something."

Blu said, "We need a couple of lanes if you got them."

"Course I do," he said.

The old man wore his usual outfit of flannel shirt, blue jeans, and a ball cap with a rebel flag on it. The hat didn't bother Blu. Lucy's father was African American and Pops had adopted him into the family and was teaching him the taxidermy side of the business.

Crome and Blu shot their nine millimeters. Once Blu had proven to himself and Crome that the Ruger was a good alternative, they got into a friendly competition.

Pops took score and Crome beat Blu by one shot. Blu had been the sniper but Crome was wicked with small arms fire. Back in the day there wasn't anyone better in the Rangers.

Crome didn't get anywhere in the military, meaning any kind of promotion, because he was one step away from being a Section 8 —mentally unfit for service. He was a great soldier but quite nuts.

When they finished and walked out of the range, they checked their messages. There had been two missed calls from Tess.

Townley had flown into Charleston along with several mercenaries. Blu was glad his own team had already circled the wagons.

Chapter Thirty-One

As if following Blu's playbook, Townley checked into Charleston Place. He'd reserved half a floor for his henchmen and they appeared to mean business.

Jimmy Z. sent Blu a text six hours later. He'd been contacted about providing firepower. Blu had suggested that he go through with the deal, but to let him know what they wanted. Turned out they wanted AR-15's and handguns of various makes and models. Each merc had his own preference, much like Crome still wanting Glocks no matter how well the Ruger shot.

Powers had enlisted in Blu's army, with the promise of a consulting fee large enough to pay for a semester of books for his daughter who was in college.

Brack Pelton agreed to work for minimum wage.

It was Colette's partner that had become the wild card. Her name was Dallas and she had dark hair, a brown shade of skin that wasn't entirely from the sun, and coal black eyes. She was solid, strong, and menacing. A good five eight, she wore a t-shirt, jeans and boots and Crome was smitten all over again.

Because she didn't carry her service weapon on the plane, she requested a Glock and Crome nearly buckled at the knees. He gave her the one he had along with his holster and dug his backup out of one of the saddle bags of his bike.

Townley had as many mercenaries as he cared to pay for.

Blu's merry army consisted of two Ranger thugs—himself and Crome, an ex-Marine—Brack, two semi-on-duty cops—Powers and Dallas, and three ex-investigative reporters—Tess, Harmony, and

Darcy.

What his team lacked in evil they made up for in cunning. He couldn't have asked for better operatives. He just wished he didn't care about their wellbeing as much as he did. If any of them got hurt, he would spend a lot of days trying to forgive himself after he killed the one who harmed them.

He also had Brother Thomas and his congregation. They had proven to be resourceful in keeping Ariel hidden from view despite men like Dreg looking for her in their backyard. Blu wasn't sure how Sherman and Dreg had gotten so close, but they hadn't found her yet so that was a good sign.

Apparently no one was talking.

And lastly, he had two of Juanita's friends who worked at the Palmetto Inn giving him intelligence. They would prove to be the most valuable as Blu couldn't get as close as they could to Townley.

The first hint of movement came when a call to Blu's phone from a woman who spoke Spanish told him Townley and three men got in a black SUV and headed out.

Jimmy had already informed Blu the weapon sale would go down today. Ten AR-15's, ten Mossberg shotguns, and ten pistols of various makes and models.

Apparently there would be ten of them to Blu's immediate eight. He didn't count Brother Thomas or Juanita, although he had a feeling both would do whatever needed to be done.

Juanita's friend also gave them the SUV's plate number. It was a rental registered to one of Townley's businesses. Obviously he didn't care about a link. He was going to openly fight and not hide behind anything.

Blu had to admire that, while at the same time wonder why the man was being so reckless and bold. Confidence was one thing and it came from superior planning and managing the details. Overconfidence came from using money to bowl over obstacles. Sooner or later that plan blew up.

Townley was due.

*   *   *

Baxter called Crome an hour later.

"Whattaya got?" the biker asked.

"Your man's been busy since he got to town."

Crome watched the waves crash onto the beach behind his rental. Dawn was coming up in front of him. He inhaled a lungful of vapor.

On the exhale, he said, "Give it to me."

He listened to a laundry list of activities. Apparently the tycoon never slept and the man was spending a considerable amount of money in town on his plans for Blu Carraway Investigations' demise.

When Baxter finished with the report, he said, "This guy's got enough clout to remove you both from the face of the earth with no trace you were ever here."

"I doubt it," Crome said. "But he can try."

The call ended.

Dallas came up behind him and put an arm around his bare chest as he stood there wearing only his jeans.

"You really got to even your color out," she said, referring to his farmer's tan.

"I ain't got time for that nonsense," he said.

She kissed his shoulder. "Come back to bed."

He turned and found she didn't have any clothes on. Life really didn't get much better than this. The possibility for more danger and a woman in his bed. He didn't ask for a lot in this world and therefore usually got what he wanted. He was made for this.

"In a minute." Crome looked at his phone, the one Blu made him carry. The one he usually hated but had lately begun to depend on. It was the one thing in his life that peddled the danger his addiction needed and it had a huge supply at the moment.

He scrolled through his recents list and tapped on the number called "BLUE." It always made him smile that Blu's previous client misspelled his name with the phone number she gave him.

*   *   *

Blu listened as Crome relayed what Baxter had told him.

When he finished, Blu asked, "You believe him?"

"Mostly. The man's playing an angle and I ain't sure what it is yet. But I think we can't ignore him."

Between Townley running ragged in his town and Baxter's need to sell them up the river, Blu didn't know which one had a greater hold on their private parts at the moment. He couldn't dismiss either of them.

Tess handed him a cup of coffee and sprayed on odor free bug repellant.

"Townley's been busy," he said. "It's time to get to work."

She kissed him. Even first thing in the morning, she was perfect. It wasn't just how she looked. She knew exactly what he needed in every moment. He on the other hand barely remembered his daughter's birthday. Making sure he was the best he could be for Tess was a stretch even for someone with forty-six years of experience behind him.

"What?" she asked.

"After this is over, why don't we get away?" he asked. "Leave Charleston behind and take a trip."

"Where?"

"Wherever you want," he said.

Standing on her tiptoes again, she gave him a longing kiss. When he was just about to forget his own name, she turned and walked back inside his house. "I'm holding you to that, Mr. Blu Carraway."

All he could do was hope that she would. If not, he didn't know what that could mean. Lucky for him, he had two of the most powerful men in the world planning his demise. The distraction kept him sharp and not lamenting a life without Tess.

Pelton showed up at Crome's bungalow exactly on time at eight a.m. The kid took his new job seriously and Crome wouldn't knock him for it. Tardiness was for amateurs. Professionals stuck to timelines, even Crome.

The two had worked semi-successfully together in the past. It was semi-successful because they actually got along and didn't try to outwardly kill each other. The problem was both of them could be characterized as "reactors". If they weren't careful, they could bounce themselves from one end of Charleston to the other like a pinball machine while chasing leads.

Outside, on the back patio facing the Atlantic Ocean, Pelton said, "Darcy found out Townley's been meeting with the Charleston old money."

That wasn't good. Townley was trying to sway the city's standing on the battle that was about to occur. Blu Carraway Investigations, et. al., didn't need to fight their neighbors as well as the invaders.

"Your wife's already working on it, huh?" Crome asked.

With a smile on his tanned face, Pelton said, "Of course. Whose F-150 is in the drive?"

Crome threw him the key fob. "The Agency's. You drive."

"You couldn't have gotten a Bugatti?"

The kid and his wife could afford ten of them and not make a dent in their net worth. He was just trying to get a rise. It felt good to work with someone who didn't care about whether or not they got into a fight or with whom. "Sorry. Maybe next time. Where's Shelby?"

"With the dog sitter," Brack said.

"Trish?" Crome asked. "You put a tracker on her?"

It was no secret that Pelton's dog sitter, Trish Connors, had such a deep affection for the mutt that she wasn't above dog-napping.

"Very funny," he said, not smiling.

"Well, we get done with this job and you find you need help hunting her down, we'll look into it for ya."

"I'd hate to interrupt your plans to run, I mean take a leave of absence."

The kid pulled no punches. He usually came back with direct hits and this time was no different.

"Fair enough," Crome said, backing off. Self-control was something new to him but he found it worked out a little better than overreacting.

Harmony topped the steps. "Sorry I'm late. I'm surprised you two aren't throwing punches by now."

She wore a sleeveless shirt, shorts, and sandals all in various pastels. She also carried a tote bag over her shoulder.

"Come back in five minutes," Crome said.

Pelton laughed. "Yeah, so you can call an ambulance for the Road Hog, here."

Harmony said, "I can see this is going to be a fun day."

"What's in the bag?" Pelton asked.

She opened it for them to see. "Clothes. If we're going to do this, we need to really do it."

What she referred to was how the three of them planned on taking two cars to shadow Townley.

"You get a rental?" Crome asked.

"Yep," Harmony said. "A silver Ford Explorer like a million other ones on the road."

Crome was convinced Townley remembered exactly what she looked like in California and would recognize her again. Behind the wheel of an enclosed vehicle and disguised was the best place for her.

As Blu pulled his Grand Cherokee forward, around Dink and Doofus, and approached the small bridge that connected his island to the mainland, his phone buzzed. He put his new-to-him SUV in park and looked at the display. It was Andeline.

He accepted the call.

Before he could say anything, she said, "Hey Gorgeous."

"'Hey Gorgeous', yourself," he said.

"If only you thought that, Mr. Carraway, I could show you a way of the world you have never experienced."

Her being an ex-prostitute and Madame, he did not think replying to her comment would be in his best interest, so he kept quiet.

"No reply?" she asked. "Fine, then. Be a sour grape. This isn't a social call, anyway. You'd know if it was. Because I wouldn't be calling, I'd be at your front door."

"You've been over here several times, And," he said.

"Yes, but always with your girlfriend," she said. "I'd like to try it once when Tess was somewhere else."

This conversation wasn't going anywhere but downhill.

"I'm just playing, Blu," she said. "Jeez. Lighten up."

"Sorry, And," he said. "I've got a lot on my mind."

"I know, Sugar," she said. "That's why I'm calling."

Crome had already told him what Darcy had found out. He wondered if this was the same information from a different source. It wouldn't necessarily help, but it would be confirmation.

She said, "You got a price on your pretty head."

"You already told me that."

"Sure I did," she said. "Except I think your friend from California decided it would be better to try and bankrupt Kincaid than knock you off first."

Up until this very moment, he'd considered Adam Kincaid invincible. Now, a small crack of doubt began to propagate in his belief.

"What makes you say that?" he asked, and heard the lack of confidence in his words as he spoke them.

"I already know Darcy Pelton is aware of and probably told you that Townley has been meeting with the Charleston elite. What she probably didn't say because she is too smart for her own good and the best networker in the city is that the goal of these meetings is for him to move his sorry ass into a position of power in our fine city."

"They aren't listening to him, are they?"

"They're listening to his billion dollars."

None of this sounded good. In fact, it sounded downright terrible. But then he remembered something about Andeline that most others overlooked. While she was one of the best sources of information in the city, when she felt threatened, she fought back.

"What have you done about it?" he asked.

"Funny you should ask," she said. "I have more than a few friends in this town. And what they like less than someone playing with their money is blackmail."

"Wait a minute," Blu said. "Townley is trying to blackmail them?"

"Yep."

Blu's not-so-limited experience with the Charleston elite gave him perspective on how they worked. They were secretive, knew how to move their money around, and demanded the utmost loyalty. Someone coming to town to threaten them with blackmail for their sins in exchange for their support would never work as a long term solution.

"So what are they going to do about it?"

"They're going to help you kick, and I quote, 'that California carpetbagger out of our fine city.'"

There was only one Charlestonian who still spoke like that. Pushing ninety-five years old, conservative to the end, and a product of the Great Depression, Preston Marquis III held a tight control of the city through mostly backroom dealings. Thirty years ago, he was one of Andeline's best clients. Now he was her best information source. Who said sentimentality was dead?

"How is old Preston?" he asked.

"I should have married him when I had the chance," she said.

"Then you wouldn't be Andeline," he said. "You'd be Preston's third trophy wife."

"Why Mr. Carraway," she said, "that is positively the nicest thing you could have said to me at this moment. Maybe I could be your trophy wife instead."

"Maybe," he said. "Tell you what, And. You get me and Darcy

in a room with the old man and I'll set you up with my partner. He's like my brother, you know."

"I love your biker friend with all my heart," she said, "but it's not the same thing."

"You're probably right. You need constant attention. It'd be hard to get that from Key West."

"So you think your friend is going to take off when this is over?"

"All signs point to yes."

There was a sigh. "I wish he wouldn't do that."

"Me too."

"You have a lunch appointment with Mr. Marquis at the club. He's expecting you to bring a guest. I wasn't going to suggest Mrs. Pelton unless you didn't mention her first."

"I owe you, And."

"Yes, you do." She ended the call.

The guitar riff from Four Non-Blondes' "What's Going On" started up as he put the truck in drive.

Chapter Thirty-Two

Crome listened from the passenger seat of the F-150 as Pelton talked with Blu.

The kid said, "You ever worked with my wife before?"

There was a pause, followed by a chuckle.

"Well, there's always a first. Good luck and watch your six."

Crome knew what Pelton was talking about. The story went that before they were married, Brack and Darcy worked together to find his uncle's killer. They got set up and ambushed and Darcy ended up shot and in the I.C.U. At the time, she was the premiere investigative journalist in the city with an aggressive reputation. She hadn't slowed down since she left the news arena and married Brack; she just turned her focus toward her family business. Now it appeared as if Townley was going after the Charleston elite, of which Darcy's family were members. If she felt threatened, she would go after him. And Blu would be her backup.

Crome said, "We should probably back them up."

"The last thing my wife or your partner would appreciate is us second-guessing them."

The kid had a point.

Pelton pulled to the curb and dialed a number.

The first thing Blu learned about Darcy was that she liked to be in control, which started with her need to use her own vehicle. At least she was going to let him drive.

He met her at the downtown office of Wells Shipping, her

family's multi-billion dollar business. The reception area, with high ceilings decorated by crystal chandeliers and walls lined with marble and brass, was the most opulent he'd come across in the city and that was saying something for Charleston.

The attractive, youthful receptionist told him to take a seat in a leather couch while he waited for Darcy. As he sat there, his phone chirped. Andeline sent him a text.

He read it and put his phone away as Darcy walked up.

She wore a smart business suit which made him glad he'd made the last minute decision to change into khakis and a decent polo before the meeting. He'd left his main gun in the SUV.

He stood and offered a hand, wanting to show her respect and keep the business tone. She ignored his gesture and stepped in to give him a kiss on the cheek.

"We're practically family," she said. "No need to be so formal."

The other reason he was trying to stay formal was so he could keep his mind focused on the task at hand. If he felt responsible for her well-being, he might not be able to do what needed to be done.

She'd just blown his plan to pieces, smiling while she did it.

Pelton had married well.

"Where's your gun?" she asked.

"In the car." His main one was, anyway. He'd strapped a backup to his ankle.

"Let's get something straight," she said. "You have clearance to be here with open carry if you so choose. If we're going to do this, we're going to do it right."

"Damn the torpedoes," he said.

"No," she said. "Cover all the bases."

"Now that we have that covered," he said, "are you ready?"

"No one is ever ready for a meeting with Preston Marquis."

"I'll give you that," he said.

They walked to a parking garage behind the building and got in her truck.

She said, "You know Tess loves you, right?"

It caught him off guard. He didn't know what to say.

Darcy, her hair pinned up, as her husband once told him, to keep her neck cool in the Deep South heat, said, "I'm only telling you this because you're a lot like my husband. I loved him from the first moment I saw him but I ran away. He finally got smart and came after me."

"You two are meant for each other," he said.

"I know that now. Don't make the same mistakes we did."

Brack had told him to watch his six. He didn't anticipate getting ambushed by the man's wife.

"Thanks," he said. What other response could he give?

"Good," she said. "Now that we have that straight, you lied to me about not having a gun on you, right?"

"Yes."

"I figured as much. Let's go."

He started her SUV and they were off.

"You know Blu has a way with the ladies," Crome said.

"I do," Pelton said, seemingly unfazed.

"And you don't mind your wife riding in a car with him?"

"Nope."

Crome took a hit of vapor. "Well I would."

"Because you'd question any woman that married you?"

Exhaling, Crome almost choked. "That was pretty good, kid."

"You met my wife," he said. "What do you think?"

"I heard both of you gunned it out with some killers in Atlanta," Crome said. "I wouldn't mess with her."

"You are smarter than you look," Pelton said. "Where are we headed?"

"Market Street."

The heart of the tourist district.

"Market Street?" Pelton asked. "You need a t-shirt?"

"Nope," Crome said. "We need to meet Andeline."

"And she chose the location?"

"Yep. When it comes to her I don't ask a whole lot of

questions."

"I don't blame you." Pelton steered toward Seventeen North that led them into the city.

Preston Marquis had a suite that overlooked the harbor. Blu kept his attention focused on anything strange as they walked into the semi-private hotel and rode the elevator to the top floor. At one time, Marquis had made it to the top fifty on Forbes' richest list.

Darcy knocked on the door.

It was answered by a black woman in a servant's uniform. Darcy announced them and the woman led them inside.

Blu followed the women, taking in the room.

Who rented a suite for lunch? Someone who didn't want the lower class visiting his home. Darcy wouldn't fit the definition, but Blu did and he knew it.

The old man stood in the living area to greet them. He wore a dark suit and tie, his bald head gleaming in the midday sunlight. His mustache was white with flecks of grey and black and his back had a slight stoop.

Darcy walked toward the man. "Mr. Marquis." She shook his hand and then said, "May I introduce Blu Carraway."

Blu shook the man's hand.

Marquis said, "So you're Kincaid's boy? I expected something a little bigger and more polished."

Blu stood six three, a good half a foot over the old man. And he was solid thanks to the workout regimen Heath and Roger had developed for him. This guy was trying to rattle him.

"Looks can be deceiving," Blu said.

"I hope for your sake you're right." He turned to Darcy. "How's your mother?"

"A pain in the butt," Darcy said, changing up the conversation.

"That's her job, my dear."

"She does it well, then. Why are you being such a pill?"

Marquis eased into a chair. "Because I'm old and I can get

away with it. Have a seat."

Blu and Darcy sat.

"So you want to know about Mr. Townley? Talk about a pain in the ass. The man comes to town with his big California dreams and tries to whisk us off our feet. Well I, for one, am not buying what he's selling. Sounds like typical politician hubbaloo. He should be kissing babies he's so slick."

"What tipped you off?" Blu asked.

The old man waved a hand in the air. "He doesn't need anything we have here. I've traveled the world. Charleston is unique but not for everyone. This man would fit in as well here as I would in his town."

"He has taken a special interest in a client of mine," Blu said.

"Ariel Braam," Marquis said. "Yes I know. Do you know why?"

"Something about a ten million dollar deal she rejected."

"Men like Townley, like me, don't like rejection. We like owning things, owning people. It makes us feel self-important. This isn't about a ten million dollar deal. It's about a woman who wants to stand on her own two feet and a man who doesn't want her to."

It was a perspective Blu had not considered. Most men wouldn't. He suspected Darcy, and Tess, and Harmony, and Colette had all already come to the conclusion the old man had from the start. With age came wisdom, and even a little understanding of the fairer sex.

"He's not going to stop until he either owns her or she doesn't exist," Darcy said. It wasn't a question.

"I believe he's moved past the option to buy," Blu said.

The woman who answered the door came back into the room carrying three salad plates.

"I forgot to ask what you all wanted to drink," she said.

"Sweet tea is fine," Blu said. "Thank you."

Darcy said, "Same here."

The woman hadn't forgotten, but had tried to respect their conversation time with Marquis. She nodded and went back to the kitchen area.

They ate mixed greens with a mild vinaigrette while she brought three glasses of tea. Marquis' glass looked different. Blu bet the man must not be allowed sugar.

"There's more to this," Darcy said, between bites.

"Yes there is," the old man said.

"The security detail bothered me from the start," Blu said.

"It should." Marquis pushed his plate forward a few inches and wiped his mouth on a napkin. "You know nobody in the business pulls a Benedict Arnold on their own ward unless there's a significant payout."

"There would have to be," Blu said. "Who would want them guarding their lives after word got out they set up a past client."

Darcy finished her salad and took a drink from her tea. Setting the glass down, she said, "Which leads me to something I found out."

The men looked at her. Both knew she had a knack for discovering details no one else did. It was how she'd been so successful as an investigative journalist and how she had been instrumental in navigating her family's business through the world of shipping, doubling their profits in two years.

She said, "There's a consolidation taking place. One organization in the private security arena. Jake Jarnel is leading the hostile takeover."

"How'd you come by this?" Blu asked. His sources had already told him, but he was curious as to how she'd come across it.

"It started with an innocent email, one of those that on the surface looks like either spam or a mass distribution. After that, they got perpetually more focused to the point of singling out not just clients who currently have private security teams, but the specific decision makers."

The old man laughed. "You got tapped, didn't you, Mrs. Pelton?"

"For my parents," she said. "I began to look into who was behind it all and came to the conclusion it was an outfit in California."

"How's Townley involved with Jarnel?" Blu asked.

"Townley's using Jarnel's consolidation team to stiff-arm people like Ariel."

The servant came back with three more plates, the second course which consisted of shrimp and grits and steamed broccoli spears.

Blu lifted his salad plate so she could set the main course down. "There's a lawsuit in there somewhere."

Marquis said, "Let me guess, because Ariel's detail had a private contract with her, only they are liable."

"Exactly," Darcy said, then to the servant, "this looks amazing."

"I hope you like it, Darlin'," the woman said.

"So we work on Townley," Blu said.

"Yes," Marquis said. "If you can, the world would be a better place without him. Same with Jarnel, but he's more slippery."

The meeting with Andeline turned into a lecture about Crome's desire to head to Key West and what a bad idea that was. He let her talk and didn't say much and afterwards sat in the F150 thinking as Pelton drove.

His phone rang, interrupting his thoughts. It was Dallas. He said, "Where the hell you been?"

"You miss me already?" She sounded playful, but he knew she was using him to avoid dealing with the loss of Colette. He knew because he was using her for the same reason.

With everything going on, they couldn't afford to have any renegades in their midst. Wait a minute, did he just think that?

She said, "While you're trying to figure out how to answer my question, I'll tell you that Charleston PD has Townley under surveillance."

That was definitely something. "How'd you find that out?"

"It's called professional courtesy," she said. "I'm sure you've heard of it."

Now she was just being mean.

"I have," he said. "Like it would have been courteous to let me know where you traipsed off to this morning."

Dallas began to say something.

Pelton said, "Traipsed?"

"Shut up."

Dallas said, "Did you just tell me to shut up?"

"No, I told Pelton to shut up."

"He's there? Tell him his wife and Blu make a cute couple."

He was not about to say that. "What are you talking about?"

"They're meeting with someone by the name of Preston Marquis. The police also have them under surveillance."

"What about me and Pelton?" Crome asked.

"Not as far as I can tell," she said.

"This sounds like a setup."

"It is," she said. "Your friend Powers is ticked off which is good for us. It seems they don't care who they bust on a murder charge. If someone dies, they will make an arrest. It doesn't matter if it's you or me or Blu or Brack or Townley. They'll take one or all."

Maybe Blu Carraway Investigations had finally outgrown this town.

Chapter Thirty-Three

Blu opened the passenger door for Darcy and caught movement in his periphery. "Duck."

She didn't question him.

As she slid down in her seat, he slammed the door, pulled out his Ruger, and crouched in a shooter's stance.

Two men approached fast and split up.

Blu rolled away from the truck, ducked behind a parked car and raised himself up.

One of the men had almost made it to Darcy.

Blu had him in his sights. "Stop."

The man stopped.

The side window of the car Blu was using for cover blew open. It was from the second man.

Blu fired and hit the man closest to Darcy three times before turning on the shooter.

An alarm wailed from somewhere.

The shooter vanished.

As Blu walked to Darcy's truck, he pulled his phone and called her.

She answered and he said, "I'm coming to you. Don't shoot."

"You hit?" she asked as if she said those words every day. Maybe being Brack Pelton's wife meant doing things a little differently.

"No. Sounds like the police are on their way."

He came up beside his truck and looked in the window. Darcy

had slid herself into the foot well and had a thirty-two in one hand and held a phone to her ear with the other.

Holding up a hand to let her know he didn't want her exposed yet, he did a scan of the area. There was no movement. With his gun still in his hand, he stooped and checked for a pulse of the man on the ground. There wasn't one. But there was a gun in the guy's hand. It wasn't really a clean shoot, but he wasn't a cop. The dead guy's partner had fired first. The bullets in the car would prove that. They'd also prove there was another gun in the area.

Of course Blu and Darcy would have to give up their weapons. So would the dead guy, but who cared about that.

What was cause for concern was how they were tracked to this location. He could not—would not—believe that Preston Marquis had traded him and Darcy to Townley.

Something else was going on.

As the siren got louder, Blu called Andeline.

"Who knew about our little meeting with Marquis?" he asked.

"Just me and him and you and Darcy."

"Well we just ran into two guys with guns."

A cruiser rounded the corner.

Blu immediately lowered his gun to the ground. Into the phone, he said, "Call my lawyer and tell him I'll be in lockup."

Ending the call, he placed his phone on the ground next to his gun, got on his knees, and raised his hands.

Darcy opened the car door as the police got out of their cruiser, saw Blu, and did the same thing.

The two officers had weapons drawn and pointed at them. Scenes like this were not the time to offer any resistance.

Crome got off the phone with Andeline—a call he almost didn't take—and looked over at Pelton with a not so good feeling.

"Um," he said.

"What?" Pelton asked.

"Before I get into it, your wife is okay."

Pelton pulled over to the side of the road. "Okay."

Good. The kid didn't overreact. At least not right away.

"Apparently when she and Blu were in the parking garage after their lunch meeting, two men drew down on them. Blu took one of them out but the other got away. Your wife crawled onto the floorboard of the truck."

"Where are they now?"

"They were taken into custody. Andeline already called Blu's lawyer."

Pelton tapped the steering wheel. "We can't do anything about that right now."

"What are you suggesting?" Crome asked.

"No one is going to get at them where they are," Pelton said. "My wife is safe for the moment. Let's take the opportunity to hunt down Townley."

"Your call."

After a few seconds, Pelton said, "Yeah. That's what I wanna do. Show them we don't scare easy. Take it right to them."

Crome liked it.

Harmony called Crome right at that moment. "I just heard."

"Can you get over to the police station and check on them for me?" Crome asked, fingers crossed.

"What are you going to do?"

"Me and Brack are staying on Townley's tail. I want that bucket of donkey piss to get what's coming to him."

Camera footage in the parking garage corroborated Blu's story enough for reasonable doubt to cover the gray area of him killing the man who wasn't shooting at him first. He could tell that Powers didn't buy his suggestion that he had bad aim. Everyone on the police force knew Blu had been trained as a sniper, although even he would label himself the mediocre shot of his old unit.

The hole in the argument was that the worst shot amongst the trained snipers was still a damn good shot. Blu preferred hand-to-hand combat to splattering brains from a thousand yards anyway.

Darcy Pelton had been one tough customer through the whole ordeal. Most anyone else after a gunfight needed to take some time to unscramble their brains. She was anxious to get back to work and on Townley's trail. The man had made a grave mistake threatening the Wells family. Blu would not want Darcy or her husband as enemies.

It seemed as if the city of Charleston was coming down on Blu's side. Normally extremely welcoming, the holy city didn't take kindly to outside agitators with selfish agendas.

In front of the police station, Harmony met him and Darcy, giving both of them cheek kisses and hugs. Working with women on a professional level meant altering traditions. Crome would have greeted them with loaded pistols and an awaiting napalm air strike. Just tell him where to drop it.

The women preferred pleasantries first.

Then Harmony said, "I found a stripper who thinks she got the clap from one of Townley's goons."

Before Blu finished processing the declaration, Darcy said, "She tell you where they're hiding out?"

"Yep."

Slinging her purse over her shoulder, Darcy said, "Let's go."

Blu, whose name was on the investigation agency's marquis, found himself along for the ride, almost an inconvenience to the women doing the work.

Baxter called Crome while they were driving around hunting Townley.

"Yo."

"I got some bad news."

That wasn't anything new. Baxter always had bad news. The benefit was in how soon the bad news was learned. Given enough of a warning, any situation could be rendered harmless. Such was the reason for having a friend like Baxter.

"What's that?" Crome said.

"Townley's got Death, LLC on retainer."

In a spoof on Murder, Incorporated, the gangster era killer syndicate from the thirties, Death, LLC was made up mostly of highly trained thugs.

"And they're headed my way, right?" Crome asked.

"Yes."

"Thanks, Baxter. I owe you."

"As long as you know that." The call ended.

"Trouble in paradise?" Pelton asked.

"Not as long as you still got that itchy trigger finger."

Blu did not like hearing what Baxter had told Crome. While he agreed that most of the members of the new syndicate were goons, there were a few really dangerous characters. One in particular liked knives and preferred up-close-and-personal hits. The man enjoyed watching the lights go out in his victim's eyes.

Harmony dropped Darcy off in front of her family-owned office building downtown.

Darcy said, "I would have expected the first person I got arrested with would have been my husband. You beat him to it."

"I'm honored," Blu said.

"You should be." Darcy gave Harmony a cheek kiss. "Keep your shorts on, kiddo."

It was a not-so-subtle inside joke.

Harmony said, "Why start now?'

Darcy gave her a wink. "I'll call you all later."

With that, she walked inside the building and Blu felt a sense of relief. Even though they'd been arrested, she hadn't been harmed. Now he only had Harmony to worry about at the moment.

"You don't have to worry about me," Harmony said, reading his mind.

"Why not?"

"Because I know how to shoot."

They opened the doors to her rental SUV. "That doesn't solve every problem."

"No," she said, "but it prevents quite a few."

Not in Blu's experience. At times he'd found it wasn't the knowing how to shoot that prevented them. It was knowing who and when to shoot that made all the difference. He'd have to figure out a way to coach Harmony on this. If he left it up to Crome, all she'd learn was to shoot first and run to Key West when it blew up in her face.

"Where to now?" he asked.

"Your girlfriend wants to see you," she said.

"Point taken."

"I'm certainly not the one to give relationship advice," Harmony said, "but you should probably set time aside for both Tess and Hope."

"You're right," Blu said. "You're not the one who should be giving advice."

She gave him a sideways glare.

"But," he said. "It doesn't mean you don't know what you're talking about."

"I thought so," she said, all smiles and happiness returning to her visage. "And by the way, Sherman won't be a problem anymore."

"What do you mean Sherman won't be a problem *anymore?*" All of a sudden, Blu wasn't sure his first assessment of Harmony being off her rocker wasn't spot on.

"He got busted in a trafficking sting with two fifteen-year-olds," she said matter-of-factly.

"Did you...?"

"Set him up?" she asked. "Maybe."

"Is he in jail?"

"As we speak."

"Did he give up Townley?"

She gave him another sideways look, this one an open-lipped grin that showed her perfect teeth not unlike Jack Nicholson's

Joker face.

"You've been a busy little bee," he said, settling into his seat.

"I wanna make a good impression, boss."

Closing his eyes, he said, "Keep up the good work, Ms. Childs. You may yet have a bright and shining future with an upstart investigation agency."

"Don't kid yourself, Blu. After twenty years, nothing is an upstart."

He chuckled and found himself letting go. Soon after, he was asleep.

Chapter Thirty-Four

Blu felt lips on his and opened his eyes, afraid it was Harmony attacking him in a way that would hinder their business relationship. Lucky for him, it was Tess.

She pulled back. "How are you?"

"Good now."

Harmony said, "When he's not getting himself shot at and arrested."

He stepped out of the truck and stretched. "All part of the job."

Tess, wearing a sundress and her librarian glasses, put a hand on her hip. "We need to find out who set you up."

"I already know who set us up," Blu said. "Marquis."

"But why?"

"He's a scared old man," Blu said, "and Townley's got something on him."

"Then we've got to start there."

"Darcy's on it," he said. "When she gets finished, there will be one less one-percenter in the lowcountry."

"So what do we do now?"

Blu realized they were on the crushed shell in the parking lot of the Pirate's Cove. "Eat lunch."

It might be their last meal together. The way things were going, Blu wouldn't be surprised about anything.

Harmony said, "I'm going to leave you two lovebirds alone and head out. Call me later."

*   *   *

Crome watched the road and vaped as Pelton drove. Dallas rode in the backseat.

She said, "I got it! You're Brack Pelton. You signed with Hank Phillips Racing eight years ago and then fell off the planet. What happened?"

What little Crome knew of Pelton was that she'd been right. He had signed with the second ranked team in NASCAR at the time and then his wife got sick and died. Instead of continuing, he dropped out of society, joined the Marines, and fought in Afghanistan during the beginning of Obama's second term. Crome looked over, saw the apprehension in Pelton's face, and said, "We all got pasts. Give the kid a break."

Dallas, her long dark hair all over the place in a form of controlled chaos, sat with her legs sprawled over the backseat. He tried real hard not to get distracted.

She said, "No problem. But you shoulda seen this guy drive."

Pelton said, "Thanks."

Crome said, "Where the hell are we going?"

Without a destination in mind, the kid seemed to be heading somewhere in particular, even taking evasive maneuvers as if dodging a tail.

"To check on Ariel."

"Why there?" Crome asked.

"You got a better place?"

"Not at the moment."

The truth was they were stumped. With the one attack on Blu and Darcy, the one guy dead and the other in the wind, there were no leads. Townley had vanished and they didn't have a bead on him.

Pelton used the truck's Bluetooth to make a call.

The answer that played through the sound system was, "Brother Brack!"

"How's your guest?" he asked.

"Doin' fine, just fine, mm-hmm."

"We're on our way there. You need anything?"

"Who you got wit you?" the preacher asked.

Pelton told him.

Crome got the impression that Brother Thomas might have been worried that Blu was with them. This meant that Blu's ex-girlfriend Billie could be visiting with the preacher. She was, after all, in the choir. This would be interesting. No one had seen her in over a year.

After another few detours, Pelton wheeled the truck into North Charleston and then onto the parking lot of the Church of Redemption. The preacher had moved with his flock out of downtown Charleston. Most had left when the property values skyrocketed and the tourist district expanded into their neighborhoods. The problem was, lately, all property in Charleston County was at a premium. There was so much expansion that the city was set to burst. Another reason to head out of town when this was all over.

From what Crome could tell, the church had managed to get a fair chunk of change for its location; enough for the good preacher to buy a property double the size. Thanks to Brother Thomas' driving force, a lot of people were getting the help that they needed. Crome respected that. He'd even caught a few services when he wasn't too hung-over.

The large white steeple stood out as a beacon of hope to the city.

Not necessarily a believer, Crome nonetheless thought it better to acknowledge the Higher Power than ignore Him. The twelve-step program he'd dabbled in helped him see that.

Of course, all this would go out the window when he dropped his kickstand in Margaritaville.

They got out of the truck.

Even this far inland, if he inhaled deeply enough, he could smell the ocean. He might leave this city, but he would never get too far from the sea again as long as he lived.

The preacher opened two large, heavy doors to greet them.

Six three, three-hundred-and-fifty-pounds, all held together by a black suit and a minister's collar, Brother Thomas did not go unnoticed anywhere he went.

"Welcome!"

Pelton introduced Dallas to the pastor who took her hand and smiled.

"You have a nice place here," she said.

"Thank you, kindly. Do come inside."

The three of them followed him inside the church.

As they stepped in, Crome got a call. He looked at the display, saw Jimmy Z.'s name, and answered.

A hurried Jimmy said, "The Charleston town council rejected Townley's offers. He's pissed at you and coming after Ariel. They know she's at Pelton's friend's church and they're coming for her now."

"Thanks."

Pelton looked at Crome. "Problem?"

"The worst." Crome dialed Blu and talked when he answered. "We're at the church. Townley's goons are on the way here now."

"On my way," Blu said.

The call ended.

"Where is she?" Crome asked.

"Sittin' inside at the piano."

Blu ended the call with Crome, dropped money on the table on top of their half-eaten lunches. "I gotta go now."

Tess had been around him long enough to know he didn't overreact. It was another thing she loved about him.

"I'm coming with you," she said.

Trained killers with weapons were about to storm a church. There was no way in hell she was getting anywhere near the place.

"I'd like you to stay here and call Darcy and Harmony."

"Harmony's already on her way, you know."

He didn't know, but he could assume. Still, she was pretty much a Blu Carraway Investigations employee. Tess was his girlfriend. She might not understand what that meant, but he had it crystal clear in his mind.

Paige came over to the table. "You better go."

Blu looked at her, confused as to how she knew what was going on.

"I worked with Brack for five years," she said. "I know the look."

With a nod, Blu was off.

"Wait a minute!" Tess called.

He turned to face her. "I don't want you to come with me. Not to this."

She looked at him through her librarian glasses, hands on hips. "So now I'm your secretary?"

He wrapped his arms around her. "You know why I have to do this. It's bad enough everyone else is in harm's way. Knowing you are here and not there will help me stay focused."

Their lips met. He knew there was a chance they many never kiss again and took the time to enjoy the moment.

When they separated, she said, "I love you."

"I love you, too," he said, turned, and ran outside to his truck.

Pelton saw them coming first. Crome got the call, screwed the illegal suppressor on the end of his Glock, thumbed the safety off, and sighted in the door.

The description was two men, military postures, short hair, and stupid loafers. If there were two visible, that meant there could be another pair or two lurking about. Not ideal, but not undoable. The kid had proven himself every bit the killer Crome and Blu were. That meant three apiece. Unless the entire army had come.

He tried to remember who Blu had told him was in Death, LLC. One of the names stuck out—Hector Kuvey, the knife thrower. He'd have to be shot on sight. A trained man with a knife could kill a whole regiment in the dead of night. An expert like Hector could do it all from ten feet away. His throw was so accurate, he aimed for the neck. It killed and silenced at the same time.

Crome was on the north side of the church, Pelton the south. Dallas covered the Preacher and Ariel.

It was too late to try and evacuate Brother Thomas and Ariel. Luckily, they were the only other two in the building. Crome had given explicit directions that no one was to come through the door behind him or in front. Anyone entering those doors would be shot.

Pelton had the same setup.

Blu and Harmony, both on their way, understood to send a text before they entered.

The door in front of him opened. Crome fired two shots, dropping the man as he came through.

At the same time, the door behind him opened.

Crome spun and unloaded his clip. Something hit him in the neck and he fell backwards.

Blu charged through the city in his Grand Cherokee SRT and hit a hundred miles an hour on I-26 as he barreled toward North Charleston. Off the interstate, he ran every light, flicking his high-beams and honking his horn, his flashers on.

Without caring about tipping off whoever was there, he pulled into the lot and parked next to his F-150. He texted Pelton and Crome and let them know he was there and got no replies. Harmony and Powers were still five minutes out.

Not knowing what was going on inside, Blu exited his truck at a run and made it across the clearing to the front door.

He opened the door but stood back. No shots were fired at him. He slipped in, crouching with a backup Glock aimed forward. Brother Thomas had said he had Ariel in the kitchen with the doors closed and locked.

Blu made his way, concerned that he hadn't come across anyone thus far.

As he turned the hall to enter the kitchen, a hail of gunfire erupted in the South end of the church. It was Pelton.

No time to come to the kid's rescue, Blu's first objective was to protect Ariel and Brother Thomas. He sent the pastor a text and gave the kitchen door a knock.

Dallas opened the door and Blu slipped in.

Ariel raised herself up from the floor behind a counter in front of the sink.

Just then, the door behind him flung open.

Chapter Thirty-Five

Hector stood over Crome, a huge, black handled knife in his hands. "I'm going to gut you like the pig you are."

From the floor, Crome felt the blood trickling down his neck. Hector had hit him with one of his throwing knives. It was his trademark kill shot and Crome realized several things at once. The knife Hector had thrown at him had penetrated his skin but wasn't stuck in him. He knew this because he'd fallen on it.

Another detail Crome knew was Hector had made a grave mistake.

The whack of the bullets punched harder than anything Blu had experienced before. He felt himself go down.

Ariel screamed.

Dallas aimed but got taken down by a second shower of bullets.

Brother Thomas pushed Ariel behind himself as Townley walked into the room. He looked down at Blu who could only stare at him. The pain was intense. More than anything, Blu hated to lose.

Townley stepped over him. "This is what happens to people who come against me."

Dallas lay slumped on the floor.

Brother Thomas said, "You really don't wanna do this."

"I'd sure hate to have to kill a man of God," Townley said, "but you leave me no choice."

With gritted teeth, Brother Thomas said, "Do what you gotta do, then. Get it over with."

Townley raised the AR-15 in his hands, took aim at the preacher, and—

From the floor, Blu raised his gun and shot Townley four times in the back. The AR-15 dropped out of the lawyer's hands as he fell, face forward.

The door behind him banged open and Blu watched Crome enter the room, a black-handled knife in his hand.

Dallas coughed and tried to raise herself up. The vests she and Blu wore stopped the bullets from penetrating, but not the force of impact.

Crome picked up the rifle and moved past his victim as he dropped to his knees.

Looking down at Blu, Crome said, "You get shot or what?"

Blu tried to speak but all that came out were gasps. It hurt like hell.

Ariel said, "I'll call an ambulance."

Brother Thomas knelt down to help Dallas.

That was the last image Blu had, of the larger-than-life preacher kneeling over her, his strong hands holding her.

Crome called Pelton who apparently answered while he was still engaged with the enemy.

The kid said, "Could use—" Blam! "—little help—" Blam! "—Crome." Blam!

Crome didn't reply. He dropped the phone into a pocket, handed Ariel a pistol, and said, "Shoot anyone who comes through that door. I'll knock first when I come back."

Before she could reply, he slipped out of the room with a pistol in one hand and Townley's AR-15 in the other.

No one greeted him.

Gunshots were getting louder and more staccato.

Pelton was in real trouble.

Apparently Townley had split the men up, a larger team to provide distraction and a smaller one with Hector, and himself.

Crome thought about all of that as he ran toward the shooting, which suddenly stopped.

A man said, "Give it up. We've got you surrounded."

Just before Crome reached an intersection, the point of no return if he had to guess, he heard Pelton say, "Semper Fi."

Crome hit the intersection at full speed and mowed down three guys in front of him with the AR-15.

Three others turned to fire at him. He and Pelton blew them away.

Crome's boots slid across waxed linoleum and he plowed into a table set up to serve coffee. The table collapsed and glass pots, cylinders of sugar and creamer, bags of coffee, and one heavy-as-hell coffee maker fell to the ground along with Crome. It made a horrendous crash and did good job ringing Crome's bell. He lay stunned for a few seconds.

Pelton stood over him. "Took you long enough."

Crome had tagged the wall before the floor and had to shake cobwebs out of his head.

A gun fired behind them.

Pelton and Crome turned to see Harmony standing over a man who grabbed at his chest. It was another one from Death, LLC.

Before Harmony had a chance to decide what to do next, Pelton raised a pistol and shot the man, killing him.

She looked up at Pelton and then at Crome, surprise in her eyes.

Crome didn't feel any remorse. These men had come to kill. They deserved no mercy. This was as perfect an example of the type of job Blu Carraway Investigations handled. Either she dealt with them and got over it or she wouldn't.

Looking around the room, Crome saw the three men he'd killed, the three he and Pelton had killed together, the one Harmony had shot, and five other dead men. To Pelton, he asked, "You hit?"

"Naw," he said. "But I owe Brother Thomas another piano. It saved my life, but you can't play it anymore."

Chapter Thirty-Six

Blu woke up in a hospital room, Tess sitting in a chair next to his bed holding his hand.

She rose up and looked at him. "Hi, there."

"Hey yourself." He tried to get up, felt a stiffness all over and stopped.

"Take it easy," she said. "You've got a bunch of cracked ribs. So does Dallas."

He took a few breaths to get himself focused again. "Everybody else okay?"

"Yes," she said. Her blue eyes looked at him through those librarian glasses. He felt other parts of himself stir.

She caught his hand as it tried to trace her leg. "I'm not going anywhere but we've got to give you some time to heal."

"How's my client?" he asked.

"She's great. Appreciative of you and Crome."

"She hasn't left town yet?"

"Are you kidding?" Tess said. "She's planning a benefit concert for North Charleston. A ton of her friends are coming in to perform. It's already sold out."

"How long have I been out?"

"About four hours."

Crome had a score to settle. Jake Jarnel had vanished and was on the run. His plan to rule the world's private security imploded in the most spectacular fashion in Charleston. If Crome had to guess, he'd believe Jarnel regretted ever partnering up with Blake Townley.

Kuala Lumpur, Malaysia

Ring Anuwat met him as he passed baggage claim and followed the sign to ground transportation.

They stood on the balcony of Crome's suite in the five-star hotel overlooking the other tall buildings. Directly below, about twenty floors down, was a rooftop with some decorative foliage.

"So what are you here for?" Anuwat asked.

"I wanted to clear things up for Blu," Crome said. "He's still a person of interest in five murders here, ya know." He inhaled vapor and exhaled it into the night.

Anuwat leaned on the rail. "How you plan on doing that?"

The vapor countered the translator's cologne which was pretty stout. The man's silk clothes and what looked like a real expensive watch were well above what should have been his means. Especially given the gambling debts Crome had found out he'd accrued. The guy would be willing to sell out his own mother to pay back even part of the huge vig he owed to some very dangerous men.

"Tell me, Ring. You really think you were going to get away with it?"

The man visibly stiffened up, one hand still on the railing, but the other now by his side.

"There was no way anyone from here knew Blu was in the city but you, yet within twenty-four hours, he was set up for murder."

"That doesn't mean anything. You guys have enemies all over the world."

Crome said, "It was you."

Anuwat went for something in his pocket.

Crome threw the vape pen and tagged the man in the eye with it. Both of Anuwat's hands went to the injury. All the training in the world didn't work without self-discipline. Auwat had proven he didn't have much of that. When Crome lifted him off the ground, Anuwat realized he was in trouble and began to fight. But it was too late.

Crome pitched the man off the balcony and watched him drop twenty stories and land behind the potted trees on a rooftop below.

The only luggage Crome carried was a small backpack. He didn't plan on being in town longer than necessary. In fact, his return flight left in two hours.

Picking his vape pen off the floor, he took a hit and exhaled. "I thought chickens could fly."

Epilogue

Late February, Charleston South Carolina

Crome had been gone for going on five months now. Blu guessed he was in Key West, but wasn't sure and didn't really care. His partner and friend needed time to heal from Colette's death and from Maureen's kidnapping and he'd deal with things in his own way.

Tess walked into Blu's living room from the kitchen with a bowl of popcorn and two Coke Zeros. "Have they announced her yet?"

Looking at the screen, Blu said, "Right now."

Together, they watched Ariel accept a Grammy, her third, for the album she recorded with Phineous at the Kincaid compound. She dragged the lanky photo analyst up on stage with her.

"Look at Phineous up there!" Tess exclaimed.

Blu was happy for him but sad because he'd have to find someone else as good as Phin was. It wouldn't be easy, but not much in this life was.

Tess kissed him.

Okay, so maybe life wasn't so bad.

DAVID BURNSWORTH

David Burnsworth became fascinated with the Deep South at a young age. After a degree in Mechanical Engineering from the University of Tennessee and fifteen years in the corporate world, he made the decision to write a novel. He is the author of both the Brack Pelton and the Blu Carraway Mystery Series. Having lived in Charleston on Sullivan's Island for five years, the setting was a foregone conclusion. He and his wife call South Carolina home.

Books by David Burnsworth

The Blu Carraway Mystery Series

BLU HEAT (Prequel Novella)
IN IT FOR THE MONEY (#1)
BAD TIME TO BE IN IT (#2)
CAUGHT UP IN IT (#3)

The Brack Pelton Mystery Series

SOUTHERN HEAT (#1)
BURNING HEAT (#2)
BIG CITY HEAT (#3)

Henery Press Mystery Books

And finally, before you go...
Here are a few other mysteries
you might enjoy:

MURDER AT THE PALACE

Margaret Dumas

A Movie Palace Mystery (#1)

Welcome to the Palace movie theater! Now Showing: Philandering husbands, ghostly sidekicks, and a murder or two.

When Nora Paige's movie-star husband leaves her for his latest co-star, she flees Hollywood to take refuge in San Francisco at the Palace, a historic movie theater that shows the classic films she loves. There she finds a band of misfit film buffs who care about movies (almost) as much as she does.

She also finds some shady financial dealings and the body of a murdered stranger. Oh, and then there's Trixie, the lively ghost of a 1930's usherette who appears only to Nora and has a lot to catch up on. With the help of her new ghostly friend, can Nora catch the killer before there's another murder at the Palace?

Available at booksellers nationwide and online

Visit www.henerypress.com for details

COUNTERFEIT CONSPIRACIES

Ritter Ames

A Bodies of Art Mystery (#1)

Laurel Beacham may have been born with a silver spoon in her mouth, but she has long since lost it digging herself out of trouble. Her father gambled and womanized his way through the family fortune before skiing off an Alp, leaving her with more tarnish than trust fund. Quick wits and connections have gained her a reputation as one of the world's premier art recovery experts. The police may catch the thief, but she reclaims the missing masterpieces.

The latest assignment, however, may be her undoing. Using every ounce of luck and larceny she possesses, Laurel must locate a priceless art icon and rescue a co-worker (and ex-lover) from a master criminal, all the while matching wits with a charming new nemesis. Unfortunately, he seems to know where the bodies are buried—and she prefers hers isn't next.

Available at booksellers nationwide and online

Visit www.henerypress.com for details

ARTIFACT

Gigi Pandian

A Jaya Jones Treasure Hunt Mystery (#1)

Historian Jaya Jones discovers the secrets of a lost Indian treasure may be hidden in a Scottish legend from the days of the British Raj. But she's not the only one on the trail...

From San Francisco to London to the Highlands of Scotland, Jaya must evade a shadowy stalker as she follows hints from the hastily scrawled note of her dead lover to a remote archaeological dig. Helping her decipher the cryptic clues are her magician best friend, a devastatingly handsome art historian with something to hide, and a charming archaeologist running for his life.

Available at booksellers nationwide and online

Visit www.henerypress.com for details

BOARD STIFF

Kendel Lynn

An Elliott Lisbon Mystery (#1)

As director of the Ballantyne Foundation on Sea Pine Island, SC, Elliott Lisbon scratches her detective itch by performing discreet inquiries for Foundation donors. Usually nothing more serious than retrieving a pilfered Pomeranian. Until Jane Hatting, Ballantyne board chair, is accused of murder. The Ballantyne's reputation tanks, Jane's headed to a jail cell, and Elliott's sexy ex is the new lieutenant in town.

Armed with moxie and her Mini Coop, Elliott uncovers a trail of blackmail schemes, gambling debts, illicit affairs, and investment scams. But the deeper she digs to clear Jane's name, the guiltier Jane looks. The closer she gets to the truth, the more treacherous her investigation becomes. With victims piling up faster than shells at a clambake, Elliott realizes she's next on the killer's list.

Available at booksellers nationwide and online

Visit www.henerypress.com for details

CPSIA information can be obtained
at www.ICGtesting.com
Printed in the USA
FFHW011945270219
50700269-56094FF